Krazy About Kentucky

Big Blue Hoops

Jamie H. Vaught

Wasteland Press
Louisville, KY USA
www.wastelandpress.com

Krazy About Kentucky: Big Blue Hoops
by Jamie H. Vaught

First Printing-October, 2003
ISBN: 0-9746290-5-7

Cover Photo Courtesy of UK Media Relations
(photo by Breck Smither).

Printed In The U.S.A.

Acknowledgments

Like my previous three books on UK basketball which were published in the 1990s, this book, *Krazy About Kentucky: Big Blue Hoops*, wouldn't have been written without the help of many cooperative individuals. I'm grateful to Delores Taylor, of Corbin, who was a tremendous help. A very dependable and trustworthy person, Taylor spent hours in transcribing the exclusive, tape-recorded interviews. In addition to the brief interviews, she transcribed thirteen lengthy interviews of people -- players, coaches and even the First Lady of Wildcat hoops -- who have strong connections with UK. Just like my other books, *Krazy About Kentucky: Big Blue Hoops* is primarily another entertaining look at UK's hoops program through the eyes of players and coaches.

Publicists at various universities were very helpful along with the schools' basketball media guides. Before leaving his UK post as media relations director in the athletics department in the summer of 2003, Brooks Downing arranged some interviews and provided photos. Mandy Polley and Matt Steinke, both of UK, also helped. Annabelle Vaughan, who is the assistant athletics director for media relations at North Carolina State, was very helpful, setting up the interview with coach Herb Sendek at his office in Raleigh. Thomas Whitestone, the sports information director at Charlotte, furnished the photos and background material on Mike Pratt.

Several public relations folks from NBA teams kindly arranged the interviews and provided the photos. They were Kim Turner (Utah), Phil Mickey (Utah), David Benner (Indiana), Krissy Myers (Indiana), MaryKay Scott (Indiana), Harold Kaufman (New Orleans), Scott Hall (New Orleans), Arthur Triche (Atlanta), Tim Hallam (Chicago), Sebrina Brewster (Chicago) and Matt Lloyd (Chicago).

Special thanks go to sports editor Jim Kurk of Henderson's *The Gleaner* for editing the manuscript. Kurk is a former colleague of mine in Somerset during the 1980s when he ran the sports department at *The Commonwealth-Journal.* Sportswriters Kevin Patton, Jerry Boggs and Neill Morgan also contributed in various ways. Before concluding, I would like to thank my wife (Deanna), my mother (Betty), and the rest of the family for their support. And I hope I didn't omit anyone else who lent a hand for the book. If I did, special thanks go to them as well. Enjoy the book!

J.H.V.
August 2003

Contents

Chapter 1

Between Ivy and Barnhart

Back in early March of 2002, when University of Kentucky president Dr. Lee Todd was looking for someone to take over embattled Larry Ivy's athletics director job on a temporary basis, one of the names he had in mind was ex-Wildcat basketball standout Terry Mobley.

But Todd didn't get a straight answer from Mobley, a longtime administrator at UK, who had reservations about taking over the AD position. "I'm not sure this is something I'm interested in," Mobley told his boss.

Todd later got in touch with Mobley again and said, "Well, would you reconsider?"

"Well, sure," was the reply.

And the rest is history.

Mobley, 58 at the time, finally agreed to the temporary spot as the school's top boss in the athletics department. "You don't say no to your superior," he explained.

Mobley, a native of Harrodsburg who played for legendary coach Adolph Rupp in the early 1960s, had mixed emotions about his interim role as AD.

It was a very awkward time for him. He saw Ivy, an old friend of 25 years, lose his AD job. In addition, Mobley was in the middle of a major fund-raising campaign of $600 million as the school's chief development officer, a position he really enjoyed.

"We were moving into the final stages (of the fund-raising campaign) and I just felt like as an university employee that perhaps my services could be better utilized there," commented Mobley, who has worked at UK since 1977. "It had nothing to do with what had gone on here (athletics) or the inability to do it.

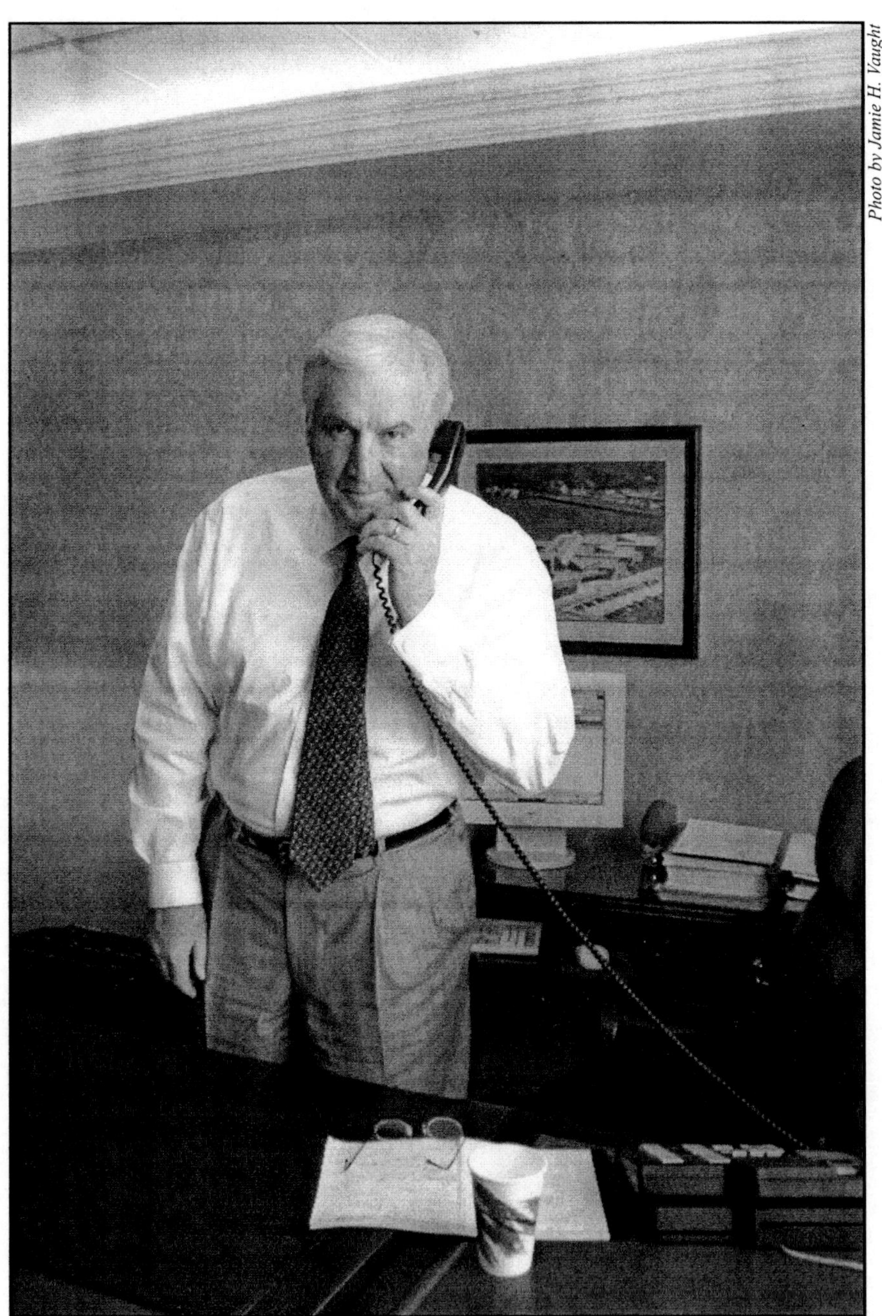

Photo by Jamie H. Vaught

Terry Mobley, who played for legendary coach Adolph Rupp in the early 1960s, served as UK's interim athletics director for several months in 2002 after Larry Ivy resigned his AD position.

"You never like to see bad things happen at an institution that you love, which is especially in my case, and when you have a place this size change is inevitable, but you hate to see it happen to a longtime employee. Apparently, it was felt that a change needed to be made and you don't like to assume a position because of that and you don't like to assume a position especially when it involves a friend. But I understand that those things are going to happen so it was a tough day for everyone."

Mobley liked to call his interim AD role "my day job and my other one my night job and my weekend job."

Sounds like he had been working 24 hours a day? Well, not quite, but close, he said.

Mobley said putting together a new athletics budget for the 2002-03 school year was one of his bigger challenges as it included no bowl revenue of an estimated $1.5 million which was lost due to NCAA sanctions in football. "It is never a lot of fun when you meet with your good folks and tell them we've got to reduce expenses," he added.

While he enjoyed working with the employees in the athletics department during his five-month tenure as interim AD, Mobley was glad to return to his old job when UK hired Mitch Barnhart in mid-July 2002 as the new AD. A former assistant athletics director at Tennessee, Barnhart had been serving as athletics director at Oregon State since 1998.

* * *

The 1950s, when President Eisenhower occupied the White House, saw the U.S. enjoy economic prosperity where many folks found new, comfortable lifestyles with new cars, televisions and appliances in fulfillment of their American dreams. During that time Mobley and his older brother, Tony, were two of millions of youngsters fortunate enough to enjoy their boyhood, growing up among the rolling hills of Mercer County in central Kentucky. They lived in a farming community called Rose Hill, located just outside of Harrodsburg.

"It was a peaceful time in my life because I had no worries," said Mobley, whose father doubled as a Southern Baptist preacher and a farmer. "You know, I would work and do odd jobs, mow yards or what have you. I had loving parents. I played basketball, baseball, football, those things that you do in small communities. It was not a time of turbulence in my life at all.

"I can remember watching (comedian) Red Skelton on TV. I can remember watching Gillette Cavalcade of Sports on Friday night and that is about all I can remember. There were some color (TV) sets in my later years in high school, but what we had was very definitely black and white and we were happy to have that."

Basketball played a big part in Mobley's life. The youngster would play the sport outside without a concrete floor whether it was raining or not. It didn't matter to him. He just wanted to play, even when the ground was wet with mud. "I guess at the age of four or five I started shooting baskets," he said. "My dad had put a basketball goal up on the side of a barn. So that is where I first started.

"I remember going to the sink in the kitchen and washing the mud off of the ball and putting clear shoe polish on it to make it look new again." It may be hard to fathom, but Mobley said his mother, who was a homemaker, didn't get upset after he messed up her kitchen. "Oh, no. I don't think so," he added. "She was just glad I was doing something at home instead of some place else."

* * *

By the time Mobley was around 10 or 11 years old, he began to play organized basketball. He remembers his first game. "I was in the fifth grade and we had some pretty good players from the fifth and sixth grades and our first coach was a gentleman by the name of Evan Harlow, who was the principal of that elementary school," Mobley recalled. "He took a group of young kids and organized a team. As a matter of fact, we were undefeated in the fifth grade. So that is my first memory at Harrodsburg of organized basketball."

Besides playing basketball, Mobley had another interest. Like many kids who grew up listening to legendary announcers Claude Sullivan and Cawood Ledford describe the Wildcat action on radio, he loved UK, following the teams by the time he was in the first grade. "I was pretty inbred as far as Kentucky basketball is concerned," he said. And he got to see his heroes play in person. If his parents didn't go to the UK games, their friends would usually invite the youngster to go with them to Lexington. "There were a lot of people from Harrodsburg who had season tickets and I saw all the games I needed to see," said Mobley. "(We) drove to Lexington to come to UK basketball games expecting them to win. I mean it wasn't a question of it. It was how much." After the game, Mobley and friends would stop at Frisch's restaurant before driving back home. "I got a Big Boy and a milk shake," he recalled.

Later, he played basketball at Harrodsburg High School where he was coached by Aggie Sale, a former All-American at Kentucky and 1933 Helms National Player of the Year. Mobley couldn't have been at a better place than Harrodsburg if he was to going to play at UK. After all, it was Rupp who had tutored Sale in the early 1930s. Sale also had ties with UCLA coaching legend John Wooden as they were teammates on a semi-pro barnstorming squad, based in Kentucky, while Wooden coached at Dayton (Ky.) High School. As it turned out, Sale's knowledge and experience paid off for Mobley, who became a star, guiding the Pioneers to their first-ever trip to the state tournament in 1960.

However, before earning its Sweet Sixteen trip to Louisville, Harrodsburg had to scrap and fight against bigger foes, especially the Lexington schools, to capture its regional crown. Said Mobley, "Back then Harrodsburg was in the same region as all the Lexington schools. We had 220 kids in all of the high school. We had like 60 students in each class. So the likelihood of a small community or town like Harrodsburg sending someone to the state tournament was pretty remote when you had Lafayette with (coach) Ralph Carlisle, Henry Clay with Baldy Gilb, Dunbar with S. T. Roach. Of course, you had Bryan Station and Lexington Catholic."

During the 1959-60 season, Lafayette spent most of the time as the state's top-ranked team with stars Jeff Mullins and William Moore, but the Generals were knocked out early in post-season action. "Dunbar wound up in the district (tourney) beating them somehow," Mobley said. "It is interesting that we are sitting here doing this interview because the regional tournament my junior year was played right here in Memorial Coliseum." In the regional action, Mobley's Harrodsburg squad, after defeating Franklin County in the opening round, faced coach Roach and Dunbar in a crucial matchup. "There were 11,000 people in this place and we upset Dunbar, which had a very good team, 52-50," he said. But the contest wasn't without controversy as the Kentucky High School Athletics Association conducted an investigation after a post-game incident involving angry Dunbar fans.

Later, in the state tourney, Harrodsburg didn't advance very far. "Bell County beat us in the first round," Mobley said. "We should have beaten them. They had a good team, but we were just happy to be there." The loss, as it turned out, marked the last game for Sale as Harrodsburg's coach. Said Mobley of his mentor, "(He was) our coach all the way through to my junior year. He had always said that if he ever made it to the state tournament, he would retire." Sale, who had a sporting goods store, later became involved in politics, serving as a state legislator before he died in 1985.

Over the years, Mobley and Roach, who later became a longtime member of UK athletics board, have continued to needle each other about their early days. "We kind of kid around them. He remembers them well," Mobley commented. "We were undefeated – 20-0 -- my senior year and we played Dunbar in the regionals again and they beat us. So they got even my senior year, but they had good teams back then."

After completing his senior year with a 23-point average, Mobley, a two-time all-state performer, played in the annual Kentucky-Indiana all-star games. And the future Wildcat Randy Embry, a 5-10 guard from Owensboro, was on the all-star squad as Kentucky's Mr. Basketball. "They (Indiana) beat us at Louisville and we beat them at Indianapolis," recalled Mobley, who roomed with Embry for three years at UK.

* * *

With the Cotton Nash-led Wildcats coming off a remarkable 23-3 campaign with a final No. 3 ranking in the previous season, bigger things were expected of the squad as the 1962-63 season approached. With Nash returning after leading the SEC in scoring with 23.4 points the previous year, the demanding fans were enthusiastic, believing the Cats would be heading for their first national championship since the Fiddlin' Five team won it in 1958. Now a junior, Nash was expected to carry the load. He was the big man on the campus, having appeared on the cover of *Sports Illustrated* magazine in its special college basketball issue. And Mobley, as a sophomore, would be playing on the varsity team for the first time. He didn't play as a rookie due to NCAA rules, which forbid freshman eligibility at that time.

But on the first day of December things went awry for the Cats, who were ranked No. 3 in the preseason, in their season opener at Memorial Coliseum. Facing unranked Virginia Tech and assistant coach Guy Strong (who played on UK's 1951 national championship team), Kentucky struggled to find another scoring threat besides Nash to keep the defense honest. Even though Nash pumped in a game-high 34 points, the Hokies stunned Kentucky in a major upset. Despite the setback, Nash's sophomore teammate, Mobley, began his UK career on a good note, hitting 11 points in a reserve role. He was probably good enough to start, but Rupp had other ideas. "Coach didn't like to start sophomores. He would start a senior any time before he would start a sophomore," Mobley explained. "So (future U.S. Congressman) Scotty Baesler was starting as a senior when I was a sophomore. I was actually coming in as a substitute then and later on my sophomore year I started. But when you're coming off the bench, you don't know how many minutes or how many points you're going to get."

The Wildcats would go on and lose eight more games in the season, including a 68-66 loss to coach Dean Smith's North Carolina club, and finish fifth in the SEC without appearing in the NCAA tournament. With the squad at 16-9, it marked Rupp's worst year at Kentucky at that time. It was a horrible year.

* * *

For Mobley and his teammates, the following season of 1963-64 was much more bearable. They helped Kentucky finish No. 3 in the country with a very respectable 21-6 mark. Mobley, a junior at the time, started 25 of UK's 27 games, averaging 9.4 points, fourth highest on the squad. He had several good games.

For the Mobley family, December 9 will always be a special date. It's Terry's birthday. But that day in 1963 – his 20th birthday -- will always be a memorable one for a special reason. He had a great game against the Tar Heels of North Carolina. Mobley wasn't gun shy, scoring 21 points, in leading Kentucky to a 100-80 win at Memorial Coliseum. The Tar Heels "had (future NBA star) Billy Cunningham," he said. "It was on my birthday and that's why (I remember)." He added that he didn't have much of a birthday celebration after the game. "I went back to the dorm and studied," Mobley laughed.

Three weeks later, the Wildcats traveled to the Sugar Bowl Tournament in New Orleans where they got caught in a rare snowstorm. "They had the first snow that day they had in like 76 years so traffic was horrendous, but we finally got to the arena," recalled Mobley, who played a heroic role in UK's tournament title. In the finals of the tournament, he found himself at a couple of critical moments. With less than two minutes remaining, Mobley scored a field goal which deadlocked the game at 79-79. Later, with the game still tied at four seconds left, he poured in a game-winning shot, a short jumper, as the unbeaten Wildcats defeated a tough Duke club, led by Lexington native Jeff Mullins, keeping their winning streak alive at 10 games.

"Duke had a great team. There was no question about that," Mobley commented. "We got down 14 in the first half and then Cotton (Nash) got hot in the second half and we just gradually kept coming back. (At the very end), we called timeout and coach Rupp set up a play that was to go to Cotton. Of course, everybody in the fieldhouse knew that was where it was to go. So Duke actually sagged back and had him covered. Of course, time was expiring so I didn't have many options but to go ahead and shoot it. So we ended up winning 81-79. Then the polls came out the next week and we go to No. 1 in the country." Nash, who was selected the tourney's MVP, finished with game-high 26 points and Mobley added nine points.

However, Mobley almost didn't make it to the championship game. The night before, he couldn't do anything, scoring just one point in UK's 86-64 victory over Loyola (La.). "I was sick the first game," he said. "I started, but then they took me out for the first half. I had a groin muscle pulled and the team doctor had given me some muscle relaxers. It just absolutely relaxed me too much. They had to take me out of the game.

"Then they asked me if I was okay for the Duke game. It still didn't (feel right), but I think I played the whole game. It wouldn't be a great game, but it turned out okay."

After the holiday tournament, top-ranked Kentucky didn't stay unbeaten very long. The Wildcats saw themselves on the losing side for the first time that season when Georgia Tech, then a member of SEC, upset UK 76-67 in Atlanta. A couple of nights later, UK lost again, this time to Vanderbilt in Nashville, dropping its record to 10-2. The Wildcats, who also featured All-SEC standout Ted Deeken to go along with Nash, went on to complete the regular season with 11 victories in the next 13 games.

But the Wildcats didn't enjoy their trip to Minnesota where they dropped two games in the NCAA tournament. Mobley had another career performance with 21 points against Loyola of Chicago in the consolation game for third place in the Mideast Regional. Since Kentucky was out, it was a meaningless game as far as the Bluegrass folks were concerned.

* * *

Like Rupp, there are a lot of Cotton Nash stories. Mobley remembers one about his old teammate when "King Cotton" challenged Rupp, threatening to sit out the Sugar Bowl tournament. The Wildcat star needed game tickets for his family and friends.

Walking from the famed Jung Hotel (where President Lyndon Johnson several months later spoke at a fund-raising dinner) in New

Orleans, located not far from the French Quarter, Rupp and his staff boarded the team bus and the Wildcat boss asked student manager Hub Metry, "Is everyone here?"

"No," said the manager. "Cotton is not here."

"Where is he?"

"Well, I'll try to go find him," said the manager.

The manager went back to the hotel and saw Nash chatting with his family in the lobby. King Cotton had a lot of folks coming in that night. Some of them were from nearby Lake Charles, La., where Nash starred in high school basketball.

"You tell Coach Rupp I'm not playing tonight because I asked for these tickets for my family and he hasn't given them to me," an angry Nash told the manager. "I know he has them and tell him to go ahead, but I'm not playing."

So the manager ran back to the bus. While the players, sitting and waiting for the bus to depart, listened and watched all the commotion that was developing between Rupp and the team's star, the manager said, "Coach Rupp, Cotton says he isn't playing tonight. He is gonna stay with his family because if they can't go to the game he would rather be with them."

Rupp got mad and used choice words, calling Nash everything. Finally, when the coach calmed down, he asked, "Well, how many tickets does he need?"

"I don't know," said the manager.

So the manager returns to the hotel.

Said Nash, "Well, I need 14."

And the manager goes back to the bus and tells Rupp what Nash wanted.

A frustrated coach says, "Hell, no, that is way too many."

The manager walks to the hotel and repeats the coach's message.

"It is either 14 or I'm not playing," was Nash's curt reply and the Wildcat star then went up to his room.

Mobley, who was on the bus, then saw Coach Rupp take a batch of tickets out of his pocket. "It was a whole lot more than 14," recalled Mobley.

Rupp then took four of the tickets inside with his assistant, Harry Lancaster, delivering them to Nash's room. And Cotton finally boarded the bus.

They didn't speak on the way to the arena.

"I lost my cool," explained Nash in an interview in the mid-1990s.

"I knew there were some available. Finally, I just said that if I couldn't get tickets I would just take them (his family) out for a movie and show them a good time. I don't know if I was serious. I was just kind of angry.

"My parents made a trip every holiday season because my dad couldn't get any time off to see me play. My dad was in Massachusetts and had driven down to Lexington to see the holiday tournament (UKIT) and stayed long enough to see the Sugar Bowl tournament. The trip had been over a thousand miles from Massachusetts. So when the team got to New Orleans, I automatically assumed that we would get tickets for our families."

Said Mobley, "Not many other players would have challenged coach Rupp, but he did. Everybody wrote about he and Cotton having a bad relationship, but that was totally incorrect. I mean, Cotton was good enough that he would kind of challenge him occasionally, but they didn't have a bad relationship. Cotton was a great player and good to play with."

Mobley and Nash are neighbors in Lexington, living within a walking distance of each other.

* * *

While practicing for his senior year at Kentucky, Mobley suffered a near-tragic accident in a pre-season workout in mid-October. He underwent surgery to repair torn tear ducts resulting from a fingernail cut to his eye. It was a major setback for Mobley, whose experience and leadership were crucial for the young Wildcats, who featured two promising sophomores, Pat Riley and Louie Dampier.

"We were scrimmaging, playing before formal practice started, and Louie Dampier and I collided with one another, going after a loose ball," Mobley said. "But to make a long story short, Louie always played with long fingernails and he came across my eye and it severed my tear ducts, my upper and lower tear ducts. They rushed me over to old Good Samaritan Hospital and I had surgery."

And it happened on the day before the squad's Picture Day. That would usually mean that Mobley couldn't have his official team photograph made with his teammates. However, Rupp, a complex man who can be kind-hearted at times, decided the pictures could wait.

"Coach Rupp told the photographers there won't be a team picture today," Mobley said. "He said one of my boys is in the hospital and I'm not gonna take a team picture until he is back. So if you looked at the pictures of anything that came out two days later after the Picture Day there was no team picture. And he sent the photographers up to Good Samaritan Hospital for the individual pictures and of course I was all bandaged up."

Because of the injury, Mobley had to miss two weeks of practice and it probably cost him a spot in the starting lineup. As a result, Rupp named long bomber Dampier as the starter in place of Mobley in the season opener against Iowa. Kentucky won that game at home, but it later failed to earn a berth in the NCAA tournament, finishing with a dismal 15-10 worksheet for the season. Mobley's season highlight was his performance against Auburn at Memorial Coliseum. His 18 points helped UK to a 73-67 victory over coach Bill Lyons' Auburn club. After the season, Rupp and his staff awarded the team's leadership award to Mobley.

* * *

The early part of the 1960's decade was not very kind to Rupp, who more than usual had lost a good share of games. Beginning with the 1959-60 season, the Baron posted records of 18-7, 19-9, 23-3, 16-9, 21-6 and 15-10 (before he had the popular 1965-66 Rupp's Runts, who went all the way to the national finals before losing to Texas Western.) The Kentucky fans weren't all that pleased with his coaching job. They began to wonder about him. Some speculated Rupp, who was in his early 60s, had slowed down and was struggling to keep up with the changing times.

Mobley, however, doesn't completely agree with the theory. "Well, he couldn't have slowed down too much," he said. "He almost won it all in 1966. So I think any coach goes through those (down) years. I didn't feel like he had lost anything actually. The game was beginning to be played a little differently. Coaches were beginning to full court press like you still see today. It was that the other teams were catching up and we just weren't as dominating as we were.

"Coach Rupp, if you didn't start, you weren't gonna play much. I mean the only time he would substitute is if you made several turnovers or got in foul trouble. I remember a reporter one time asked him, 'How come you never spend much time in practice on the full court press,' and Rupp said, 'That's because I don't ever plan on being behind.' And that was kind of the way he thought. I don't know if that was a time issue but his mind was still as good as ever."

Rupp also had a habit of calling his players by their hometowns and Mobley was no exception. "Most of the time he called me Harrodsburg which was fine with me," recalled Mobley. "He had all kinds of nicknames. He actually was pretty good with names, but he would put a name on somebody. Some guys he would call by their first name and some by their last name. There were some guys who got called a whole lot worse than that."

Mobley was fortunate that he enjoyed a good player-coach relationship with Rupp. Some players simply couldn't handle the legendary mentor's personality as a master psychologist. "He would get on you just like he would everybody else," said Mobley, who served as a pallbearer at Mrs. Adolph Rupp's funeral in 1998. "He was very humorous in his criticism, but you didn't dare laugh at it. I mean I incurred his wrath like everybody else did. But as long as he was treating everyone the same, you accepted it. I never really had an unpleasant experience with him.

"He was a brilliant man. A lot of people, I think, underestimate how smart, intellectually, coach Rupp was. But he played with your psyche a little bit. He could compliment you or he could get on you. I didn't seem to be bothered by all that. I mean it was a job as far as scholarship to college (was concerned). While we were sitting around one night during Christmas when all the other students were gone and we had been practicing all day long, we figured we were getting paid about 33 cents an hour. That's about what that scholarship was worth.

"But he was complex in the fact that he could be funny. He could be tough on you. He could be very demanding. I think most of the players pretty well had him figured out. It was gonna be a tough four years and if you could take it, you would stay (in the Wildcat program). Of course, lots of guys didn't and left. I think of him as being smart, witty and tough to play for."

Asked if he ever broke a curfew, Mobley replied with a smile, saying, "Not that I recall, but I probably did. We would have threatened the manager or trainer with their lives if they had turned us in anyway. I don't recall ever being in any kind of trouble."

* * *

Mobley has another Rupp story. He remembers a trip to the Queen City to see to an NBA game where the old Cincinnati Royals once had stars Oscar Robertson, Jerry Lucas, Wayne Embry and (ex-Wildcat) Adrian Smith.

But the problem was that Mobley and his teammates, Cotton Nash and Ted Deeken, had taken the trip without Rupp's knowledge or permission, and the coach didn't like that at all.

"I remember coach Rupp calling us in the next day and he wanted to know where we were (the night before)," Mobley said. "Of course, he already knew. I guess he had either listened to it (the game) on radio or TV and he knew where we were, and we were smart enough to tell him the truth.

"I don't recall us breaking curfew but it was the fact that we had gone out of town and didn't let him know. So he gave us a little tongue lashing and we went on with that."

* * *

Another Rupp experience.

During his senior year, Mobley had been invited to speak at the Billy Graham Crusade in Louisville to represent students from the state of Kentucky. A large crowd of around 20,000 was expected. But he had a problem. He was very worried, afraid that he couldn't arrive at the special event at Freedom Hall on time after a pre-season practice on the UK campus. He would have about an hour or so to drive. Not much spare time, if any. He would have to rush. And he didn't inform the coach about his speaking engagement. Because of that, Mobley believed Rupp wasn't aware of the player's plans for the Louisville trip.

Anyhow, Mobley was having a good practice and Rupp took him out during the middle of a scrimmage. He called him over to the side of the playing floor.

"Harrodsburg, aren't you supposed to be speaking in Louisville tonight?" questioned Rupp, who had seen a newspaper ad featuring the crusade.

"Yes, sir, I am."

"Well, you are cutting it kind of close, aren't you?"

"Yes, I am but I wasn't going to ask to be off of practice."

"I knew you wouldn't ask off of practice," Rupp said. "If you'll go in and shower up, I'll have a state patrolman take you to Louisville to get you there on time."

And Mobley made it to the crusade without any difficulties. He said he hasn't forgotten Rupp's kind gesture. The coach had "a heart there. You just didn't see it."

* * *

Many folks in the UK camp, including Mobley, aren't real happy when they hear about Rupp and his alleged racism. It gets pretty tiresome when the sportswriters or broadcasters, especially on the national level, continue to talk about racism without good background knowledge, Mobley commented. "Same old stuff. If he was racist in any way, none of us ever saw it," he explained. "I'm kind of sick and tired of it."

Before the Kentucky-Texas Western NCAA title game, a historic landmark which marked the growing influence of black players in college basketball, the top-ranked Wildcats had to play No. 2 Duke in the national semifinals. "People forget that Duke didn't have any African-American players. So (why not) write about them," he said, adding that Rupp also tried to recruit prep stars Wes Unseld and Butch Beard, both from the state of Kentucky. "But there was this fear of taking them on the road in the South at the time. It had nothing to do with Coach Rupp not wanting to coach them."

* * *

Interestingly, Mobley has an older brother who once had ex-Hoosier coach Bobby Knight working for him as a part-time instructor at Indiana University. Retired in 2002, Tony Mobley once served 26 years as the dean of IU's School of Health, Physical Education and Recreation and that's where Knight's class had been offered for many years.

In 2000, Tony received some national attention when quick-tempered Knight, who had been slapped with the school's new zero-tolerance behavior policy, declined to teach a course in coaching. The course had been well-received in the past and it wasn't unusual to see at least 75 students enrolled for that course. In regard to Knight's class, Tony was also mentioned in the coach's best-selling autobiography, *Knight: My Story*, which hit the bookstores in 2002.

"He just felt with that policy that he didn't want to expose himself to any situation that might arise," Mobley was quoted as saying in an Associated Press article. "He just thought that if a student became upset with something, and wanted to make an issue, that somehow it might fit under that policy. It was a chance that he wasn't willing to take."

Before getting his advanced degrees, Tony Mobley attended Georgetown College where he received his bachelor's degree.

"He was a good basketball player (in high school), good baseball player and ran track," said Terry. "But he was a better student than he was in athletics. So he went to Georgetown on a full academic scholarship."

* * *

Shortly after graduating from UK, Mobley taught five classes of 11th grade American history and coached basketball at Lexington Lafayette High School. He served as an aide to Rupp's son, Herky, a former UK player who was the head coach of the Generals. "(Herky) asked me to go out and be an assistant," Mobley said. "I thoroughly enjoyed coaching, but it just wasn't something that I aspired to do for the rest of my life. I admire those that do, but I was ready to do something else."

So he then started to work for IBM Corporation for several years in Lexington and Washington, D.C., trying to find a vocation that he would enjoy. He returned to UK in 1977.

"(School president) Dr. Otis Singletary approached me about a position in the Development Office back then," said Mobley, who is married to his high school acquaintance from Owensboro, Becky, with three children and three grandchilden. "It sounded better than continuing to move quite frequently. So that is how I got here."

Chapter 2

Casey at the Court

Over three decades ago, when the editors at *Sports Illustrated* decided to use Kentucky star Mike Casey on the magazine's cover along with two other collegiate standouts for its pre-season college basketball issue, Casey said they had to get permission from coach Adolph Rupp. As you'll recall, the Baron, during his coaching days, limited the media's access to his players.

After getting Rupp's OK, the magazine made arrangements to have Casey fly one morning in early November to Chapel Hill, N.C., home of the North Carolina Tar Heels, where the photo shoot was held. With Casey, North Carolina's Charlie Scott and Davidson's Mike Maloy posing for a cover photograph for the magazine's Dec. 2, 1968 issue, the folks at SI figured their teams had a legitimate shot to dethrone powerful UCLA from college basketball's national championship map. At the time, the Bruins were in the midst of their unbelievable string of consecutive national titles from 1967 to 1973.

At the shoot, Casey said the trio had a nice time, sharing some stories. And he didn't stay very long there as he returned to Lexington later that evening. It was one interesting moment of Casey's outstanding career at UK. In anyone's right mind, who could forget an experience with a national sports magazine, especially *Sports Illustrated*? The magazine cover gave the Wildcat junior, who was coming off a superb sophomore year as the team's leading scorer for UK's fifth-ranked 22-5 club, a good dose of national exposure.

* * *

Now in his 50s, Casey is a well-known figure in the UK basketball family, but that doesn't mean many older fans recognize him today. With his gray hair, many simply just walk by him, not knowing he was the Kentucky star in the early days of black-and-white images from the

Photo by Jamie H. Vaught

Former Kentucky star Mike Casey talks on the phone in his Louisville area office.

newspaper photos and television sets. They just simply remembered his name when he was a young Wildcat. But many Kentuckians have fond memories of him. He was their big hero. Casey, who grew up in Shelby County, was their hometown boy.

While traveling as a sales representative for the Balfour Company, which specializes in class rings, among other things, Casey has had some interesting moments. He recalled an incident at a school where a receptionist nearly fainted when she heard Casey's name in an introduction. But when she first saw him, she didn't know him. "We went to the school, but we didn't have any business with them. (When I was introduced to her), she stood up and just grabbed her heart, backing up all the way to the corner and I thought the lady was having a heart attack," said Casey from his Louisville office. "You know that's just how people are about Kentucky basketball players. They are actually crazy about them -- believe it or not, as old as I am.

"My name still gets me in a lot of doors. A lot of young people don't remember me but their parents and some of their grandparents (remember). I've been in sales now for about 24 years and people still remember you, which is nice and they may not recognize you right off the bat. But they see your (business) card or you tell them who you are, then it brings back a memory to them or something like that."

* * *

Like most former Wildcats, Casey still follows UK basketball. He attends several Wildcat games at Rupp Arena every year. "I go to a lot of them," Casey said. "I go to most of the good ones. I don't go to the 9:30 (p.m.) games because at 10:30 I'm looking for some place to lay my head. But I go to most of the good games – the Tennessee, Alabama, Florida and LSU games. I don't go to exhibition games or anything like that.

"Of course, it is a pretty tough conference now," he added, referring to the Southeastern Conference. "I remember when we were there it was Tennessee basically and you know you could throw in Florida one year and (then) maybe Alabama. Now it is pretty tough (from top to bottom) – Arkansas and so forth. I think it is the toughest conference in the United States."

* * *

As a youngster growing up on a farm, Casey began following the

Wildcats on the radio, especially the 1957-58 club, which finished with a 23-6 mark. Known as the Fiddlin' Five, Kentucky, which posted a final No. 9 ranking before the post-tourney action, went on to capture the school's fourth NCAA title, beating Temple and Seattle in the Final Four in Louisville.

"I used to listen to Cawood (Ledford) on the radio," Casey said. "We didn't have any TV at all back then. We lived a mile and a half from the main road in Finchville (before the family moved to Simpsonville in 1960). Of course, everybody had radios and I would start listening to Cawood and those teams.

"I really got interested in the '58 team – Vernon Hatton, Johnny Cox, (John) Crigler and that bunch. I used to listen to them and I told my dad one day that I was going to school there if I ever get the opportunity. And I was fortunate enough to do that."

Casey's mother and father had to work on a farm to make a living. His father, Dutch Casey, also held other jobs, including a stint serving as a law enforcement officer. "My father drove a truck also to help supplement the income," Casey said. "We were, I guess you would call, sharecroppers with my grandparents on my mother's side. Then after we moved to Simpsonville we bought our small farm, a 100-acre farm, and had a dairy there that my mom and dad ran there.

"My father was also deputy sheriff for two terms and then got elected jailer (for) one term and then he was only in the office three weeks when he dropped dead of a heart attack."

Casey also added he never had the opportunity to watch the Cats play their home games at Memorial Coliseum.

* * *

As a senior at Shelby County High School, the 6-3 Casey, who had already privately committed to the Wildcats, was considered one of the nation's top basketball players in the prep ranks in the 1965-66 campaign. He and another star, 5-10 senior guard Bill Busey, helped the Rockets win the Sweet Sixteen tournament with a near-perfect 33-1 mark. A clutch shooter who was named Kentucky's "Mr. Basketball" after the season, Casey averaged 28.5 points for coach Bill Harrell's talented squad.

Casey has a favorite memory of his senior season. It happened during the semifinals and finals of the state tournament. Ironically, on the day when he and his Shelby County team were fighting for the state championship, Kentucky's "Rupp's Runts" and Texas Western (now

Texas-El Paso) fought for another championship – the NCAA – at College Park, Maryland.

Recalled Casey, "That morning we played a very good Thomas Jefferson team which had Ron Gathright and Nat Northington. And Nat went on to play football at Kentucky there for a couple of years. Then that evening we played Louisville Male the night Kentucky played Texas Western. Anyhow, that was the first year that both Jefferson County teams were represented in the state tournament and I believe, if my memory serves me correct, we are the only team to beat both Jefferson County teams in a state tournament on the same day. That year I think probably four out of five on each team got (NCAA) Division I scholarships. So we beat two very fine teams – Thomas Jefferson in the morning and Louisville Male that evening." (Thomas Jefferson's Ron Gathright, and Male's Ted Rose and Gene Smith later joined Casey and Busey on the all-star team in the Kentucky-Indiana summer series.)

And, while practicing during halftime of the Sweet Sixteen title contest, Casey managed to take a quick break to catch a glimpse of the Kentucky-Texas Western matchup, which was televised. "We came out at halftime and they had a small screen there at Freedom Hall. There were about 17,000 people and I remember we were warming up. I looked over and I was watching the screen," said Casey. "It was a real small one, not anything like they have today. It was probably maybe a 4 by 10 or something like that -- nothing real fancy. But I remember watching them (Wildcats). It was on the floor and I was warming up for the second half of our game and they were finishing up. (The Wildcats) were getting beat pretty soundly there and about that time they were down 12 or 13 (actually 11) and the clock was ticking away on them there. So I did get to watch part of it warming up at halftime."

* * *

Even though Casey was pretty much set on going to Kentucky, many major schools still recruited the Rocket superstar. Like Rupp, they loved his natural athleticism. He had all the moves, and could shoot and rebound. "I got probably around 300 letters from different colleges," commented Casey. "But I told most of them I was going to Kentucky and (told them) to concentrate on somebody else.

"Louisville made a big push toward me at the very end. (Peck) Hickman was the coach and John Dromo was the assistant coach. My mom had worked at a plant in Simpsonville and a couple of the owners were big U of L alumni. They were putting pressure on my father and myself. They wanted me to come. But I stuck to my guns and coach (Harry) Lancaster called me the last two weeks before I signed (with Kentucky) which made it official."

Tennessee coach Ray Mears, who was one of the more colorful coaches around, also pursued Casey as well as Casey's standout teammate, Bill Busey. Mears and his assistant, Jerry Parker, visited the Shelby County duo. After the meeting, both men from UT came away very disappointed. They struck out. Said Casey, "They flew up (to Kentucky). They had a little private jet that they used. Coach Parker had arranged it and they flew up and talked to us – Busey and myself. But I just told them I was going to the Big Blue and again I was just being honest with them and telling them concentrate on somebody else.

"Mears had Jerry Parker -- one of his former players and captain of his team (Mears' first squad at UT in 1962-63) – who spent a lot of time in Shelby County. He really wanted Busey to come down (to Knoxville) and be the point guard on offense. But he (Busey) had his heart set on going to Kentucky. Bill made up his own mind."

Casey added there was no special deal for him and Busey to attend Kentucky. "There was always a rumor that it was a package deal, but it really wasn't," he said. "You know they (Wildcats) signed Clint Wheeler and Benny Spears from Ashland the same year. But nothing was ever discussed." Wheeler, a 6-7 swingman, and Spears, a 6-2 guard, played for Blazer High where they received all-state honors. (Wheeler's older brother, Bill, lettered at UK in football in the early 1950s.)

* * *

Rupp saw Casey a few times during the youngster's senior year in high school. And the Kentucky coach also spoke at Shelby County's post-season basketball banquet. Casey remembered his first face-to-face meeting with the legend. "The first meeting was when we played Ashland at Shelby County our senior year and there were 13 college coaches from all over the country there that night," Casey said. "They were there for Spears, Wheeler, Busey and myself. And there were a couple of other players whom they were looking for. Jobie Miller (of Shelby County) went on to play at Austin Peay, and (Ron) Ritter (of Shelby County) signed with Austin Peay, but it didn't last very long.

"But that was the first time I got to meet (Rupp) in person. He came down a couple of times after that and went by the coaches' office. You know they called me (from class or practice) and I got to talk to him a little bit there. Then he spoke at our banquet. He was our official speaker and we signed that night with the letter of intent."

That evening actually marked Casey's first public commitment to UK. Before Rupp's appearance at the high school dinner, Casey didn't make a verbal commitment to UK publicly. But everyone had already known where the youngster was going to spend his college days. Unlike today when the prospects can sign early if they wish, Casey didn't have the early signing periods in November to deal with back then. "In the papers it said Mike Casey was headed for the University of Kentucky and you know it was pretty well assumed that I was going there," Casey said. "And then I just made it official that night when he (Rupp) was there."

Earlier, to concentrate on basketball, Casey privately told Rupp and Lancaster that "I was coming and just leave me alone and not to worry about me changing my mind. I was glad I did that because, you know, I think most everybody knew I was going there. That was where I wanted to go and I got that. We didn't announce it. It was off the record and we just wanted to leave it that way. They (the high school) didn't have it set up where you could announce early or anything like that."

* * *

The 1966-67 season was horrible. It marked Rupp's worst season of his Hall of Fame coaching career. His Wildcats, who were coming off a 27-2 campaign, broke even at a 13-13 record with returning standouts Louie Dampier, Pat Riley and Thad Jaracz, a 6-5 center. As a freshman, Casey saw UK's troubles from a very close distance, but he couldn't help the varsity team. Like other rookies at the time, he wasn't allowed to play on the varsity.

"That was a tough period," said Casey, who played on a strong freshman team filled with several prep All-Americans. "Riley got hurt that summer (before) his senior year. His back just caused him all sorts of problems. And to be honest with you, it wasn't a very fun year. They had the (Bob) Tallent incident where he got kicked off the team after the Tennessee game.

"Of course, the freshmen couldn't play with them and we couldn't help out that year. With Riley's injury and we didn't know how much (Larry) Conley and (Tom) Kron meant to the team until after they had already graduated and how they were so stable in holding the team together and the little things they did.

"We practiced with the varsity. We scrimmaged them and we beat them the first two or three times we played them. We kicked their butts pretty good and after that it was dog eat dog, and you could see there was a little jealously there. We had a great freshman year. We were 17-2 (actually 18-2) and it was coach Rupp's worst year at 13-13.

"It was a bad, bad year all the way around for Kentucky standards in basketball. It wasn't a fun year for the varsity and I'm glad I didn't have to play. They worked hard but it was just one of those years where things didn't go right. Everything they tried just didn't seem to work."

Casey's freshman teammates included Busey, Wheeler, Dan Issel (Batavia, Ill.), Mike Pratt (Dayton, Ohio), Terry Mills (Barbourville, Ky.), and Jim Dinwiddie (Leitchfield, Ky.). Casey led the freshman team in scoring, averaging nearly 24 points a game.

* * *

Casey's varsity debut was a blazing success and the Wildcat fans, listening the game on the radio, were very enthusiastic with the sophomore's remarkable first-game performance at Michigan. In the very first game played at the new $7.2 million, 13,684-seat Crisler Arena, Casey gunned in 28 points and grabbed 14 rebounds in UK's 17-point victory. (His 28 points broke a school record held by ex-UK star Cotton Nash since 1961 for most points scored in first varsity game. Nash had 25 against Miami of Ohio. And Casey's record still stands at this writing.)

The Wolverines, meanwhile, were led by future NBA player and coach Rudy Tomjanovich, who had 27 rebounds and 17 points. Many years later, Tomjanovich said in a 1998 interview with the *Michigan Daily*, the student daily newspaper, that he definitely remembered that first game at the new gym, saying, "They blew us out, but that was a great memory of going against Adolph Rupp and those guys."

According to Casey, that game, not surprisingly, turned out to be one of the more satisfying games of his collegiate career. But he also had several other outstanding performances during his sophomore year, including a 31-point outburst against Pete Maravich and his LSU teammates, and a 30-point outing against Mississippi State.

"We were only picked like third or fourth in the conference our sophomore year," Casey said, "because they (the Wildcats) were coming out of that bad year of 13-13. We were young and inexperienced and we started clicking there about halfway during season. We got it all together and won the conference that year and then got upset during that game (in the NCAA tournament)." Casey was referring to that game which took place in the 23-team NCAA tourney where Ohio State stunned Kentucky 82-81 on the Wildcats' home floor in Lexington in the Mideast Regional finals.

Before meeting the Buckeyes, hot-shooting Kentucky – led by Casey's roommate, Dan Issel, who poured in 36 points – had defeated an angry Marquette team 107-89, also in Lexington. Casey added 19 points in the rout. Fuming Marquette coach Al McGuire complained loudly about UK getting an unfair competitive advantage by playing at home. "He threw a fit because we got to wear the home uniforms and he wouldn't stay where the other team stayed and all that," said Casey of the controversy. "But Al was a motivator and he played the trump card that year against us. They were all black and we were all white."

* * *

Three years later, Casey had a conversation with McGuire in Athens, Ga., where Kentucky and Marquette were squaring off in the consolation game of the 1971 NCAA Mideast Regionals. A couple of nights earlier, Western Kentucky, led by 7-foot star Jim McDaniels, had knocked UK out of the Big Dance. "I didn't get to talk to him until my senior year when we were playing down in Athens," he said. "We were playing for third place and I was getting my ankle (treated). I had twisted my ankle and I had it in the whirlpool and he came in. He was sitting on a stool and we got to talk. He really kept things in perspective. That is one thing I liked about him and (ex-Louisville coach) Denny Crum. When the game was over with, it was over with. Just go on and we gonna suit them up for the next game and be ready. You know we, as Kentucky fans, are die-hard. We don't forget (our enemies) too easily, and that is one thing I admire about coach McGuire. When it was over with, it was over with. You know if you wanted to go out and have a drink, I'm sure he was ready to go have a drink.

"He grew up on the rough side of town and I guess he was from New York. He knew all the angles and he worked them, believe or not, because I have heard some tales and some of the things he sent out to players. He'd get brochures from other schools, cut out pictures and say this is our chemistry building or this is our physical education building. But Al was a great coach. He was great for basketball. He was a great announcer. And he will be sorely missed."

In 1977, the maverick McGuire guided his Marquette team to the national title before retiring as a coach. For many years, he served as a colorful TV broadcaster. He died of acute leukemia in 2001 at the age of 72.

* * *

Like his sophomore year when he was named a first-team All-SEC selection, Casey also had another All-SEC season as a junior. He was the team's second-leading scorer with a 19.1-point average, behind All-American Dan Issel's 26.6 points. In a non-conference home game against a formidable North Carolina club, which later finished with a No. 4 ranking, Casey pumped in 26 points in a Kentucky setback. U.S. Olympic standout Charlie Scott, the first black basketball player at North Carolina, paced the Tar Heels with 19 points.

Even with the talented junior trio of Issel, Casey and Mike Pratt, the Wildcats, however, still failed to reach the Final Four. A fired-up Marquette team, ranked No. 14, avenged its NCAA tourney loss to UK in the previous year by stopping Issel and seventh-ranked Kentucky 81-74 in the opening round of the NCAA Mideast Regional. The Warriors' sticky defense limited Issel to 13 points, nearly 14 points below his average. Casey took the game scoring honors, hitting 24 points with a perfect 10 for 10 from the line, before fouling out. Three other Wildcats – Larry Steele, Phil Argento and Pratt -- also fouled out.

So the disappointed Wildcats, especially the junior trio of Issel, Pratt and Casey, had to wait for another try for the Final Four in the following spring of 1970. Would they win a national title before they graduate from UK?

* * *

Summer of 1969.

That was a very unfortunate time for Casey and the Wildcats. The star player had an accident in Shelbyville. He had a car wreck, breaking his leg and crushing UK's high hopes for the national championship in the upcoming season.

"I was going to Lexington that night to play because we had some pick-up games. It was like 6 o'clock or 6:15 in the evening," commented Casey. "We had been cutting hay all day and we did another job, too, at work and I was just going off the exit. The county fair was going on. It used to go on the last week of July every year and I was going off to tell my dad (at the fair) where I was going. He was on duty that night at the fair. And I went off that exit there and my left rear tire blew. It just threw me into this concrete embankment that had a light pole on it. It came right through above my ankle. And I was pinned in there until they cut me out."

Looking back, Casey said the wreck could've been a lot worse. "First of all, I was lucky to be alive even though the only thing I had was a broken leg," he said. "You know you are dealt blows in life and you have to live with them. I had to go three months in a cast – a leg cast all the way up to my hip and then a knee cast. When they cut it off to the knee, I got to work out. I started shooting free throws and lifting weights and stuff like that. You know that was 30 some years ago. But in today's time, you would probably be out a month. They would have you with all kinds of treatments. With medical technology, it is amazing what they do."

So Casey had to sit out a year, forcing Rupp to find a suitable replacement as the 1969-70 Kentucky club aimed for its first national championship since 1958. And the Wildcats survived without Casey, going all the way to the NCAA Mideast Regional finals before losing a 106-100 heartbreaker to Jacksonville in a high-scoring affair. Issel and Pratt took a heavy scoring load for the 26-2 team, averaging a total of 53.2 points a game. Despite the squad's failure to win the national crown, it was one of Rupp's greatest teams ever at UK. Issel has said he believed Kentucky would have captured the NCAA title if Casey hadn't been injured.

Casey said he has often wondered if his presence would have made a difference in UK's run for the championship. "Well, not being disrespectful to the players who took my place that year, I felt like if I could have been healthy, I think we would've made a run at it whether we would have won it or not. I think we would have been there," he said. "Dan (Issel) had his outstanding year. We didn't have any outside scoring. You know Mike (Pratt) was at forward and Dan was the center. And we didn't have anybody to play out front (in the backcourt) even though the guys – Jim Dinwiddie, Kent Hollenbeck and (Bob) McCowan – were outstanding. They (Wildcats) just didn't have anybody (to replace) a 20-point per game scorer. You know it is hard to fill from one year to the next."

* * *

Kentucky, by the way, made history in the summer of 1969 when Rupp finally got his first African-American player on basketball scholarship, signing 7-foot Tom Payne of Louisville. Casey and some of his older teammates, including Issel and Pratt, had a part in getting the Shawnee High School product to UK. They helped Rupp recruit Payne.

"We were recruiting them anyway whether they were black or white," said Casey. "Since we were juniors that year, he (Rupp) would usually put some of the older players or the starters with them (high school stars) when they would come to town."

Payne, by the way, was not the only black star UK had recruited in the late 1960s. "We tried to recruit (Jim) McDaniels, Jim Rose, (Clarence) Glover, and (Jerome) Perry," Casey said. "Those guys had all signed (with other schools)." McDaniels, Rose, Glover and Perry all went to Western Kentucky, which surprisingly knocked out Kentucky from the 1971 NCAA tourney championship picture by a score of 107-83.

Casey initially thought Payne made a wise move to attend UK because of his strong family background. "His daddy was a captain in the Army," he recalled. "His dad was very strict on him. So he kept his thumbs on Tom."

But the elder Payne died several months into his son's freshman year. Without his father's guidance, Payne -- who wasn't eligible to play on the freshman team because of academics – slowly began to lose direction in life. He had no one to tell him what to do. And the younger Payne was married. "He had a lovely wife and a little baby girl," Casey added.

Payne became eligible as a sophomore and played for the Wildcats, replacing popular Issel at center. He had very tough shoes to fill and Casey, who was a senior at the time, saw a lot of racial abuse. For Payne, that made things more difficult, especially when the Wildcats traveled on the road in the South, facing other SEC schools.

"I look back a lot of times at some of the torment he had to go through – the name-calling and I remember this just like it was yesterday," Casey said. "Down at Ole Miss they had an old theater, upstairs and downstairs. (After) we all ate together and practiced, we went to a movie. We went upstairs in the balcony. Now this was 1970-71 (season) and you don't think that is that far back. But they came up there and told (Payne), 'You are not allowed up here.' So we all left. We said we were all one on the team."

Understandably, Payne had trouble controlling his emotions at games filled with verbal assaults. "Tom let it get to him and these people were mean to him," Casey said. "I mean the "N" word was used. Tom wanted to retaliate and I can see that. If I had been in his shoes, I would've (done the same) myself. They were cruel to him everywhere he went. Not only in one or two places, but just about every place that we went. And that was just part of the South.

"So it was a tough situation for Tom. Tom had a tough time adjusting to it and rightly so. Probably Tom was not ready for Kentucky."

Pratt, who signed a pro contract with the Kentucky Colonels in 1970 after his senior season, said he never had a chance to see Payne play on the varsity. But he added, "I know Casey reached out for him and did a lot. Hollenbeck did a lot. Casey and Hollenbeck were together that year and I heard their stories. Casey and I got close and we talked a lot."

In a 2001 interview with Louisville *Courier-Journal* held at the Green River Correctional Complex in Central City, Ky., where Payne was held for rape convictions, the ex-Wildcat spoke out and told reporter Brian Bennett that his past crimes and problems were the result of racial abuse during his college days. "I read the article," Pratt said. "I'm very sorry that Tom feels that way."

The author of this book also had an interview with Payne arranged. However, through his prison spokesman Ron Beck, Payne backed out of his commitment just a few days before the scheduled book interview in prison. No reason was given, but it was speculated that he didn't like the Louisville newspaper article and didn't feel like doing any more interviews.

* * *

While many articles and books unfairly have painted Rupp as a racist, Casey has another viewpoint. He also discussed the Baron's treatment of Payne. "You know the part about coach Rupp being a racist – I never heard him put down the black players," he said. "I remember someone made a comment in the paper the other day, (saying) we didn't want to go to Kentucky because coach Rupp was a racist. Coach Rupp was already gone when the player signed to play with U of L and it is just how things carry on.

"They didn't say anything about us when we were at Shelby County and we played (against predominately black teams). Thomas Jefferson was all black and Male was all black. They didn't bring that out and we were all white. We had a couple of blacks on the jayvee team, but nobody ever brought that out.

"Coach Rupp did everything he could to help that young man (Payne). I mean he got every break in the book. (In the 1971-72) there were a couple of other (black) players -- Darryl Bishop and Elmore

Stephens." Football players Bishop and Stephens joined Rupp and the Wildcats as walk-ons after the season had already begun.

Casey believed that had Payne remained at Kentucky for his junior and senior years, instead of leaving early to sign a lucrative contract with the NBA's Atlanta Hawks, things might've been much smoother for him. "If he had stayed his last two years, he would have been an All-American because he really worked at it. He really did."

After the 1970-71 season, both Casey, who had lost a step or two after that automobile wreck, and Payne received All-SEC honors as the Cats finished with a 22-6 mark. Their Kentucky teammates Larry Steele and Tom Parker also earned All-SEC accolades.

As SEC sports history will show, Perry Wallace became the conference's first black basketball player with a scholarship in 1966. Casey remembered competing against Wallace, a 6-5 forward, when their teams clashed. Casey said Wallace, who earned All-SEC honors his senior year, "withstood (racial bias) and you know Perry was very intelligent. You don't get into Vanderbilt unless you are very intelligent." After getting his bachelor's degree in engineering at Vanderbilt, Wallace continued to focus on academics. With a law degree from Columbia University in 1975, Wallace is a professor of law at American University in Washington, D.C., specializing in environmental law, corporate law and finance.

* * *

Like many of Rupp's former players, Casey sometimes did things that the Baron, a stern disciplinarian, didn't like, such as breaking the team rules. The legendary mentor would get mad and ornery. One form of punishment involved Rupp's taking the prized tickets away from his players, who were allowed four tickets for each game. "I was in his doghouse several times," said Casey. "When you mess up, you pay the fiddler and I paid. I got mine taken away a couple of times. Of course, back then, the tickets (were scarce.) If you got a ticket to a basketball game at Kentucky, you were on top of the world and coach Rupp knew that. So if you got out of line or you misbehaved, coach Rupp would pull those tickets real quick.

"I did break curfew and got caught a couple of times. Coach Rupp had his ways of finding out. In Lexington you couldn't go anywhere without somebody recognizing you. If he caught you, then you paid the fiddler."

And Rupp had help. He had someone to keep close tabs on his players. A trainer and academic advisor for the team, Claude Vaughan, served as one of coach Rupp's closest confidants. Vaughan, who also taught economics at the university, was a sort of watchdog for Rupp. Casey once got himself in hot water with the trainer.

"I got in trouble with him my junior year," recalled Casey, who majored in physical education with a minor in geography. "I broke curfew one night and he was in my bed. I sort of nudged him out a little bit and I paid for it the next day. After we got through practicing (the next day), coach Rupp and I were in his office. So I paid for it dearly for the next six weeks. You don't understand when you are 20 years old why somebody is out checking on you six weeks before the season. But you know Claude was doing his job.

"He was very outspoken. He knew he had a job to do and he was gonna to do it. Coach Rupp expected him to do it and he wouldn't let coach Rupp down. He was very fond of and close to coach Rupp. A lot of players didn't like him. I would say that I was one of the ones who were on his good side and got to know him real well.

"I remember sometimes I would skip class and before I would get back to (Memorial) Coliseum to practice he already knew about it and that just blew my mind. I didn't know that the professors were keeping tabs on us. Claude had a job to do and that was to keep us eligible and make sure that we go to class. He helped to keep a lot of us eligible."

In 1971, Casey was selected to the Academic All-American team. And he managed to complete his bachelor's degree requirements in five years, including his redshirted season of 1969-70. "In my last year, I only had to do 12 hours each semester and (I did) my student teaching," he commented before adding, "My hat goes off to youngsters who can get it done in four years and still maintain a good career."

Casey said he never got to use his degree since he didn't coach or teach.

* * *

A Rupp story.

"My favorite story about coach Rupp? There are a lot of them. Some of them you can print and some of them you can't," Casey said. "I guess one of the funniest (stories) was after we got beat by Florida our junior year down there (in Gainesville) and we got put to bed that night at 6:00 without any supper. We always played Florida and Georgia on the same trip – Saturday and Monday. And I remember we were all starved. But we got beat and coach Rupp was upset with us. He just didn't give us anything to eat that night. We got up Sunday morning and went to Athens. We played them (Georgia) on Monday night. Buddy, we took it out on them and we never wanted to go to bed hungry again."

For the record, after losing to the Gators, led by All-American center Neal Walk, by one point, the Cats bounced back to defeat Georgia 85-77.

* * *

While at Kentucky, Casey got to know several teammates who went on to become a national success. He has a story about Riley, who later became the head coach of several NBA championship teams. Called by Rupp "one of the most complete athletes I ever coached," Riley was three years ahead of Casey.

"I remember him being an All-American and he and Louie (Dampier) roomed together," Casey said. "Everything Riley did, he was very immaculate about it. We would go over to see him or go by there and he would make us take our shoes off. He had a towel there by the door where you put your shoes. He was an immaculate person, like he is today. I guess he is probably the best-dressed coach in America. And he has been very successful."

And Casey had several roommates at Kentucky. "Most of those guys got married on me," he laughed. According to Casey, his roommates included Mike Pratt (freshman year), Dan Issel (sophomore and junior years), Larry Steele (redshirted year) and Kent Hollenbeck (senior). "I stayed single all the way until I got out of college," he smiled.

On Issel, who became the UK men's career leading scorer with 2,138 points, Casey said, "I guess one of the funniest things about him is that if Dan didn't get the ball, he had a tendency to pout a little bit and you could tell. Adolph (Rupp) could pick up on it. Dan always had a tendency to just stand around if he wasn't getting the ball. And Coach Rupp called timeout and I never will forget this. He said I want to introduce you all to somebody. He said, 'This is our center Dan Issel and we need to get the ball to him a bit more.' So I think the next seven or eight times down the floor, we got the ball to him and finally he said, 'Boys, that's enough, that's enough!' Issel wanted to get his shots like we all did at that time."

Before the 6-8 Issel finished strong as the team's second-leading scorer (16.4 points) during his sophomore year, he had a major health problem to deal with. "Dan had a tumor taken off the roof of his mouth the size of a half a dollar and that slowed him down and that is why he took awhile (before he blossomed as a star)," Casey said. "He got off to a rocky start with that operation. If you look at the statistics the last half of his sophomore year, Dan started coming into his own there."

* * *

In the 1970 ABA draft, the Kentucky Colonels selected three Wildcats – Issel, Pratt and Casey. While Issel and Pratt signed fat contracts with the Louisville-based Colonels, Casey chose to finish up his career at UK. Casey was eligible for the draft because he was a member of the graduating class (fourth year in college). Also, he was picked by Chicago in the eighth round of the NBA draft. The Colonels, by the way, picked Vandy's Perry Wallace in the draft as well.

But in the following season, Casey had to try out for a spot on the Colonels roster even though he was a big-name Wildcat star. The ABA club also had another high-profile rookie -- All-American Artis Gilmore from Jacksonsville – along with other first-year players. But unlike Casey, Gilmore had a no-cut contract reportedly worth $2.4 million (It has been reported that Gilmore's total compensation package, however, was much less than $2.4 million). According to Casey, he signed a one-year contract for $125,000 but it was not guaranteed. He would have to make the team and it wouldn't be a cakewalk as Kentucky was already loaded with outside shooters – Louie Dampier, Darel Carrier and Issel. New Colonels' floor boss Joe Mullaney, who had been the head coach of the NBA's Los Angeles Lakers for a couple of seasons, also was looking for someone with quick hands and feet to play defense.

"I went through six weeks of summer camp – Artis Gilmore and myself," Casey said. "As a matter of fact, I averaged 27 points a game during that time. We played about 12 games -- we played Carolina, Indiana and Virginia. Gilmore was the only one that had a no-cut contract, which I understood. But I never will forget that night he (Mullaney) had to go in and make the final cut (in eliminating Casey from the squad). We had beaten Indiana with (star rookie) George McGinnis and his bunch."

In the September 18 exhibition rookie game between the Colonels and the Pacers, Kentucky's first-year players overwhelmed Indiana by a score of 127-95 in front of a good crowd of over 6,000 at Freedom Hall. For the Colonels, Casey poured in 14 points and grabbed nine rebounds. But Casey's performance wasn't good enough as Mullaney chose to keep other rookies – Mike Gale and Pierre Russell – on the roster in addition to Gilmore.

So Casey's pro hopes were dashed. That meant he wouldn't play with his college teammates in the ABA. He was very downhearted. He had thought his chances with the Colonels were good. "That was one of the hardest things I had to endure because everybody thought (I would make it) after 27 points and we were undefeated (in the summer camp)," Casey said. "I remember I had to walk out and tell my mom and dad that I got cut. Nobody could believe it. It all boiled down to one (factor or two). I had $125,000-a-year contract and Mike Gale had a $17,500 (pact), which was the minimum at that time. And Mike Gale was a real good defensive specialist. They had Dampier, Carrier and Issel, and Gilmore was a rookie that year. So they had enough scorers.

"But it was hard. (I was cut) even though we had about 400 season tickets sold in Shelby County because one of the guys who helped represent me had 400 signed up. That was part of his deal to get so many people – season ticket holders. But it got down to just basic business, dollars and cents. You know it was disappointing. It was a business decision, but it is cold how they do it. That's, you know, part of life and you have to go on."

* * *

One year later, in 1972, Casey went to Memphis in hopes of playing pro basketball. He wanted another chance. Casey was going to the struggling Memphis franchise, which had undergone major changes with new ownership and management, and he agreed to a one-year contract for $17,500 if he made the squad.

Interestingly, the new owner was none other than controversial Charles O. Finley, who controlled the 1972 world champion Oakland A's. And the owner himself wanted someone with a big name in the front office. So he hired Adolph Rupp to be the team's new president. Finley also wanted Memphis to have new colors and a new nickname, changing from the Pros to Tams. The green-and-gold Tams represented the tri-state area of Tennessee, Arkansas and Mississippi.

"I had been to Mexico and playing down there for about a month and then got a call from coach Rupp, asking that I come and try out for them," explained Casey of his Memphis stint. "Johnny Neumann (All-American from Ole Miss) was there and I stayed around for about a month there, but got cut." Memphis newly-hired coach Bob Bass, who later became the front office executive for the San Antonio Spurs and the New Orleans

Hornets, said cutting Casey from the roster was a very difficult move for him as the former Wildcat nearly became the team's 12th player.

On the team's sparkling new uniforms, Casey said, "I remember they gave us all a green-and-gold 'Tams' to wear. It had the 'Tams' on it. It was cute."

While in Memphis, Casey didn't see much of Rupp, who traded stories and discussed basketball with Bass. "He was down there to make a personal appearance or something and he would stay a day or two and then leave," commented Casey. "We were practicing twice a day so he didn't stay around too long. They used him more as a consultant. I enjoyed my stay in Memphis. We stayed right in downtown at Howard Johnson's and we would walk over to the old (arena). It was quite an experience." The ex-Wildcat also added that he never had a conversation with Finley.

After two unsuccessful attempts in pro basketball, Casey decided that was enough. "I never did go to the NBA because I thought my chances were better in Louisville being in proximity to the Colonels and Shelby County and all that," said Casey, who also conducted summer basketball camps with Issel, Pratt and Rupp in the early 1970s. "But as I look back now, I got drafted by the Bulls and the Cleveland Cavaliers (in 1971), and I probably should have followed those (players) who had gone up there (in the NBA) and tried out."

* * *

Not long after he graduated from UK, Casey once considered a job offer to be the head coach at Shelby County, his high school.

"At one time I almost became a high school coach, but that was it," he said. "They offered me a head coaching job there. As you look back now, teaching and coaching was $7,300. And that was probably big money back then. Now it's $25,000 to $35,000 starting out. That is as close as I came to being a high school coach there. But the timing wasn't right and I didn't want to do it. You know if your heart is not right in something, you had better not do it."

* * *

A divorced father with one grown daughter, Laura, who is a UK graduate, Casey is appreciative of his valuable experience as a Wildcat performer and a college student at Kentucky.

"It is something that I will never forget," he said. "I got to play probably for the greatest coach of all times. He was the winningest coach. We played in (the school's) 1,000th win. We had cakes out in my junior year. Every time we would turn around we had a cake celebrating something." Rupp also notched the 800th Wildcat victory of his coaching career that season.

"It was a great experience," he continued. "If I had to do it over again, I would do the same thing."

With one exception, though. Casey said he would've "probably changed my major and gone into business. I've been in business ever since I got out. But I have no regrets. Life has been good to me. I get dealt some setbacks from time to time, but you just have to pick yourself up and go on. You can't get knocked down. I wouldn't trade it for anything in the world."

Chapter 3

Wildcat from Buckeye Country

Historical images from March of 1970.

Coming off their amazing World Series championship performance in 1969, the New York Mets prepared for a new campaign in spring training...

On weeknights, long before the days of cable TV and the Internet, Americans made a habit of listening and watching folksy Walter Cronkite report the evening news....

Richard Nixon ran the country from the White House, while Leonid Brezhnev was leading the Soviet Union...

The American soldiers fought against the Communist troops in the Vietnam War, while many college students, including Bill Clinton (who was studying overseas at Oxford University) and Hillary Rodham, protested the war.....

Shirley Chisholm, the first black woman elected to the U.S. Congress, worked on the Capitol Hill, speaking out for women's rights, civil rights and the poor.

A rare Republican governor in Kentucky, Louie B. Nunn held the state's top post...

Fast-food establishments, like McDonald's, began to populate the nearly-completed Interstate Highway system throughout the nation.....

While the 26-2 Wildcats, who finished the regular season as the nation's No. 1 team, failed to win the NCAA tourney after dropping to Jacksonsville 106-100 in the regional finals, coach John Wooden's UCLA squad captured another national title with star Sidney Wicks...

The NBA's rival, the three-year-old American Basketball Association, went to war, signing collegiate stars to lucrative contracts with UK's Mike Pratt and teammate Dan Issel joining the Kentucky Colonels.

Photo Courtesy of Charlotte 49ers Sports Information Department

Ex-UK star Mike Pratt is shown here during his head coaching days at North Carolina-Charlotte (now Charlotte) during the late 1970s and early 1980s, giving directions during a game.

* * *

Many years later, in 2001 to be exact, when Pratt was asked about the Colonels' big announcement that he and Issel had signed fat contracts, he said he actually didn't get a $400,000 contract that was reported by the media, including Louisville's *Courier-Journal* which ran a big front-page article. The Colonels also announced Issel got an estimated $1.4 million.

"First of all, none of the dollar figures that were in the newspapers in those days about the two leagues' (bidding war) were correct dollar figures," Pratt told the author in an exclusive interview held in Louisville. "In talking with everybody involved at that time all those numbers were inflated and that was part of the hype – the battle between the two leagues. The money wasn't there then. Only a few guys made $100,000 and they were the guys who were already playing. So, none of those numbers were real numbers."

Issel agreed, saying the Colonels and the ABA exaggerated his contract figures for public relations purposes. "They played it up," commented Issel in an interview in the late 1990s. "It wouldn't be as big as they said it was. Of course, that was right when the ABA was getting competitive with the NBA and going after (top) players. They said the five-year deal was for $1.4 million, but there were a lot of investments that had to work out and things like that. My actual salary was $75,000 a year. I loved the fact that I got to stay in Kentucky and play professional basketball. So that was kind of a dream come true going right up the road and playing in Louisville."

Interestingly, when the duo of Pratt and Issel, along with their agent, had reached the final agreement with the Colonels, they were vacationing on a spring break in Florida, just days after their disappointing season-ending loss to Jacksonville. Pratt said the Colonels were practically the only pro team that he and Issel had negotiated with. The Colonels' franchise was operated by five new owners – Stuart Jay, Wendell Cherry, David Grissom, David Jones and future governor John Y. Brown Jr. – who had recently purchased the team.

With the verbal deal with the ABA franchise nearly finalized, Pratt said the Colonels "put us in John Y. Brown's jet, the fried chicken jet, and took us to Florida (on spring break) and paid for everything – my wife, myself, my daughter, Dan and his wife. We were in Florida, and (we) got back and forth on the phone (during contractual talks) and agreed to it. Then they brought us back (to Louisville) on Eastern Airlines first class, picked us up and took us to the hotel. A couple of hours later, we had a press conference and announced the signing.

"They kind of hid us out (in Florida) from the NBA people before we signed the contracts. My dad (Pete) got a couple of calls from agents that represented NBA people wanting to know where we were and wanted to talk to us. My dad was told not to tell anybody where we were and he didn't know where we were, but my mom knew where we were. But they were told not to tell anybody. So, basically the deal was cut and dried."

According to Pratt, a 6-4 forward who was a three-time All-SEC selection, Armand "Mondo" Angelucci did a lot of contract negotiating with the Colonels, representing the former Wildcats. "He was a friend of coach Rupp," said Pratt. "He represented both Dan and I. He got us down to Louisville to talk to the owners of the Colonels. Mondo cut the deal with them and never let us talk to any of the NBA people and it was a done deal. He really wasn't an agent. He represented us as an attorney and obviously he was very good."

The first Monday after the signing Pratt had to go back to Lexington and do some student teaching. His anxious students obviously knew about Pratt's new status as a pro player, asking him about his big contract.

"I just told everybody, 'Don't believe everything you read in the paper,' " recalled Pratt, who grew up in Dayton, Ohio. "Having grown up as a blue-collar middle American back then, money was never (a big influence). We never had a lot. (But the pact) certainly gave me a good start on life."

* * *

At Meadowdale High School in Dayton in the mid-1960s, Pratt was a good athlete. Not only was he a basketball star, he excelled in football and baseball, earning All-City honors.

But Pratt's basketball skills, with his strong physical build, attracted many college coaches, including UK assistant Joe B. Hall. The Dayton product was a tough competitor, averaging 16 rebounds and 25 points during his senior year. With his deceptive moves, he was quicker than he looked. Only twice in the last three years of his high school career was Pratt held under double figures.

To beat out the local college recruiters in Ohio, especially Cincinnati assistant coach Lee Rose and Dayton head coach Don Donoher, Hall had to travel to Dayton many times to see the youngster in action. He wanted Pratt to understand that Kentucky still wanted him. Hall really liked what he saw in the muscular forward.

"Joe recruited me," said Pratt. "He told me that he used to drive from Lexington to Dayton to see me play. Then he would go from Dayton to Chicago, and watch George Janky and Dan Issel and then come back through and make (another) stop. That was his swing and Joe saw me play all the time. Joe was always around."

And Hall's never-ending recruiting efforts paid off as the Dayton youngster signed with the Wildcats, joining a big group of future Cats such as Travis Butler (considered by some the No. 1 prospect in Alabama), Mike Casey, Jim Dinwiddie, Mort Fraley, Issel, Terry Mills, Randy Pool (Tennessee's top prospect), Benny Spears and Clint Wheeler.

Rupp valued and trusted Hall's judgment on high school players so much that the "Man in the Brown Suit" sometimes didn't even see or visit some prospects, especially the ones from out of state, in the latter part of his coaching career.

"Joe recruited me all the time," Pratt said. "Coach Rupp would call from time to time, but he never saw me play. Issel told me, 'Coach Rupp never saw me play, either.' You know he had a chance to see Mike Casey play because he was right there (in Shelby County)."

Pratt said telling other recruiters from Dayton and Cincinnati – his other top choices -- that he wasn't coming to their school was extremely difficult.

"I was born and raised to play for the University of Dayton and had friends who played there," he explained. "I grew up wanting to play for the Dayton Flyers. Probably one of the most difficult things I had to do was to tell Don Donoher that I wasn't going to Dayton and to tell Lee Rose that I wasn't going to Cincinnati.

"I got a ton of letters, and I visited a few of the schools, but I wasn't going to where my parents couldn't get in their car and drive and see me play."

So the Lexington location made Pratt's decision to sign with the Cats easier. UK was within driving distance of Dayton – a three-hour drive. Along with Hall's active recruitment, it helped that Kentucky also had a memorable year of the now-famous Rupp's Runts in 1966. He saw them play several times in Lexington.

"I wasn't going to go too far (away from home)," said Pratt, who had no previous connections to UK whatsoever. "I wanted my family to see me play. They wanted to see me play.

"I got interested in Kentucky because they got so much publicity and I liked the way they played. I loved their passing and the cohesiveness of the team. I thought with Casey and Issel and the other guys who were signed that year, and with what Kentucky already had, that we would have a chance to make a run at the national championship. I wanted to do that since we never won a state championship (in high school)."

* * *

It wasn't too long before Pratt, who also has a younger brother, got to face his favorite childhood team, the Dayton Flyers, who had a date with the Wildcats in the annual University of Kentucky Invitational Tournament during the 1967-68 campaign. A still-tough Dayton squad was coming off a remarkable performance the year before, finishing as the NCAA tournament runner-up. And Pratt, then a sophomore who had been hospitalized with the flu, surprisingly found himself emotionally charged when he saw the Flyers warm up on the Memorial Coliseum floor. Ironically, Pratt would earn his first varsity start as a Wildcat against his hometown university.

"It was a good game," said Pratt, who gunned in 15 points and grabbed game-high 15 rebounds in UK's 88-85 win. "We played against (All-American) Don May, Bobby Joe Hooper and all the guys that I had either played against in high school or played against in the summers. It was a big game and it was not a game we wanted to lose. It meant more than just a December game. The year before, Dayton had been to the NCAA championship game (losing to UCLA in Louisville). That year (1967-68), they would end up winning the NIT, which was a very prestigious tournament because only 24 (actually 23) teams went to the NCAA. So the NIT was very, very prestigious. So we are talking about some really good teams.

"It was a game I didn't want to lose and have to go home the next summer (and face the guys who would tease him). I wanted to win this game. Playing well was icing on the cake. It was a big win for me and for us."

Pratt's teammate, Casey, added 27 points to pace the Wildcats. Kentucky went on to win the UKIT the next night, beating coach Frank McGuire's South Carolina squad 76-66.

* * *

In the following year of 1968-69, the Wildcats met two individuals from a respected Army team who someday would become big celebrities – a young coach by the name of Bob Knight and his player named Mike

Krzyzewski. Coming off a 20-5 NIT season in the previous season, Army was UK's opponent in the UKIT championship game. And Kentucky managed to overcome Knight's "slow-down" tactics and win 80-65.

Many years later, in the early 1980s, both Pratt and Krzyzewski, now the head coach at Duke, would run into each other at various functions, usually in North Carolina, and talk about "the old times." Pratt, who was coaching at North Carolina-Charlotte at the time, would tease him about that game in Lexington. They both remembered the contest like it was yesterday. Coach K had six points in the losing effort.

"I used to laugh about it and he used to laugh about the game," Pratt said. "He was a guard and he was not the star guard. Doug Clevenger was probably their leading scorer, but Krzyzewski was just a solid, tough guy who played the point and Mike's team was solid and tough. They beat a lot of people and did well very in the NIT that year (reaching that post-season tourney for the third time in four years).

"I remember coach Rupp talking about this tough (Army) team, (saying) 'This is a very well-coached team and you guys are going to have to play to beat this team.' Coach Rupp was really thorough in his scouting reports. We had 30 or 35 pages of scouting reports. (It had) anything you wanted to know. We went over and over, and we were charged with keeping the scouting report and bringing it back to the game and turning it in. He (Rupp) was way ahead of his time in this part of the game because he had these big thick scouting reports. He respected not only the young coach Bobby Knight, but he also thought they were a tough, hard-nosed team.

"(Krzyzewski) said it was a real thrill to play in Lexington at Memorial Coliseum. Of course, Army didn't have that kind of crowd. That was a big game for them and a big tournament at that time. (The UKIT was) probably the premier holiday tournament maybe outside of New York City. It was not a cupcake tournament by any stretch. Coach Rupp got the best teams he could get. So we had to buckle up and play to win that tournament."

* * *

At UK, Pratt had a lot of good games. But there is one game that stands out that he's probably best remembered for. It took place during his senior year. His 42-point outburst against 11th-ranked Notre Dame at Louisville's Freedom Hall in December of 1969 ranks among the school's best individual performances in history. While Pratt scored the most points in the contest, there were a couple of other standouts – both All-Americans -- in the offensive showdown witnessed by a crowd of over 17,000. In top-ranked Kentucky's 102-100 victory, Issel poured in 35 points (along with 16 rebounds), while Austin Carr gunned in 43 points. And Pratt's parents, who practically attended every home game during his Wildcat career, got to see their son's stunning MVP performance against the Fighting Irish, who were coached by Johnny Dee.

"It was a very satisfying game," Pratt recalled. "It was a full house and you couldn't get a ticket. It was a real big ball game. You know I did score a lot of points and got quite a few rebounds. It really was a thrill because you only got to play in Louisville once (a year) and they were so good and they had so many players who went on to play professionally. It is something I will always remember because a lot of people remember it and they bring it up to me."

Pratt has fond memories of the old Freedom Hall. He really liked the Louisville arena before it was refurbished in the mid-1980s. "I still remember it as one of the prettier places that we played," he said. "It was dimly lit and just had that excitement, that atmosphere to play in. They allowed people to smoke in Freedom Hall and it all drifted out into the middle over the top of the basket. You may have seen it before in Madison Square Garden (in the old days) that the smoke came upstairs and the lights were real dim. The lights weren't bright like they are now. It was a bigger version of Memorial Coliseum."

* * *

During his UK career, which includes three SEC regular season championships with a three-year overall record of 71-12, Pratt got to see a lot of Rupp. He has many memories of Rupp. He remembers one Rupp episode in Tuscaloosa, Ala., in 1970 when the Cats traveled to play the Crimson Tide in a new arena (now called the Coliseum) and won 98-89 behind Issel's 47 points.

"We were playing in Alabama on a Monday night my senior year. We had practice on Sunday and we went to Alabama's new facility. It is the same they are in now," Pratt said. "We had a short practice and then we ended our practice by coming together and coach Rupp would say a few things. So I remember standing there and looking out the corner of my eye and I see this fellow over in the end zone in the corner of the gym. He's got a houndstooth hat that I knew of in Alabama. I kept watching him and coach Rupp is talking."

While motioning the Alabama man to come on over to where he was standing on the hardwood floor, the Baron then introduced the fellow to the team.

"Boys, I want you to meet a good friend of mine, the best college football coach in the country, Paul 'Bear' Bryant," said Rupp.

Bryant went through the team huddle and said, "How're you doing, guys? You guys are a great team. You are No. 1 in the country. You know you have a good game tomorrow night."

After exchanging pleasantries, Rupp said, "Thank you."

And Rupp then ordered assistant Joe B. Hall, standing nearby, and the team, "Let's shoot foul shots." So the players split up to shoot free throws, and Pratt watched the legendary duo walk off the floor, leaving the coliseum.

"Do you know where they were going? They were going to Bear Bryant's house to have dinner," Pratt said.

Pratt added that he had heard they were not friends. Bryant once coached football at Kentucky in the late 1940s and early 1950s, compiling an eight-year mark of 60-23-5 with four bowl appearances. "I always heard that they didn't get along," he said. "Maybe they didn't when they were at Kentucky. But I'll never forget that (moment)."

According to a 1996 book, *Coach: The Life of Paul 'Bear' Bryant*, by Keith Dunnavant, Bryant once sent his private airplane to Lexington in the mid-1970s to bring cancer-stricken Rupp to Tuscaloosa for a basketball game. The Baron was treated like royalty, according to the book.

* * *

Less than a month later, Pratt got to see another football legend. That brief encounter occurred in the somber dressing room, just moments after Jacksonville, with towering 7-2 Artis Gilmore and 7-0 Pembrook Burrows, had upset Kentucky in the NCAA Mideast Regional finals in Columbus, Ohio, the heart of Buckeye Country. One of the four Wildcat players who fouled out, Pratt had just finished his collegiate career on a sad note, scoring 14 points on poor 4 of 13 field goal shooting (in addition to 13 rebounds).

"I'm sitting on a bench and right next to me was coach Rupp," recalled Pratt. "Coach was not saying anything after the game, just sitting there. In walks Woody Hayes and sits down next to coach Rupp, and says a few words. (Then he) comes over to me and says, 'Tough game.' You know there is Woody Hayes in a short-sleeved white shirt and dark tie with the Ohio State baseball cap, just like I pictured him when I was a kid. He was coaching there (at OSU) then in 1970. But he came in to say something to coach Rupp. Then he came around and said a few words to me. Then (he went) out the door.

"Things like that I remember because it was so much fun playing for coach Rupp. It meant so much to play for a legend because now when you talk about it, people always want to know about coach Rupp because he is a legend. So I had the opportunity to play for a legend in the coaching world and then to have a chance to get up close and personal to two football legends because they came to see my coach. That was quite a thrill.

"I could spend two days telling Adolph Rupp stories that I personally know and the ones that former players have told. Some of them are very funny and some are maybe not so funny."

After the setback to Jacksonville, Rupp and his players were hurt, stunned, speechless and crying. As the nation's top-ranked team, the talented Wildcats had been expected to advance to the Final Four. Rupp believed his team had an excellent chance to win the Big Dance with perennial national champion UCLA lacking big men like Lew Alcindor (now Kareem Abdul-Jabbar). Some observers have labeled the 1969-70 Wildcats as Rupp's best team that never won a national title.

"I think that Jacksonville loss really hurt him because he thought that even without (injured Mike) Casey we had a pretty darn good team," Pratt said of Rupp. "(UCLA was) more size-wise like we were. They were a little bigger than we were. We were not a big team when I was at Kentucky. I was 6-foot-3 and played forward. Larry Steele, at 6-4, played forward and (Dan) Issel was 6-8, but we could run and shoot. The other thing was that we could pass. That made our team a lot like Rupp's Runts because we could move, catch, shoot and pass and we did very good. We shared the ball very well.

"Losing to Jacksonville was definitely a heartbreaker and foul troubles are always part of the game. The sophomore class was led by (Kent) Hollenbeck, (Stan) Key, (Mark) Soderberg and (Tom) Parker. Those guys really almost pulled the game out after Steele, Issel and I (along with Terry Mills) all fouled out. These guys did a special job and almost won the game. We went home after the game in a snowstorm and it was a very difficult time. It was heartbreaking for all of us. Even as good as Jacksonville was, we still thought we could beat them."

After surprising Kentucky, Jacksonville defeated St. Bonaventure, which played without the services of injured star Bob Lanier, 91-83 in the national semifinals.

But Jacksonville's height didn't scare UCLA as the Bruins, sparked by Final Four MVP Sidney Wicks, overcame their slow start to win the national crown 80-69.

* * *

While Pratt said he never broke the curfew, he managed to get himself in trouble with Rupp several times. It was mainly because of poor basketball.

"I was in his doghouse probably because of performance quite a few times, but the (good) thing about coach Rupp you always had a chance to get out of his doghouse by performing," he said. "A couple of times academically I got lazy and he had to get on me. Everybody could get in coach Rupp's doghouse, but you could get out it. The way you got out was to correct your problem. But if you kept making the problem, you would get in big trouble.

"He didn't play his bench a whole lot. If there was one thing about his game I could say during my three (varsity) years, we had some pretty good players on the bench. Later on in my life as a coach, I looked at that (bench) and I said, 'Man, I might have played those guys a little bit more than coach Rupp did.' But he believed in five or six guys and once you got his trust, you were there. (If) you had a bad game, he would say something to you. He would make sure you knew you had a bad game, but you never broke that trust. You went back (in) and got the playing time. You got all the playing time you wanted."

And when Pratt married his hometown sweetheart after his freshman year, Rupp, not surprisingly, wasn't all that pleased. Pratt's father even came to Lexington to discuss the potential sticky situation with Rupp. Even though the Wildcats had married players on the varsity team, they still weren't sure about Rupp's reaction.

In the meeting, Rupp commented that he couldn't do any more to help Pratt other than his scholarship, but the elder Pratt said that was no problem. "He's got a summer job. I can help him and everything will be okay," the father told Rupp.

"Fine. We'll see how it works out," said the Baron.

Said Pratt, who had a baby daughter while in college, "Gary Gamble and Steve Clevenger were married and they played. They were on the varsity and I was a freshman at that time."

Pratt, who also has a son, has since remarried in the late 1990s.

* * *

While he played in the ABA's wild life for only two years, helping the Colonels post a league-best 68-16 mark in 1971-72, Pratt still has some thoughts and entertaining stories about the pro league.

"It was quite a league," said Pratt, who compiled an ABA career average of 5.6 points in 143 games. "The ABA was a very talented league. What we didn't have then, compared to NBA, was television (coverage). Having played forward in college, I had to move to the guard spot. We had some talented guards, quick guys who were smaller than me. They were really good. It was not a power (league). It was a quickness league. The NBA was a power league. They had power centers. We didn't have that many centers in the ABA."

Some of the league's standout guards included Mack Calvin, Freddie Lewis, Steve Jones, Louie Dampier, Merv Jackson, Don Freeman, Charlie Scott, Glen Combs, John Roche, Johnny Neumann, Darel Carrier, Larry Cannon and Rick Mount.

On one particular weekend during his rookie season of 1970-71, Pratt remembered an unusual game, which included big promotional giveaways at halftime, in Pittsburgh's 13,500-seat Civic Arena. Kentucky was facing the red-and-gold Condors, one of the league's weakest franchises in home attendance, in the last game of the regular season. Pittsburgh was very lucky if they drew 3,000 fans to a contest.

"We showed up there and the dang gone place was full," said Pratt, whose team later lost 149-132 in a high-scoring affair. "We couldn't believe it. The place probably sat 15,000 and there were like 10 or 12,000 people. We found out (later) because at halftime they were giving things away. They had everything from washing machines to (whatever) you name it. They had advertised this giveaway.

"So they had a delayed halftime and they had this drawing with the ticket stubs. If you had a ticket stub, you had to be present to get something and they gave all this stuff away. Frank Ramsey is coaching us and he said, 'Guys, just relax. It is going to be a long halftime.' We came back out to warm up for the second half and you could have shot a cannon through there. There was nobody left. Once they gave all the prizes away, everybody left. People just came in to have a chance to win a prize."

Another memorable incident involved Pratt's teammate, 6-7 Cincy Powell, and others in Game 5 of the 1971 ABA championship series with the Utah Stars at the Salt Palace.

Said Pratt, "I'm in the game, and I'll never forget it because I was looking. There was a fast break situation and a foul was called. All of a sudden a lady runs out of the end zone, right on the floor, and takes an umbrella and hits Cincy Powell on top of the head. Cincy had his back to her. And pretty soon the Utah bench empties, our bench empties. There were people pulling people out of the way. There was a huge, huge fight (among the players), and it all started because a lady ran out of the end zone and popped Cincy."

When the emotionally-charged game ended, the Stars were the victors, winning 137-127, behind the outstanding backcourt play of Ron Boone, Merv Jackson and Glen Combs. Utah center and ex-NBA star Zelmo Beaty also put in a superb performance, pumping in 32 points and snatching 22 rebounds with the victory giving Utah a 3-2 series advantage. Leading the Colonels was Dan Issel, who had 33 points, a game-high, and 16 rebounds. In a reserve role, Pratt played 22 minutes, scoring 10 points and grabbing five rebounds.

As record books will show, Utah eventually defeated Kentucky for the league crown in seven games.

* * *

One of the meanest guys in the ABA, if not the meanest, was John Brisker of Pittsburgh. A 6-5, 230-pound high-scoring performer, he played three years in the ABA. He was a superstar, earning All-ABA honors in 1971, but very mean, scaring his opponents and teammates alike. The Utah Stars once staged "John Brisker Intimidation Night" when Brisker and the Condors visited Salt Lake City. After the league folded the Pittsburgh franchise, Brisker then went to NBA's Seattle Supersonics in 1972.

"The last I heard Brisker was a mercenary back in the '80s or '70s in Uganda or someplace, and (he) has never been heard from since," Pratt said. "He was a tough guy. I never saw him get in a fight but he sure looked tough. He had that look about him – that mean look in his face. But he could shoot the ball. He could score points.

"But in the ABA there are a lot of stories about bounced checks and a lot of things. It was a lot of fun. It was basketball. It was up and down the floor. It was tough. You know people would fight because this was better than digging ditches or teaching school for a living. Guys would fight you (for the ball). On that floor, it wasn't millionaires taking care of millionaires. It was guys making $12, 15, 20 or 25,000 trying to hold on to their job."

* * *

In his post-ABA days, Pratt worked for Converse Rubber Company for awhile. During that time, he also took four courses at UK, earning 12 more credit hours that he needed to get his bachelor's degree in history.

"When I got done playing pro ball, I went back (to school)," said Pratt, who was an Academic All-American choice in 1970. "I was a history major and I had all the requirements for a teaching certificate when I was in school. I really enjoy history and having a teaching certificate would also allow me to do some coaching (in the prep ranks) if I wanted to."

In 1975, Pratt began his coaching career with North Carolina-Charlotte (now Charlotte). He had stayed involved with basketball through his sales/promotional work with Converse. He loved basketball and he decided to give coaching a try.

Pratt's friendship with new UNCC coach Lee Rose didn't hurt. His new boss had just taken the Charlotte post after spending many successful years at Transylvania University in Lexington. Rose, a native of West Irvine, Ky., also had served as assistant at Cincinnati in the mid-1960s. "Lee Rose and I had been good friends since when he tried to recruit me in Cincinnati," Pratt said. "I used to speak to his basketball camp in Transylvania and we talked about getting into coaching."

Instead of heading to North Carolina, Pratt nearly went to the midwest. U of L assistant Bill Olsen, who years later became the athletics director at Louisville, once considered the ex-Wildcat for the assistant coaching post at Wichita State. "I almost got into coaching with Bill Olsen," Pratt recalled. "He was offered (a job) and was going to Wichita State. Bill talked to me about going out there with him. He took it and then turned it down. So, I might have gotten in at Wichita State with Bill Olsen had he accepted the job. But Lee took me to Charlotte and got me started. He is a great teacher. I think he is one of the special basketball coaches I have ever known."

* * *

During the March Madness of 1977, Pratt, working as an assistant coach, returned to Lexington when the North Carolina-Charlotte 49ers played in the brand-new Rupp Arena during its phenomenal run in the NCAA tournament.

And the ailing Rupp, who would pass away several months later, was there to watch UNCC, Michigan, Syracuse and Detroit battle for the Mideast Regional championship. He was especially interested in the 49ers with Pratt and Rose on the bench. Some of today's familiar names coaching in the tourney in Rupp Arena back then included Dick Vitale, who was the head coach at Detroit, and Jim Boeheim, who led the Orangemen.

Pratt's parents also attended the tournament. They had driven from Dayton on I-75 to see their son coach from the bench. And they got to chat with the Baron for the first time in several years. In 1972, when Rupp coached the last game of his long career in Dayton, losing to Florida State 73-54 in the NCAA tournament, businessman Ervin J. Nutter, a UK alumnus from Dayton, had invited his parents to attend a social function and they renewed their friendship with Rupp even though their son was playing pro ball. "Ervin Nutter, who was giving the university a lot (with his generous financial support), had a big party and he was kind enough to invite my mom and dad," said Pratt of his parents' 1972 visit with Rupp.

But, at the 1977 regional tourney, Pratt's parents almost lost an opportunity to say hi to the former Kentucky coach between the games. They had difficulties in reaching Rupp. Pratt said his mother and father had seen "coach Rupp across the way so they wanted to go over and say hello. (But) the fellows wouldn't let them go across. So my mom said, 'My son, Mike Pratt, played here a long time ago, and I want to go and see coach Rupp.' That guy looked at my mom and said, 'Lady, are you sure you're Mike Pratt's mother?' So he said okay and you better go right over to coach Rupp and she spent about 20 minutes talking to coach Rupp.

"Then she walked back over and the guy said to her, 'Well, I guess you are Mike's mom' and she looked at him and said, 'Go and see coach Rupp.' She still remembers that (encounter). She said he (Rupp) was so nice and just talked my ear off."

As far as the tournament was concerned, UNCC stunned the Rupp Arena folks as they captured the regional title, defeating the Big Ten Conference champion Michigan 75-68. Cedric "Cornbread" Maxwell of the 49ers captivated the crowd with his superb 25-point, 13-rebound performance. It was a happy moment for Pratt and his relatives, too. UNCC's surprising victory over coach Johnny Orr's club meant that Pratt had finally earned his first-ever trip to the coveted Final Four despite his glory days at UK.

* * *

While spending his three-year apprenticeship under Rose in the late 1970s, Pratt, on a recruiting trip, got to meet a young head coach by the name of Tubby Smith in North Carolina.

"Tubby coached at Hoke County High School and he was a tough, intense guy," said Pratt. "He had a fellow on his team who ended up a pretty good basketball player and a lot of people tried to recruit him. That was when I first saw Tubby coaching."

In 1978, Pratt then became the school's new head coach with Rose moving on, taking the job at Purdue. As for Smith, he departed the prep ranks a year later to become an aide at Virginia Commonwealth under the leadership of J.D. Barnett.

Interestingly, both Pratt and Smith became coaching rivals of sorts in a relatively new league called the Sun Belt Conference. Pratt also knew Smith's boss at VCU. "At VCU as an assistant coach was a tough job because the head coach was a pretty temperamental guy," said Pratt, who compiled a four-year head coaching record of 56-52 at UNCC. "I think Tubby was like all the assistant coaches then. He did exactly what the head coach wanted done and did all the dirt, all the tough jobs that assistant coaches do. You didn't make much. When I went to Charlotte, I was making $14,000 and a car. I was without a car. Tubby probably wasn't making much money, either. They just didn't pay much money back then.

"J .D. Barnett was a tough guy and ran a tough ship. (He) probably offended the coaches and players a lot because he was a tough basketball coach. (He was a) tough defensive coach and a guy who was a competitor. His teams played hard. And Tubby goes in there and I'm sure, knowing J.D. a little bit and knowing Tubby a little bit, that was a tough job, being J.D.'s assistant.

"J.D. was a special coach and I really like him. I haven't seen him for awhile. I've got a lot of respect for this guy. He had great success at Tulsa after he left VCU. But I would imagine Tubby really has gotten some stories to tell about that."

Smith spent seven years at VCU, including six seasons under Barnett, before taking a similar job at South Carolina in 1986.

* * *

One of the individuals who helped Pratt in coaching was ex-Tennessee head coach Don DeVoe, who played with Bobby Knight at Ohio State and was an assistant under Knight at Army. In addition to Tennessee where he directed the Vols for 11 years, primarily in the 1980s, he also served as head coach at Virginia Tech, Wyoming, Florida and Navy. Like Pratt, DeVoe was a native of Ohio.

"Don became a very good friend of mine over the years because I grew up with his cousin. About five blocks apart, Don DeVoe's cousin and I grew up and till this day we are best friends," said Pratt. "And when I was in college, I used to go (home) and spend time with Don and talk basketball. He was very helpful to me in the defensive side when I was coaching in college, working with me, just talking. He was coaching at Tennessee; I was at UNC-Charlotte. He was a very helpful soul."

DeVoe, who is from Sabina, Ohio, had entered Ohio State on a partial grant before he later was given a full scholarship by head coach Fred Taylor after a good freshman season. In 1962, when Ohio State finished second in the NCAA tournament, dropping to Cincinnati in the title game, DeVoe was a little-used reserve on a squad that had Jerry Lucas, John Havlicek, and Bobby Knight, among others. He eventually became a starting forward with the Buckeyes.

* * *

UNCC relieved Pratt of his head coaching position in 1982. "My boss and I got sideways and your boss always wins," he explained.

Looking back, Pratt said he, for the most part, enjoyed coaching. He loved working with his players at UNCC, missing the daily contact he had with them. "I think coaching, to me, was an awful lot of fun," he said. "I really enjoyed the practices and I didn't mind the recruiting. I really liked the teaching part.

"You know the games are games. Once you play in enough of them, I'm not so sure you get all excited about the thrill of another game of coaching. But I certainly miss the interaction with the young guys, the teaching part. I always felt that every player I had at UNC-Charlotte was like a son to me. So I really liked that association."

Later, Pratt spent some time in the NBA for several years in various capacities as a broadcaster, scout and assistant coach. He served as an assistant coach for the Charlotte Hornets for three years.

Since he is involved with his broadcasting work as a hoops analyst on the UK Radio Network, a post he took in late 2001, joining play-by-play man Tom Leach, Pratt isn't looking to return to the brutal coaching profession. "I haven't really given it much thought," said Pratt, who has worked for the ESPN and Fox Sports South networks. "No one has called and asked me (to coach)."

* * *

On his Wildcat playing career, Pratt said "it was quite a thrill for us and all of our family, all our relatives, to be part of all of those three teams because we were always in the newspaper. Coach Rupp and Kentucky, you know, have a name. We were successful and we got a lot of publicity. It was always a lot of fun because of that and it was a very special time. They (Pratt's relatives) got to meet a lot of people."

And Pratt got to be a cover boy for a national sports magazine. Not once, but twice. *The Sporting News* headlined Pratt as the "Kentucky Thoroughbred" in its Jan. 31, 1970 edition. In the cover story written by John Carrico about the second-ranked Wildcats, Rupp commented that the 6-4, 217-pound Pratt is the strongest performer he's ever had at UK. In Rupp's eyes, ex-Wildcat All-American Pat Riley had been the strongest at Kentucky. And two weeks later, on the front cover of TSN's Feb. 14, 1970 issue, Pratt was shown guarding Pete Maravich, the scoring machine from LSU. Maravich was the subject of that week's cover story.

"I thought it was pretty neat," Pratt said of *The Sporting News*' front page coverage. "(Mike) Casey was on the cover of *Sports Illustrated* so they let me be on the cover of *The Sporting News*. I still have a couple of copies. As a matter of fact, when I was coaching with the Charlotte Hornets, George Shinn, the owner, had picked up (a copy) and brought it to me. A copy of that was on sale at some flea market. He said, 'Hey, look at this, I didn't know you were on the cover. I bought this for $2.50 or something down there at a flea market I was at.' Anyway, I thought that (front cover) was a neat honor and it's something that not everybody gets."

* * *

With Kentucky's strong basketball tradition, it's no surprise that there are Wildcat fans everywhere. And that includes games even at Thompson-Boling Arena in Knoxville when Tennessee faces an opponent other than UK. Several years ago, when Pratt covered a Tennessee-Alabama matchup for the Fox Sports South network, he was seen signing an autograph for a faithful fan wearing a Kentucky cap.

Pratt, who has a private business in Louisville, said he appreciates the Wildcat fans for their enthusiastic and loyal support over the years. "That is one of the great things about Kentucky fans," he once told the author in a column for Middlesboro's *The Daily News*. "They sometimes forget what you look like because we all get older, but they don't forget you as far as your name."

Chapter 4

Super Kitten

22-0.

That was the perfect record posted by UK's 1971-72 highly-regarded freshman team, which was often more entertaining to watch than the somewhat struggling varsity team. Even a national basketball magazine selected the Kittens as the nation's No. 1 freshman team. At many places in Kentucky, the black and white "charcoal art" posters of the seven freshman stars along with their coach, Joe B. Hall, were on display. They were the talk of the town.

"It was an exciting time. That was the last year that freshmen couldn't play on the varsity," recalled super kitten Bob Guyette of his rookie year. "We ran the ball and we played good defense. We scored a lot of points. I think we averaged over 100 points a game which is unheard of, especially with today's scores.

"You know we got a lot of publicity. We played before huge crowds. There would be people lined up in Memorial Coliseum hours before the freshman games. Some of them actually would leave before the varsity game, believe that or not."

The varsity Wildcats, who co-shared the SEC title with Tennessee with a 14-4 league mark, ended that season on a disappointing note with a 21-7 record, losing to coach Hugh Durham's Florida State club by 19 points in the NCAA tournament, as UK forced coach Adolph Rupp to retire.

Interestingly, Guyette, a pre-dental student, began his promising collegiate career on the wrong foot with assistant coach Hall, who doubled as the boss of the freshman squad. After completing his classes on the UK campus, the rookie had taken a nap and overslept in his Holmes Hall dormitory room, missing the team's first practice of the season.

"You want me to admit to that?" smiled Guyette of his early mistakes. "I'll tell you one thing that sticks out in my mind on the very

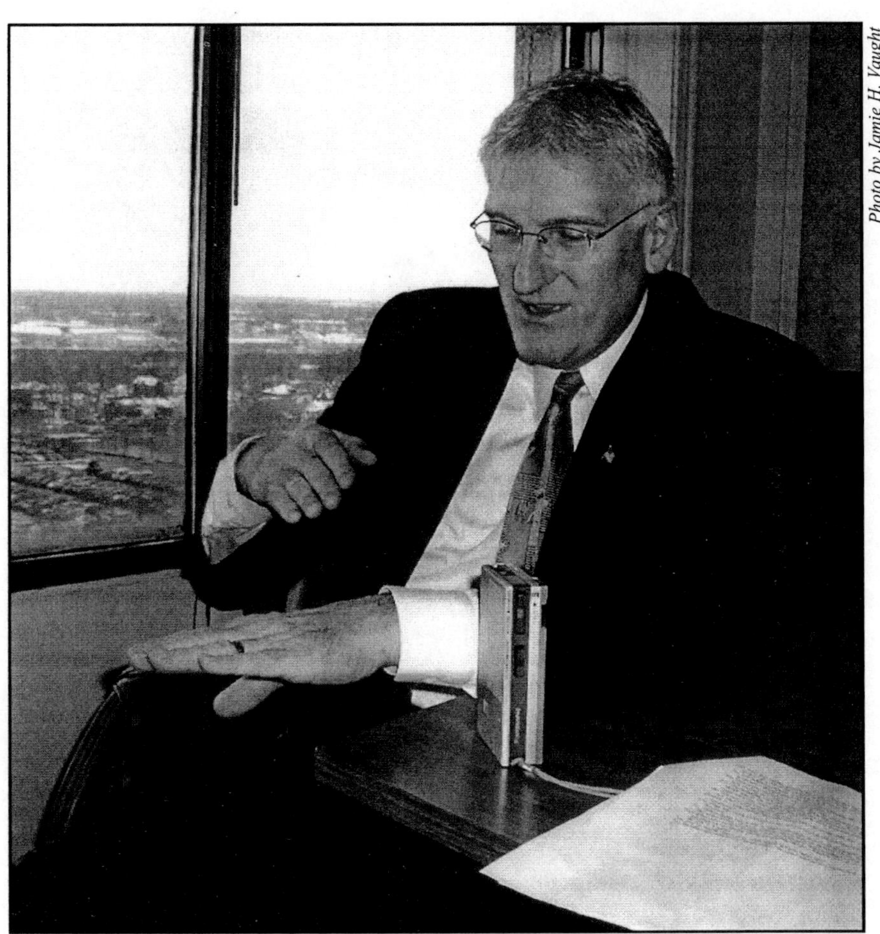
Photo by Jamie H. Vaught

A former Joe B. Hall disciple at UK during the early 1970s, Dr. Bob Guyette talks with the author in a 2003 interview at a Lexington hotel.

first day of practice in my freshman year. I had stayed up late (the night before) studying for a couple of tests and I remember falling asleep about 1:30 or 2:00 p.m. You know I had to be there at quarter to 3 or 2:30 p.m. I was going to sleep a half hour. So I fell asleep and for some reason my roommate (Steve Lochmueller) didn't come by. I remember running over to Memorial Coliseum, and getting my shoes and socks on. It was right at 3:00 o'clock, like two minutes after three.

"(But) they closed the gates and coach Hall wouldn't let me practice the very first day. I thought, 'Gosh, my career is over and here I'm glued on the first day.' So I couldn't practice on the first day with my freshman team. (Hall) made a huge deal out of that and for two months I didn't know what was going to happen. I thought he was going to send me home. But you know he was trying to make a point and I can understand that now. It is one of those things you have to learn and so that is how I started off my career (at Kentucky)."

Not surprisingly, Hall definitely got his team's attention with his disciplinary actions. "The second day he talked to everybody about if you can't come out on time and if you can't follow the rules, you don't practice," recalled Guyette. "So he made his point and I don't think anyone was late the rest of the year. I know I wasn't late."

Guyette said the freshman team was "a close-knit group. (We) really bonded." In addition to the 6-9 Guyette, who was a prep All-American from Ottawa, Illinois, the members of the Super Kittens squad included a couple of Mr. Basketball standouts – Jimmy Dan Conner (from the state of Kentucky) and Mike Flynn (from Indiana). The other "super" standouts were Kevin Grevey, Jerry Hale, G.J. Smith and Lochmueller.

According to Guyette, the Kittens almost didn't have a perfect record after facing Florida at the infamous 7,000-seat Florida Gym, better known as the Alligator Alley. "The only game that was close was the Florida game at Florida," he said. "They (the Gators) came within two or four points of beating us. But, on the road in Gator Alley, we weren't going to let that happen. That was our introduction to college ball. We played some good teams and being undefeated didn't happen very often."

His roommate, Lochmueller, by the way, was a serious freshman student, just like Guyette himself. "I think Steve and I, at least initially, were the only ones to take classes seriously," said Guyette. "We had some of the same classes together and he at that time wanted to go to dental school, too. He didn't end up going there. We had some things in common."

* * *

Guyette was the last UK signee from the 1971 high school class. In choosing UK over North Carolina, Notre Dame and UCLA, he didn't let Rupp's expected retirement affect his decision. He knew the school's hoops program would continue to be strong in the post-Rupp era because of the tradition and the fan interest. Nevertheless, Rupp's active recruitment (along with his assistants) and the school's strong dental program influenced Guyette's decision. And it didn't hurt when UK president Dr. Otis Singletary even paid Guyette a visit.

Rupp visited the future Wildcat in Illinois a couple of times, including the signing ceremony, according to Guyette, who added that assistant coaches Hall, T.L. Plain and Dick Parsons "probably came a total of five or six times." Guyette certainly remembered one occasion in the early part of his senior year when Rupp and his gang arrived late at a high school game in Marseilles, a small town located southwest of Chicago. That night would mark Guyette's first encounter with the Baron.

"It was an away game at a town about 20 miles away (from Ottawa). He flew in with Dr. Otis Singletary, coach Hall, coach Parsons and coach T.L. Plain," Guyette commented. "They got to the game a little bit late, almost at the end of the first quarter. It was during the game when he walked up into the stands. Then the whole place got quiet and (the crowd) stood up and started applauding. The referee actually stopped the game and waited until coach Rupp sat down before resuming the game.

"Afterwards he spoke to me for a few minutes and it was just a tremendous experience for me to meet coach Rupp. He was a very engaging personality and you know just when he walked into the room he just kind of let it out."

Rupp's visit certainly made Guyette feel pretty special. "It made me feel that all the work was worthwhile and that I kind of arrived and that coach Rupp was willing to fly to a poor dump town like Marseilles, Ill., to see me play a game," he said. "It gave me the confidence to know that maybe I could play at the next level."

When Guyette later informed Rupp that he was signing with the Wildcats, the Baron made another trip to obtain a letter of intent with the kid's signature on it. The signing ceremony took place at his parents' home in the river city of Ottawa.

"They came to our house and we had all the pictures (taken) and the (local) newspaper was there," said Guyette. "We had a pretty small house. We had the dinner table, took all the chairs around to one side and took some pictures. My high school coach was there, my high school athletic director and their wives. It was a big deal in that small town. And so until the last week I didn't know where I was going to go and you know it was a tough decision.

"One of the things that my dad had driven into my head was not only doing well in basketball, but also to do well academically. You know that sports only lasted so long and he felt it was important for us kids to do something beyond basketball (after playing days are over). So the academic side of it was very important to me. The fact that Dr. Singletary came (was impressive).

"When I came to visit (UK), I would go to the dental school and meet the other graduates and deans. So they knew I was really interested in the academic side, too. I didn't want to go some place where I was just going to play basketball. I wanted to go to school where I could develop as a basketball player, but also learn something."

* * *

The fact the Wildcats were filled with super prep stars didn't bother Guyette, who is now a facial and oral surgeon in the Phoenix, Arizona, area. He was a serious student-athlete with healthy confidence who was ready to meet the challenges.

"I was convinced that I was going to get to play," he explained. "I wanted to go some place that had a chance to win the national championship. I felt that if I was going to succeed, I wanted to go to the best possible place and (have) the best competition and learn the most so I wasn't afraid of that. I think that attitude has served me well now.

"When I got here, I had to fight for not only playing time, but if you did get playing time you had to fight for the ball because there was only one basketball. But you know you learn to play within the team concept and all of us had to accept a little bit of roles. We were (high school) All-Americans and Top 10 players in the country. What we realized is that if you are going to do something, we have to do it together and coach Hall was good about that. You know he put certain players in certain roles. He gave Kevin Grevey the green light to shoot and we all felt we should be shooting more." But the team members, however, accepted their responsibilities whether they liked it or not, Guyette said, adding the players made their sacrifices for the good of the squad.

* * *

Unlike youngsters who grew up in the state of Kentucky, listening or watching the Wildcats on the radio or TV, Guyette had a different team to cheer on. "With dad's influence at Notre Dame, we always followed Notre Dame football. I mean that was a big thing on weekends, listening to the radio," said Guyette, who during the 1960s was raised in a middle class neighborhood.

"We are Catholic and my dad went to Notre Dame," added Guyette of his father, Donald Francis, who recently passed away. "So that (attending Notre Dame) in the Midwest was huge. We really grew up on football at Notre Dame. Basketball-wise, you know, we tried to like the Chicago (Bulls) team, but they weren't that good back in those days. We had the Cubs and the White Sox, from a baseball standpoint."

According to Guyette, his father "was a great influence in my life. Not so much on the basketball side, but the mental side and spiritual side. So he was a great role model. (He) actually played football for Notre Dame for about two years until he broke his wrist. After that, while dad was healing up, World War II broke out. He went to the Air Force and eventually settled in a small town in Illinois. He was an electrical engineer and worked for Union Carbide for many years. My mom was also a pretty strong lady, German descent, and also a great influence in my life. I have two brothers (one younger and one older) and one sister.

"We had a pretty small house on a middle class American street with a lot of trees out in front. It was a three-bedroom house with one bathroom and my sister had one room to herself and all three of us boys were in the other bedroom. At the time, we didn't think it was a big deal. We never thought of ourselves as rich or poor. We were able to pile in the station wagon, all four kids, with the camper behind and we drove out west or down to Florida once a year. We thought that was pretty good."

To earn money, Guyette spent some time delivering hometown newspapers. During the hot summer months, he mowed the grass as well. "When I was growing up, I had a paper route that I took over from my older brother. I was about eight or nine (at the time)," Guyette recalled. "Then I had a lawn service where I cut lawns. I cut grass sometimes 15 or 20 a week. The most I had was 21 per week and in the fall we would rake leaves. In the winter, I shoveled the snow before school, after school, after basketball practice or whatever. So we were expected to work and make our own money from the time we were young and expected to do well in school, too."

Like Guyette, his siblings have done well in their careers. His brothers are engineers and his sister is a registered nurse as well as a dental hygienist.

* * *

Shortly after Guyette decided on Kentucky, he contacted several coaches, including UCLA's John Wooden, informing them of his collegiate decision. Wooden wasn't all that pleased, but was gentlemanly enough that the Bruins coach talked with the youngster for a long time. "One of the things that I really admired about coach Wooden is even after I told him (of my decision) he talked to me for another two hours on the telephone about what it is like to play college basketball," Guyette said. "He tried to help me with some of the adjustments I would be facing and really wished me good luck.

"Back in those days UCLA just recruited (players) in California except for rare occasions. You know Lew Alcindor (now Kareem Abdul-Jabbar) came from New York. There was a guy named Pete Trgovich, who was recruited from Indiana. I really didn't think much about UCLA until the very end. Coach Wooden called and wanted me to come out to UCLA. I talked to him on the phone for an hour or two and at that time I already had scheduled coach Rupp to come in because I thought I was going to sign with Kentucky. So, for a couple of days, I was going back and forth with that – whether to put coach Rupp off and go out to UCLA or sign with Kentucky. We thought about it a lot and all the effort that Kentucky put in and what it was like there (at UK). (Then) I called coach Wooden and told him, 'I'm going ahead and signing with Kentucky.'"

While Wooden offered encouragement to Guyette, Al McGuire, the colorful Marquette coach, wasn't as understanding or helpful when the youngster told him that he wasn't interested in McGuire's program. Marquette had recruited him for several years. "Al McGuire started recruiting me, I think, when I was a freshman in high school because my brother and sister were going to Marquette University," said Guyette. "So he would drive down from Milwaukee. He just pulled in our driveway and came in the back door. We were eating dinner and he came in and sat down. He gave my mom a big kiss on the lips. He ate with us and kind of got to be a part of the family."

Guyette, though, had mixed emotions about Marquette. "I knew I didn't want to go to Marquette University and so when I told him he got kind of upset about it," he said. "So that is why (I respect the Wizard) even more. When I told coach Wooden I was going to Kentucky he still talked to me, encouraging me and stuff. So I admired him for that."

* * *

In 1972, on a wintry December day, Joe B. Hall made his Wildcat head coaching debut when Kentucky visited Michigan State in the season opener. That game also marked the first varsity appearance for Guyette and his sophomore teammates. It wasn't a real exciting contest, but 13th-ranked UK nevertheless won, beating the Spartans 75-66 behind senior center Jim Andrews' 20 points and 13 rebounds, both team-highs.

But Guyette remembers something else about the trip to East Lansing, Michigan. He didn't like the airplane ride, especially its approach to the airport. "We're coming out of the clouds. It's snowing," he said. "The airplane is coming at about a 90-degree angle to the runway, trying to make a sharp turn and then has to take off (aborting the landing) and we're all hanging onto the airplane. I thought we were going to die. He (the pilot) turned the plane around and landed."

On the basketball floor, Hall and his Wildcats survived, too. The victory over Michigan State was a big relief, especially for Hall after replacing the legendary Rupp. "Coach Hall was nervous," said Guyette, who scored 11 points. "But he wasn't more nervous than I was or any of the sophomores were. I remember playing that game. I was fighting for a starting job with Larry Stamper and we were beating each other up all the time in practice. Since I was the youngest guy, I think Larry got the chance to start (although) I was playing pretty well.

"Then I got a chance to go into the game and we were playing on that artificial surface. It wasn't on wood. I hadn't played on that but maybe one or two times in the state tournament in Illinois. So I remember the first time running down the court, tripping and falling on the floor because of that surface. There was nobody around me. I felt like a fool. But we ended up playing well. We came from behind and ended up actually beating them, a good team, by maybe 10 or 12 points (actually nine).

"Also I remember I got my picture in *Sports Illustrated* at that game and I was pretty excited about the whole process. But you know coach was pretty nervous. It was his first game and I think we were all relieved to win that game on the road."

Kentucky went on to finish the 1972-73 campaign with a 20-8 record, including winning the SEC championship with a 14-4 league mark. Vanderbilt, Tennessee and Alabama (then coached by ex-Wildcat

C.M. Newton) tied for second place in the conference with identical 13-5 records.

* * *

Despite their big high school reputations and the team's No. 10 pre-season ranking, the juniors couldn't do anything right during the dismal season of 1973-74. The talented Wildcats just finished with a 13-13 mark, a very poor record by Kentucky standards. Some observers say UK's disappointing performance was caused by dissension between the team members.

But Guyette has another theory. In addition to improving SEC competition, the under-sized Wildcat players were playing out of position, he explained.

"Normally, I was playing forward when Jim Andrews was at center (the year before). I had to go back and play center at 6-9," commented Guyette. "Kevin Grevey, who was a really good shooter, didn't know how to rebound. I kept trying to teach him how to rebound. He was supposed to be my main rebounder, too. He was out there so far that I couldn't find him half the time. He was playing outside. Then Jimmy Dan Conner, who (at 6-foot-4) was really a guard, was playing the small forward. Mike Flynn was at the No. 2 position. He should have been a point guard. And we had (5-10) Ronnie Lyons who was about as big as a fire hydrant playing point guard. So we had a very small team and we lost a lot of games by four points, three points and two points. We just didn't have the size or depth to win.

"Also, the other thing, I think, the other teams were getting better. The other teams in the SEC – the Auburns, the Alabamas – had some great players who were coming along. So, unfortunately, I was on the team that lost for the first time to some other school that coach Rupp had beaten 50-something times in a row. So that part wasn't fun. It was a very long year. A very trying year. There was a lot of expectation with the freshman year that we had. But the reality was that we had four people playing out of position and the other teams were getting better."

A quick look at UK's 1973-74 schedule showed Kentucky had dropped four close encounters on the road, losing to Alabama (by four points), Auburn (by two points in overtime), Mississippi (by one point) and Vanderbilt (by two points). Behind Grevey's 21.9-point average for the year, three other Wildcats posted double figures in scoring. Guyette, who had a couple of 26-point performances that season, averaged 12.7

points, Conner 12.0 and Flynn 11.5.

* * *

When Guyette entered his senior year, he had a special request for Hall. He didn't want a roommate. He wanted to concentrate on his studies. "I told coach Hall my senior year I wanted to graduate," he said. "I wanted to just finish up strong so I talked him into (getting) my own room. So I had my own room and no roommate. I could do a little bit of studying and finish up strong. Since the room was right next to everybody else, there were always shoes and things flying up in the air in the hallway and (there was) always a lot of racket going on."

Classroom excellence didn't always come easy for Guyette, a three-time Academic All-SEC selection who was named an Academic All-American his senior year. He had to find the right balance between basketball and the classroom. "I just I had those expectations knocked into my thick head that I was supposed to do well in school," he said. "So, to me personally, I never really thought about it (time management in dealing with books and basketball). I just had to do it. I would take my books with me and I'd try to study sometimes while other people weren't studying and that made it a little more difficult. But I took it (academics) seriously and I tried to do well. And the teachers were very good. They were understanding. They would help us make up the classes (missed) when I was on the road. They understood what the situation was. The teachers, if they felt you were trying, would help you out."

* * *

Before Kentucky could advance to the NCAA Final Four during Guyette's senior year, it had to face coach Bobby Knight and his unbeaten, top-ranked Indiana Hoosiers in the Mideast Regional finals. It marked the second time the Cats and the Hoosiers had clashed that season.

"The first game was in Bloomington and we lost by about 15 points (actually 24 points, a 98-74 verdict)," said Guyette. "During that game Bobby Knight and Joe (Hall) got into an argument at the scorer's table. Bob Knight hit Joe Hall in the back of the head and sent Joe's glasses flying. As expected, a big commotion ensued.

"Luck would have it that we got to play Indiana again in the regional finals in Dayton, Ohio. The (Kentucky) players were ready but I thought it was the best job of coaching by Joe B. Hall in the four years he coached me. He had planned everything down to the smallest detail from the pre-game practice, the game itself and the celebration afterwards."

And history will show the Wildcats surprised Indiana 92-90 in a stunning upset and many journalists labeled the matchup the "Upset of the Year." Knight said in his 2002 autobiography, *Knight: My Story*, that his 1974-75 squad was the best he has ever had at IU despite three national championship teams.

With the surprising win, UK marched to San Diego for Hall's first Final Four appearance as the Wildcat boss. As it turned out, Guyette's last game at UK was in the NCAA title game when Kentucky dropped to UCLA 92-85. Despite the setback, Guyette said that's the most memorable game of his productive Wildcat career.

"We were playing in legendary coach John Wooden's last game and for the national championship," said Guyette, who finished with 16 points and seven rebounds in 24 minutes of action. "I was positive that we would win. The game was very close but a few breaks and questionable calls (against Kentucky) hurt us and we lost. I got into foul trouble early and played only about half the game, but still managed to score."

* * *

About two decades later, Guyette attempted to tease Wooden about the officiating calls that went in UCLA's favor when they met again at the coach's condominium in Encino, California, for several hours. Guyette took his oldest sons (Rob and Kevin) to visit the legendary coach.

"I tried to (needle the coach) but he had an answer for everything," he laughed. "I got a little bit different take on that. I also mentioned to coach Wooden that if he hadn't announced his retirement the night before the game or if we weren't playing in San Diego, we would have beaten them. We played in San Diego and the whole arena was for UCLA except for about 250 fans from Kentucky up in the top. Of course, that was an advantage (for UCLA). We still lost by 4 or 5, I can't remember exactly, and you know it could have gone either way.

"But he didn't believe that at all. He felt they won because of their quickness and he said if we were just a little bit quicker we would have won. We teased a little bit, but in a good natured way. I guess if we had to lose, losing to a guy like that is the best way to go."

Guyette, who was taking his sons to a team summer camp at UCLA, got in touch with Wooden after seeing then-UCLA coach Steve Lavin, who had the legend's phone number.

"So I called coach Wooden on the telephone and said, 'Hey, coach, I would like to introduce my sons to you. You probably don't remember me. My name is Bob Guyette. I played against you in the national championship (game).' He remembered everything. He remembered how many points I scored. He remembered the first score of the game."

Said Wooden, "Why don't you come over to my house?"

"No. We don't want to intrude or anything," Guyette replied.

"No, come on over this afternoon," said an anxious Wooden, who gave the ex-Wildcat directions to his home.

So Guyette and his kids got to see the Wizard. "We sat down there, I guess, from 1 o'clock to five o'clock in the afternoon," he said.

Guyette wanted his sons to learn the facts of life, including basketball, from the legend. "Of course, my sons at that point really didn't know coach Wooden," said the father, "but (I wanted them) to know the coach much more than that. What I was able to do was keep asking coach Wooden questions like 'What does it take to be successful in sports?', 'What have you learned?', 'What would you tell the kids?' You know I was trying to get them to listen to someone else, trying to reinforce the same things. Coach Wooden was absolutely great. We went through all kinds of things. He has such a great philosophy on life and is really one of my heroes. I've got his pictures and autographs all over the wall (in my office)."

On Wooden's relationship with the Baron, Guyette said, "We talked about coach Rupp. He has a great respect for coach Rupp. He felt that coach Rupp was the best basketball coach he had ever seen.

"As nice of a man as he is, coach Wooden was a competitor and he wanted to win. And he had respect for excellence in other places and he saw that in the Kentucky program. He acknowledged that to me. He felt that the Kentucky program was a great program and that coach Rupp was a worthy adversary and there is a lot of respect between the two."

Between the two Hall of Fame coaches Rupp and Wooden, their teams captured a total of 14 national titles and won 1,540 games.

Guyette is one of the fortunate individuals to have met both legendary figures in college basketball and he is grateful for that.

* * *

As for coach Joe B. Hall, Guyette, like his teammates, enjoyed a love-hate relationship with him during his four-year stay at Kentucky.

The Wildcat swingman has seen his coach get angry. He has seen him happy. There were lots of ups and downs in Hall's early years as the Kentucky boss.

"Coach Hall wanted to win," commented Guyette. "He had a tremendous amount of pressure on him to win. A lot of our practices weren't all that fun that first couple of years (1972 to '74) until we started winning our senior year. You know it was more intense than it was fun. It was a love-hate relationship. But in the end I think he taught us a lot of perseverance and that's what it takes to succeed. We did have a lot of successes at Kentucky under some pretty trying situations.

"Those four years at Kentucky playing (against) major colleges in that environment and trying to study and get good grades were the most difficult things in my life. Everything else has been easier. The dental school, medical school, residence in practicing medicine have been easier than that. So I guess during those years (under Hall) I learned how to deal with the pressure and succeed."

* * *

Rupp's unwillingness to step down from his coaching job made things awkward for UK officials and the folks in the basketball program. In fact, it was a statewide controversy. Rupp and his loyalists bitterly fought the school's mandatory retirement age of 70. Rupp didn't walk out gracefully as Hall took over the post in 1972.

"I wish the transition (coaching change) would have been a little smoother," Guyette recalled. "It did cause some animosity and things that didn't have to happen. They told us that coach Hall was going to be the next coach. I mean that is what Dr. Singletary told me and we felt that was going to happen. But you know it didn't really affect us (the freshman team). Those of us who were there thought it was time for a change. Coach Rupp had been a tremendous man, but it was getting on in time for a new coach and a new system.

"He was in poor health and struggling with his medical condition and such. He still had that desire to win and desire to perform, but I'm not sure that he was able to recruit and do other things. There was always a rumor about 'Was he going to retire or not return?' and I think that influenced things (recruiting) as well.

"You know that once I got here coach Rupp was at a time when his diabetes (flared up) and with his age, it was time to go. I would have loved to play for coach Rupp earlier, maybe 10 or eight years before. It would have been great, but at the time that I came in, it was time for the transition."

* * *

Rupp enjoyed telling stories about his players and Guyette was no exception. The Baron loved to joke about his hometown.

"He used to tell stories about flying into my hometown," said Guyette. "After I arrived at Kentucky, he once told me, 'Hell, Guyette, I have more lights in my backyard than you have on that runway in Ottawa.' Just very clever, funny things.

As many Kentucky fans know, Rupp liked to call his players by their hometowns. Said Guyette, "He called me by my last name. Toward the end he couldn't remember people's names so he would call people by their hometown at practice. He couldn't remember Larry Stamper's name so he called him Beattyville. Even in the game, I remember sitting behind the bench after our freshman games and he would walk down to the bench and say, 'Hey, Beattyville, you get in there for (Jim) Andrews. He would remember their hometowns but not their names. So that was kind of interesting to us.

"But I always found him to be very genuine, very open and a very good guy. I know I didn't have to listen to the wrath of coach Rupp because we were freshmen and we played against the varsity. You know a lot of times we would play them pretty close and he didn't like that very much. So he was always saying nice things about the freshman team, but I wouldn't have wanted to be on the varsity team.

"I was always fascinated (with Rupp). I would try to get there early to practice just to listen to coach Rupp talk. I would walk into his room and sit down. He always had time for me and would tell stories. Coming from the Midwest, I thought it was real funny how he talked. He had a southern accent, southern drawl. Anyway, he talked different and just really had some great stories."

* * *

Guyette has several stories, including the Joe B. Hall-Kevin Grevey episode in 1974 at Holmes Hall, a dormitory located next to South Limestone Street where the players lived. "There are a lot of them," he said. "Coach Hall was a big influence in all of our lives. He became a father figure so to speak. A disciplinarian and just filled a lot of roles.

"I know some of the ones have already gotten out about Kevin Grevey being out one night and not coming back in on time. For awhile, we were roommates, but at the time I was in the room right next door. I remember getting up (real late at night), walking down the hall, going in his room and seeing coach Hall asleep there instead of Kevin. That was quite a shock. I remember (captain) Ronnie Lyons coming in and out, in and out. I think he had Kevin on the other line, trying to tell him when coach Hall was leaving so he could come back to his bed. I think coach was there all night. That is always kind of a funny story that will stick with us all the time. It is funny now, but wasn't then. You know time mellows things out."

Added Hall, "I spent one night in Kevin Grevey's empty bed sharing the room with G.J. Smith. Kevin had skipped curfew. I just waited up for him. I wasn't upset. I was worried. I was always concerned about the health of my players. We had made a long trip from Mississippi that afternoon by bus. We got in about two o'clock Sunday morning and we had another game the following Monday. I told the players to go right to bed. No one is to leave the dorm. I got to the (Memorial) Coliseum and I was worried a little bit about them. I hadn't really checked to see if they were alright, so I went back to recheck them and Kevin Grevey was out." According to Smith, Grevey, his roommate, showed up in the dorm room about 9:00 a.m. the next morning.

Hall suspended Grevey for one game because he had broken curfew. Hall later said the 6-5 junior forward didn't offer any reasons for missing the curfew. "There wasn't any excuse that would take care of a situation like that so he didn't even bother," said the mentor. "There wasn't any excuse that would be justifiable so he didn't offer one."

Grevey, nevertheless, completed the campaign as the league's top scorer with a 21.9-point average and was named All-American.

Said Guyette of his times when he roomed with Grevey, "There was always something going on and it was a lot of fun," he said. "We had a lot of fun times talking and doing some crazy things."

* * *

In 1972, Reggie Warford came to Kentucky from Drakesboro, a small town located in western Kentucky. The second black player to obtain a basketball scholarship from UK, Warford went through some uneasy moments in college. During his freshman year, he was the squad's only African-American player. But he had a friendly roommate in

Guyette, who at the time was a sophomore. They both got along well. So, for Warford, it made his college life much more bearable at Kentucky, which was beginning to recruit high school black players actively under the leadership of Hall.

"In my second year I roomed with Reggie Warford," Guyette said. "I was happy to room with Reggie. I thought he was a great kid and we learned a lot from each other and that was an interesting situation."

When he lived with Warford at the dorm, Guyette said he didn't pay much attention to his roommate's race. "I didn't really think much about that (race). I just thought he was another kid. I came from the Midwest. I had black friends and white friends. You know to me, it wasn't as big of a deal. Looking back on it, I could probably have even done a better job because when I was 19 or 20 I was just not that aware of things.

"But we would travel to my hometown in Illinois. We spent, I think, a weekend or a little longer there and visited with my sister and stayed at her house. So I introduced him to my family. We kind of stayed in touch for awhile. But looking back on it now I guess it was more difficult than I was even thinking at that time for Reggie."

A 6-1 guard, Warford eventually became a Wildcat standout by the time he was a senior. In his last college game, he guided the Cats to the 1976 NIT championship with a 71-67 win over North Carolina-Charlotte (now Charlotte) in New York, scoring 14 points on 7 of 10 field goal shooting. He was the only senior on a team that had players like Jack Givens, James Lee, Mike Phillips, Rick Robey, Larry Johnson and Dwane Casey, to name several.

Warford later entered the coaching profession as an assistant, including stops at Iowa State and Pittsburgh. In 1984, he received the Most Courageous Award, which was presented by the United States Basketball Writers Association in recognition of extraordinary courage. He had rescued an elderly couple from their burning home in Lexington. (Former UK coach Eddie Sutton also accepted this award in 2001 on the behalf of the Oklahoma State hoops program after 10 members of the squad were killed in a plane crash.)

* * *

Guyette doesn't like the Tennessee orange. His intense battles with Vols coach Ray Mears and his squad were often disappointing as the Wildcats failed to win. During his three varsity years, Guyette saw his Cats play only .500 ball against arch-rival Tennessee. In other words, UK posted a 3-3 mark in the series from the 1972-73 to 1974-75 seasons.

"I hate the color orange, you know," said Guyette when asked about the Kentucky-Tennessee rivalry during his playing days. "That was always a tough situation. We had some other great rivals – Indiana, Notre Dame, North Carolina. But Tennessee was always a tough one because we lost to them a lot. The thing that always bothered me was they would become national defense champions all those years and in reality all they did was to hold the ball. We wanted to run up and down and play defense, and they are holding the ball and passing it back and forth. Finally, after holding the ball for two minutes, (they) get a backdoor layup and it just drove coach Hall nuts.

"There were a lot of hard feelings there between coach Hall and coach Mears. There was no love lost between the players, the coaching staff. When I look back on it, I think it was a good rivalry, but it was very fiery. They didn't like us and we didn't like them."

* * *

Unlike Rupp, coach Joe B. Hall sometimes didn't enjoy a good rapport with the news media. Both coaches handled the press in various ways. Guyette has an interesting perspective on media relations.

"I have been on both sides of the sports media and I tell you we could have an interview like this and it doesn't turn out the same way in the paper," he said. "I can see where people have different angles. Part of it is interpretation, part is selling newspapers. So I can see from his (Hall's) side where you lose trust.

"Now coach Rupp understood that. He got beyond that and he learned how to manipulate the press to get what he wanted to get out of it and I think that takes media relations to another level. Not many people who get there can understand how to maneuver the media to say what they want to say. So he (Rupp) was able to develop that style over the years, develop a reputation.

"Whereas coach Hall, he stepped into a situation right from the start where he was expected to take over from coach Rupp and have all the media savvy. That takes time to develop. So I think I can understand where coach Hall was coming from. Also he had the tremendous expectations and pressure on him, and that made it look different than coach Rupp's situation."

* * *

A third-round NBA draft pick by the Kansas City (now Sacramento) Kings and a fourth-round ABA draft pick by the New York (now New Jersey) Nets, Guyette bypassed both teams and played pro basketball overseas. He said he isn't sorry for his pro decision.

"I was offered a one-year, no-cut contract with the Nets. I almost signed, but at the last minute I was called by Barcelona in Spain," said Guyette, who at the time still had plans to study dentistry. "I went to Barcelona for five days, fell in love with the place and played there for five years.

"I have no regrets about not playing in the NBA or the ABA because the European experience was so unique and tremendous. (But) my sons have a different story. They wish I would have played in the NBA."

During his pro career, Guyette would return to the U.S., including Kentucky, and spend three or four months in the summer. He and his college sweetheart, Leslie Regina, who is from Falmouth, Ky., married after finishing his second year of pro basketball.

After his playing days ended, Guyette, who had already graduated with a bachelor's degree, returned to UK, enrolling in the school's dental program. Four years later, he received his dental degree (DMD). Also, he later earned his medical degree (MD).

"Upon finishing my residency at the University of Alabama in Birmingham, we moved to Scottsdale, Arizona, to set up practice," he said, adding that he has worked there for nearly 15 years as a facial and oral surgeon.

Guyette and his wife have three sons (Rob, Kevin and Brian) who are or have been participating in athletics.

Not surprisingly, Guyette keeps up with the Wildcats today. "I follow UK whenever it is on TV in Phoenix and we like to attend one home game every year," he commented. "I especially follow their progress in the NCAA tournament.

"I keep up with the Kentucky players that come in to play the (Phoenix) Suns. I spent a lot of time with (ex-NBA star) Sam Bowie. I also talked to Rex Chapman several times, but mostly I'm just a fan. I haven't talked to any of the recent graduates."

Kentucky basketball is very special, admits Guyette. Several years ago he brought his middle son back to Lexington. "He really couldn't believe the spirit of the people of Kentucky," said the father. "It is unbelievable (to see) the fan support of Kentucky basketball. It is just amazing. I have been to other states – North Carolina, Indiana and such – and I can't imagine any place that has more feeling for the basketball team than here in Kentucky. It is just a great experience to me and a lot of good friendships for life."

Chapter 5

From North Carolina to Kentucky

Not long before Katie Hanson gave birth to her fourth son, Reggie, at a Charlotte hospital in North Carolina, hoops coach Dean Smith and his Tar Heels were coming off two consecutive NCAA Final Four trips in 1967 and 1968. Reggie came into this world on October 8, 1968 as a bouncing baby boy. At the time, the entire state, also known for its rich tobacco crop, was buzzing about the Tar Heels, who had players such as All-American Charlie Scott and future college coach Eddie Fogler. The faithful fans of the Tar Heels anxiously waited for another basketball season to tip off. The team's official practice was several days away. And Reggie Hanson, as he got older, became addicted to North Carolina basketball. He admitted that he once hated Kentucky. Just like any other Tar Heel fan.

"I was a big Carolina fan," Hanson said. "I never saw them play in Chapel Hill, but I always watched them play on TV." He really admired the Tar Heel players. Names such as Phil Ford, Kenny Smith, Mike O'Koren, James Black, Al Wood, Michael Jordan and Sam Perkins come to mind. When playing pickup basketball, he used to pretend he was North Carolina. "You know I loved all those guys. They were just awesome," he said. Hanson's favorite all-time North Carolina player? "Obviously, Michael Jordan," he said with a smile.

Like most kids, Hanson didn't have the opportunity to meet with the players. "I never had a chance to meet them," he said. "I would've loved to but I didn't get that chance."

But Hanson, a future Wildcat who grew up in Charlotte, wouldn't be a Tar Heel fan all of his life. In 1982, he and his family moved to Somerset in south central Kentucky where his older brother, Arthur, was playing basketball at Pulaski County High School. Arthur had been a participant at Pine Knot (Ky.) Job Corps, a federal government-funded

Photo Courtesy of UK Media Relations

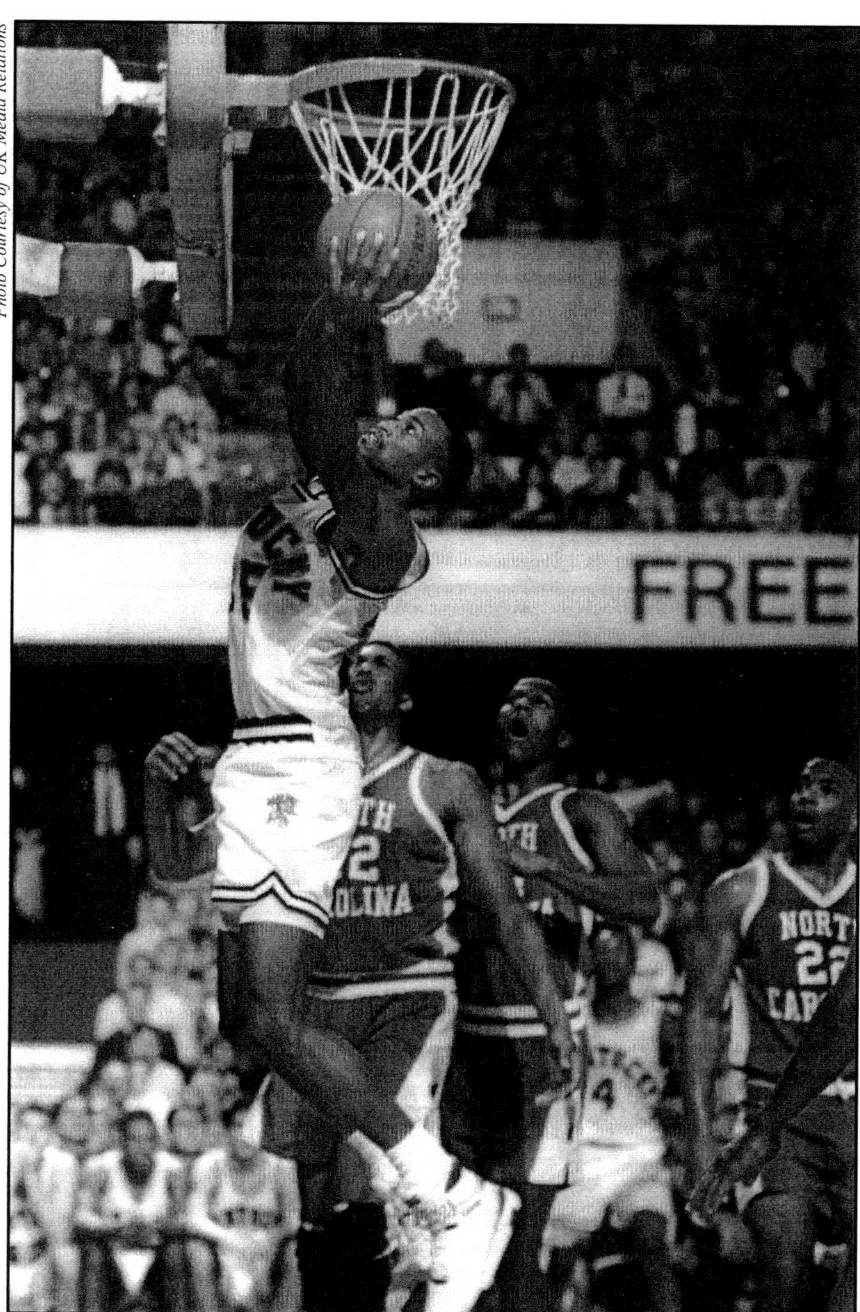

Kentucky's Reggie Hanson, then a junior playing as a 6-7 center, goes up for a layup in front of the Tar Heels in UK's 121-110 setback to coach Dean Smith's North Carolina club at Louisville's Freedom Hall. The surprising Wildcats, on NCAA probation, went on to finish with a 14-14 mark in 1989-90, which was coach Rick Pitino's first year at UK.

vocational program for economically disadvantaged youth in their late teens or early 20s, and played basketball there. While starring for the Job Corps team, Arthur caught the eye of Pulaski coach Dave Fraley with his raw talent. The coach liked what he saw on the court. The youngster had the potential written all over him. "A friend told me about Arthur," said Fraley. "He said Arthur needed some help (with education) and that he could help us."

According to Reggie, who was an eighth-grader at the time, the family decided to move after hearing of Arthur's progress at the high school even though it would mean leaving behind their other relatives in North Carolina. "(Arthur) got back in school and he told my mom that they were treating him good down there (in Somerset) and everything was working out well," said Reggie. "He told the coach that he had two smaller brothers (Reggie and Don) that played basketball. So coach Fraley came and visited my mother in Charlotte. Then my mother went down to visit (Kentucky). She came back home and thought about it for a little while. She made the decision she thought was best for our family."

Reggie agreed, "The bottom line was that it was better for our family from an educational standpoint of us having better opportunities and you know not getting caught up in the city life. I think my mother did a great job on making that move and it turned out great for all of us. My brothers got college scholarships." In addition to Arthur (who played at Cumberland College) and Don (at Georgetown College), Hanson also has another brother, who didn't play basketball, and a sister.

* * *

Three of the Hanson brothers played basketball at Pulaski High. The Hanson trio, though, never played together at the same time. "Arthur was a senior when I was a freshman and Donald was a sophomore," Hanson said. "During the regular season, we did not play together. As far as during the summer time when we were playing pickup games, we always played together." And it was Reggie who finally guided the Maroons to the promised land, capturing the 1986 state tournament title as a senior.

Before the 1985-86 campaign began, Hanson had a lot on his mind. Only 16 years old, he was already thinking about college. Where should he play? Coming off a super summer when he played as a member of the Kentucky Junior All-Star squad, traveling to Europe and Las Vegas, Hanson announced his collegiate choice in late September. He became new UK boss Eddie Sutton's first recruit. One week earlier, he and his buddy, prep star Rex Chapman of Owensboro Apollo High, had made official visits to the UK campus. Hanson had a pleasant trip and at the time pretty much decided Kentucky was the right place for him. That made his career decision easier.

With his collegiate decision out of the way, the 6-7 Hanson was able to focus on high school basketball and academics during his senior year. Averaging 23.5 points and 10.1 rebounds for the season, he led Pulaski to a stunning 32-4 mark. He couldn't have asked for a better ending of his prep career when he helped the Maroons to a state crown, defeating Louisville Pleasure Ridge Park 47-45 in the title game at Rupp Arena. For his performance, Hanson was named the state tourney's MVP after scoring 92 points and grabbing 39 rebounds in four games, including a 37-point performance against Clark County, coached by former Wildcat Guy Strong. As a three-year starter at Pulaski, he helped Fraley and the Maroons post a record of 83-13. And Hanson's statistics would have skyrocketed had the player been more selfish. But that wasn't his nature. He was a smiling youngster who desired to play as a loyal team performer.

"He would have been more of a star had he been just a little bit more selfish," said Fraley, whose son Shannon hit a game-winning shot in guiding Pulaski to the state championship. "He is the ultimate team player and he sacrificed his own game many times for the team. There are not many players with the 'team' attitude that Reggie had.

"I always enjoyed Reggie and his personality. He was a very good talent and has always been an example of leadership. I think he will one day be a very successful head coach in college as he relates so well to other people."

On Pulaski's successful run to the Sweet Sixteen, Hanson said, "It didn't surprise us because we knew we could play with anyone. We had a great year. We finished 32-4 and two of those losses came against out-of-state teams. We played (against) top competition. So they (the critics) can't look at our schedule and say we were lucky. We beat good competition."

* * *

Fraley also remembers a time when Hanson failed to concentrate on academics. His grades were poor. He was goofing off, not studying for exams or doing the homework like he should. The coach became very concerned and talked to the player's mother. "I think my favorite memory of Reggie is when he did not do so well on his grades in school and I told his mom," he said. "I remember her standing and facing him in the living room and giving him a tongue lashing, calling him Reginald (his real name). He hated that name and so I called him that sometimes."

But Hanson thoroughly enjoys a close relationship with his mother, who once worked at Oakwood training facility in Somerset where she worked with the handicapped children. He credits her for his success in life. She was the primary influence of Hanson's life when he was growing up. "She is the one who showed me right from wrong," said Hanson, who is a Baptist. "(She) disciplined me when I needed discipline, and loved me, hugged me, patted me on the back when I needed that. She instilled a lot of values in us and we grew up going to church. I really don't like to talk about religion because it is different with everyone. Religions are different, but you can still grow up having values."

* * *

Hanson, meanwhile, has a favorite story about his high school coach and his son. He frequently spent a lot of time at Fraley's household. Well, they got bored one day and they tried to find something to do. And the duo, at the time not old enough to hold a driver's license, recklessly decided to play with the coach's old green car. They wanted to have some fun, driving the car while the coach was gone, and get some driving experience.

"Shannon and I would get in the car and we would drive it up and down the driveway," Hanson said. "(Fraley) had a kind of big field in his backyard with a lot of space and we would drive it in the backyard. Just practice driving. One time I was driving by myself and I was turning around. Shannon was on the porch at the house and said, 'Dad's coming, dad's coming!' So then I tried to put it in drive to try to get (the car) up the hill to park it real quick. Well, I put it in reverse and backed up into a tree. And finally when I put it in drive and drove it up to park it, Shannon said, 'I was just joking. My dad's not coming.' But he (the coach) had a little dent in his car now. When he finally came home and saw the dent in his car, it wasn't a joking matter."

The elder Fraley was asked about the incident. "Yes, that's true, but I wasn't told immediately," he said. "I think Shannon was an accomplice on that. I don't remember being very upset. I probably wasn't pleased with them.

"Actually, I don't have many stories on Reggie as he and Shannon kept the things they did that I would not approve of hidden from me. But those were good days and those kids were special then as they are now."

* * *

One month after Hanson announced his decision to become a Wildcat, the *Lexington Herald-Leader* dropped a bombshell. The newspaper, in a series of articles, reported that cash payments and other benefits were distributed to ex-UK players during their playing days, apparently violating NCAA rules. Hanson wasn't too happy about that. Nevertheless he kept his word and signed with the Wildcats during the early signing period in November. Kentucky later got off the hook with a reprimand, as the NCAA officials weren't able to obtain enough hard evidence to indict UK for breaking regulations.

The other first-year rookies joining Hanson on coach Eddie Sutton's second Wildcat team were guards Rex Chapman and Derrick Miller. But it was Hanson who didn't play in the 1986-87 season. By the time fall semester of 1986 rolled around, Hanson learned that his ACT college entrance score wasn't high enough, making him ineligible because of the NCAA's new academic guidelines called Proposition 48. That also meant he wouldn't be able to practice with the team as well. He was devastated and crushed. His dream -- playing basketball for a major college powerhouse – had vanished, at least temporarily. He had looked forward to playing basketball for Kentucky in his first year of college. Bitter about the whole ordeal, Hanson said it was one of the toughest moments of his life.

"It was very difficult when you are used to playing ball every year and all of a sudden you had to sit out," Hanson recalled. "The (unfortunate) thing about it was that you had to sit out not because of grades (in the classroom), but because of a test score. I missed a test by one point and that is what really made it tough.

"I think the test, you know, doesn't tell what a kid can do in college. When a kid can't go to college because of an ACT test then you are just taking away the opportunity. I don't think the test makes a big difference in what a kid can do or what he is going to do. I mean I went through it and I got my degree. But I had to sit out a year just because of this test and that is not fair."

And the situation could've been a lot worse for Hanson. "I was lucky because back then you had to sit out a year plus they gave you four years of basketball scholarship," he said. "But now, you know, they take the year away from you. So it is like they try to make it tough for kids to get an education, almost."

* * *

After sitting out the year before, watching the Wildcats end the disappointing campaign with an 18-11 mark after a first round NCAA tournament loss to Ohio State in Atlanta, Hanson was ready to be active again. Even though UK's 1987-88 roster was loaded with key seniors such as Winston Bennett, Rob Lock, Cedric Jenkins, Richard Madison and Ed Davender along with sophomore star Rex Chapman, Hanson was anxious to help the team in any way he could. He had surprised some folks in the summer by playing competitive pickup basketball with NBA player and ex-Wildcat Kenny Walker. While Hanson saw limited action, playing 16 games for an average of 5.2 minutes, the Wildcats roared to a much better record of 27-6 with a final No. 6 ranking. (The NCAA later ordered Kentucky to drop three NCAA tournament games from the record, changing the team's mark to 25-5 as part of sanctions imposed on the school.)

Hanson's roommate that year was Chapman, a close buddy. They both were second-year students. They earlier met in high school and developed a trusting friendship. They liked to tease each other and joke around. They had nicknames for each other.

"He would call me 'Rebbone' and I would call him 'Slabbone,' " Hanson said. "Even to this date, we still call each other that. But no one else called me that and they (other folks) didn't really know. It was just between me and him."

And they developed a reputation as a fun-loving tandem who pulled pranks on teammates and friends. "Even the year I sat out, Rex and I came right in and we were the pranksters of that team," Hanson said. "We respected everybody on the team but we were still pranksters and they loved it."

When the youngsters wanted to get away from the campus or the spotlight, they often visited Chapman's grandmother in her north Lexington home. And she gladly fixed home-cooked meals for them. Said Mayme Little Hamby, popularly known as Rex's Granny, "The last year (at Kentucky) he roomed with Reggie, I fed Reggie all that year. The year before, he was with Winston (Bennett) and I fed Winston that year and did their laundry. Whoever he wanted to bring out, he could bring out. They didn't talk as much as they ate and I loved it. It wasn't so much the bad food (on campus), but they knew they could get what they wanted here – mashed potatoes, wieners with cheese, cakes and cookies, things like that. You know, granny foods.

"Reggie is one of the finest boys. He's sweet and kind and laughs from ear to ear. I met his mother. I sat with her during a lot of the ballgames. She's just like Reggie. Just a big smile and thinks well of people."

Bowling is one of Hanson's favorite hobbies. He and Chapman also spent a lot of time at bowling alleys. But since Hanson is married and has children, he likes to take them to bowling. "I actually like to do a lot of things with my kids since I don't have a lot of time with them especially during the season," said Hanson, who rejoined UK in 2000 as administrative assistant before becoming an assistant coach.

In addition to Chapman, Hanson's roommates included Derrick Miller and Sean Woods during his UK career. "There are stories that we keep within ourselves and we would never share (them with others)," Hanson said. "Those were good guys. As a team we hung around a lot together and went places together."

On his personality in general, Hanson likes to describe himself as a friendly person who works hard. "On the outside, people just see me as laid back, a nice person and easy to communicate with, and that is true," he said. "But a lot of people don't know that on the inside I'm highly driven, have a lot of energy. I'm a non-stop worker. I was like that when I was a player and I have a mean streak in me. My teammates and the coaching staff knew that I had a mean streak in me and that they didn't want to mess with me if I got angry and that is probably what a lot of people don't know."

* * *

Shortly after the 1987-88 campaign, things slowly began to fall apart in UK's storied basketball program. It all began with a famous express envelope, which popped open with $1,000 cash with the money apparently headed for the family of a Wildcat recruit. The hungry NCAA investigators showed up on campus and found more violations, including academics. The school was in a big mess and it got president David Roselle involved. And the 1988-89 team simply couldn't focus and, as a result, lost 19 games. Then the school forced coach Eddie Sutton to leave and Kentucky got hit with a three-year probation, including two years of no post-season tournament action.

Although Hanson started 29 of the team's 32 games, averaging at a 9.8-point clip, before suffering a season-ending injury with a stress fracture in his foot, the season however was filled with off-the-court distractions and rumors. Not surprisingly, it was a very depressing time for Hanson and his teammates. "We weren't that bad," Hanson said of the 13-19 team. "But we were young. The year before we graduated a lot of seniors. I think a lot of different things made that season bad without going into a lot (of details). Of course, Sutton had a problem of his own and then the stuff with the probation. That was a lot to deal with. There was an investigation and you had to talk to the NCAA and they questioned you like you were on trial. That was a very tough year."

When the NCAA announced the probation in the spring of 1989, Hanson contemplated leaving UK. With two seasons of eligibility remaining, he was an attractive prospect to many universities. "I'm not going to mention any schools, but a lot of the ACC schools and SEC schools contacted me about transferring," said Hanson, who because of probation would never play in another NCAA tournament game if he stayed in Lexington.

After some deep soul searching, he decided to stay home and help the Wildcats rebuild. "It all came down to me doing what I thought was best for me and this turned out to be great for me," Hanson said. "I have no regrets about it." He also heard good things about the newly-hired coach with a big reputation by the name of Rick Pitino and that didn't hurt, either.

* * *

Hanson's first impressions of Pitino?

"Very intense," he said, repeating the words two more times.

In 1989, when Pitino came to Kentucky from the Big Apple where he was the head coach of the NBA's New York Knicks club, he was "just a non-stop, non-sleep driven person," said Hanson. And it was Pitino who made the difference when Kentucky, filled with only eight scholarship players, miraculously finished with a 14-14 mark in his first year at the Wildcat helm. Many doomsayers had thought the team would be lucky to win eight games, if that many. Key players such as Chris Mills, LeRon Ellis and Sean Sutton had departed the program the season before in the wake of the NCAA probation. That left UK with just two performers with significant playing experience – Hanson and 6-5 guard Derrick Miller. "You can't get mad at the guys who left. You know a guy has to do what's going to make him successful," Hanson said of Mills, Ellis and Sutton.

At the team's initial meeting, Pitino surprised the players with his seemingly far-fetched comments. They couldn't believe what the new coach said. While they knew Pitino was a big-name coach, they were very skeptical of him. Pitino told the squad, "You know everybody is predicting you guys to win six or seven games. But I guarantee, if you do what I say and you work hard like I'm going work you, you will win more than what they are saying."

The players, including Hanson, didn't know what to think. Said Hanson, "That was the first meeting he ever had with us and we thought, 'What is wrong with this guy?'" But Pitino's work methods won over the players. "Once we started practice and saw how tough practice was and how hard we were playing, we knew that we definitely had a chance to surprise a lot of people," Hanson explained.

According to Hanson, the coach's Type A demeanor "made a big difference in us that year. His personality kind of transformed us. We took that and it made us better players. We were very fierce competitors, no matter who we played. We played (North) Carolina. We played Indiana. We played Louisville. Even though we lost 14 games, no team came in with a cocky (attitude), thinking, 'okay, this is going to be an easy game' because it wouldn't be. So I think at the time his (Pitino's) personality and everything really came through on us and helped us to be better."

For the record, Kentucky wasn't able to defeat those big-name powerhouses, but for the most part it played them close. Indiana barely defeated the Cats in a 71-69 thriller at Indianapolis in front of 40,128 fans. In Louisville, North Carolina had too much offensive firepower as the Tar Heels won in a 121-110 decision. A few days later, the Cardinals from Louisville beat UK 86-79 at Rupp Arena.

Against Louisville, Hanson had a career performance, scoring a game-high 24 points against 7-0 center Felton Spencer. The junior nearly played 40 minutes of fast-paced action without taking a break. Pitino described Hanson's superb performance as robot-like superman. In other words, the coach was saying the player was almost not human.

"I think when he says I'm not human, he was more or less talking about the fact we press for 40 minutes and I'm playing 36 or 37 of those minutes. Press and still going," Hanson said. "That's why he says I'm not human to go at that high a level for 37 minutes. I think it's pretty amazing. Once he got here and we started practice he knew that I could play with anybody. So that wasn't really a surprise to him."

Pitino earlier had warned Hanson that the player shouldn't expect to rest often on the bench. "He said (I shouldn't) expect to come out much," Hanson commented. "He said, 'I understand you are going to be tired. I understand it is going be tough for you. Don't think I don't understand. I know it, but I'm going to be pushing you and making you stay in there.'

"So that was fine with me because I just wanted to help my team to win and that helped my teammates flow as well seeing me as the leader out there, dying, but still giving 100 percent effort without quitting."

Hanson admitted Pitino's philosophy of fast-paced action with full-court pressure defense and three-point field goal shooting did wonders for his playing career after two seasons of the slower-paced game advocated by then-coach Eddie Sutton. With his highly-driven personality and never-ending work ethics, Hanson blossomed in Pitino's system and became a more effective all-around performer.

"When coach (Pitino) came and brought his style of play, his energy, his enthusiasm and his determination, that was what I needed," Hanson said. "You know coach Sutton's style was the slowdown (type), passing seven times, and you can only shoot 15 or 16 feet (from the basket). You know something like that probably would have made me leave and transfer to another school with that style of play.

"(Pitino's style) was what I needed, just the high energy, all out non-stop. That is just the way I am now. I go out there in a pick-up game now and I play the same way."

One of UK's few highlights of the season, by the way, took place on a February night when the Cats stunned Shaquille O'Neal and No. 9 LSU in a dramatic 100-95 victory before a then-record Rupp Arena crowd of 24,301.

After a successful junior year, Hanson was also full of high energy in his last season as a Wildcat co-captain. He and John Pelphrey, the team's top scorers with identical 14.4-point averages, helped ninth-rated Kentucky, still ineligible for the NCAA tournament, post a 22-6 overall mark with 14 SEC wins in 18 tries. He also ranked No. 6 in the league in rebounding with 7.2 snatches. (LSU's O'Neal topped the SEC with 14.7 rebounds.) And, for Hanson's hard work, Pitino rewarded the two-time All-SEC performer by renaming the team's sacrifice award the Reggie Hanson Sacrifice Award, which went to co-captain Deron Feldhaus.

Moments after Kentucky's 114-93 season-ending win over Auburn on Senior's Day, Tiger coach Tommy Joe Eagles declared that Pitino's club was back on top. "Kentucky is a very good basketball team," said Eagles. "They are very much ahead of their schedule. They have a good mix in their style of play and their talent, and all of the credit for them being in the position they are in should go to Rick Pitino."

As far as the historians are concerned, the game's box score will show Hanson pumped in 11 points on 3-of-10 shooting and seven rebounds. That contest marked Hanson's last game as a Wildcat player.

In Hanson's last two years at Kentucky, it should be pointed out that Pitino was not the only coach who worked with the Pulaski County product. Interestingly, three of Pitino's UK assistants – Tubby Smith, Herb Sendek and Billy Donovan -- all spent some time with Hanson before they moved on to bigger things in their successful coaching careers.

* * *

For Hanson, another career highlight came in 1998. Sandwiched between pro basketball stints in Japan, he earned a roster spot on the NBA's Boston Celtics and spent the last two months of the season playing for his former coach, Pitino, who was then the Celtics' boss.

With Japan's roundball season over, Hanson was home in Lexington when he received a call from Pitino the last week in March. "I was a little surprised," he said of the phone call. "He told me he had some injuries and he needed some guys. He was low on players and asked if I wanted to come. So I told him, 'Great.'

"I couldn't pass up an opportunity like that. You know I wasn't going to play much but I wasn't looking for that. I was looking for an opportunity to play on their level. Not many players get to play (in the NBA). So, it was a good experience for me."

Hanson said he has enjoyed a good working rapport with Pitino, who obviously loved the player's work ethics. "We got a pretty good relationship for two years there (at UK)," he commented. "We had a very good relationship, a coach relationship. So he basically knew what I was about when he called me to come up and play. I knew it could only help me (in my career)."

The former Wildcat also added that Pitino's personality hadn't changed at Boston from what he observed when the coach was at Kentucky. "He's always intense," Hanson said. "He always had high intensity. So, it's the same. I always get along with him and that's just the way he is."

In his short NBA tenure, Hanson saw action in eight games, coming off the bench. His best game came when he had four points and three rebounds in nine minutes against the Miami Heat.

* * *

After eight years of playing pro basketball, including seven in Japan, Hanson returned to the UK camp in the summer of 2000, working as a new member of coach Tubby Smith's staff. But before he took the UK position as administrative assistant (and later as assistant coach) for the basketball program, he had planned to return to Japan to play another season of pro basketball.

However, Hanson couldn't resist an opportunity to work for Smith and the Wildcats. "I've been wanting to coach for awhile so I had been talking to coach Smith a couple of years," Hanson said. "(I told him) if a job opportunity came I'd like to join his staff. I got back from Japan (in the spring of 2000) and I talked to him a lot and I put a bug in his ear. I kept saying that I want to coach if an opportunity comes."

So Smith finally hired Hanson along with former Alabama coach David Hobbs after the departures of coaching staff members Shawn Finney, who took the head coaching job at Tulane, and Simeon Mars. And a few months later, when another aide, George Felton, departed UK to accept a scout position with the NBA's Indiana Pacers, Hanson was elevated to assistant coach. Smith had once coached Hanson and was comfortable with him. The coach also didn't forget a time Hanson could have left UK when the basketball program was in shambles.

"When we had the problems and we were going through the (NCAA) probation, he had a chance to leave, but he chose to stay. We are better off because of that," said Smith, who also liked Hanson's work habits. "We have an award that is named after Reggie Hanson. We teach our players to hustle and work hard."

To become a Wildcat assistant, Hanson admitted he took a "pretty good" pay cut after leaving his overseas job as a player/assistant coach in Japan. "It is definitely quite a bit," he said of the cut. "The thing about it in life is, you know, you have to set goals for yourself and one of my goals was definitely to be a coach on this level," Hanson explained. "And you have to make sacrifices sometimes at the beginning of accomplishing your goal. (You) accomplish your goal and then reap the benefits once you get there. I did consider this – I'm taking a pay cut. If I work at it hard enough, I'll make up this money down the road."

In April 2003, when UK increased Tubby Smith's total pay, signing him to a new long-term pact, the school also upped the salaries of assistant coaches. Hanson saw his yearly paycheck increase to the neighborhood of $90,000, which is more in line with the pay of assistant coaches at other major universities.

During his Japan Basketball League career, he averaged 20.6 points and 8.7 rebounds. In 1995, he was the JBL's leading scorer, rebounder and shot blocker. Hanson also earned the league's defensive player of the year honors in 1996, while leading the JBL in scoring and steals.

According to Hanson, his mother is awfully glad that her son is back in the Bluegrass, especially coaching the Wildcats. "She's glad I'm here instead of Japan," he said with a smile.

* * *

North Carolina connections.

Ex-Kentucky star Jason Parker -- who came to UK in late August of 2000 after being denied admission to North Carolina -- and Hanson had something in common. They both are from Charlotte. They both arrived at Kentucky at nearly the same time. While Hanson was just settling in his new job, Parker was busy, registering for his fall semester classes.

When North Carolina rejected him because of academics, Parker had his feelings hurt. The Parade All-American badly wanted to play for his home state university. However, when Kentucky academic officials carefully reviewed his high school transcripts, they couldn't believe that he somehow was actually eligible. So a North Carolina miscue was Kentucky's gain. Because of Parker's awkward situation, it certainly did not hurt that Hanson's upbringing was deeply rooted in North Carolina.

Now one of the nation's best-dressed assistant coaches according to Angela Lento's Fashion Power Index, Hanson said he thought the North Carolina link made Parker "feel a little more comfortable because of the situation that he was in when he came here – the whole situation of what North Carolina didn't do and what we did do to get him here.

"When he first got here, I was telling him where I was from and where I grew up and the different parts of the city. He knew what I was talking about. We talked about it (from time to time)."

According to Hanson, Parker didn't get homesick very often during his freshman season. "He is a mature kid in terms that he isn't really going to get homesick because he loves being here (at Kentucky). He is that type of kid," said Hanson at the time. Before coming to UK, Parker spent one year away from home to improve his maturity and classwork by studying and playing at Fork Union (Va.) Military Academy, after graduating from West Charlotte High in 1999.

Parker finished his freshman year on a promising note. Named to the All-SEC freshman team, Parker started all of Kentucky's 34 games, averaging nearly nine points a game. He became the first rookie under coach Tubby Smith at UK to start his first collegiate game.

Ironically, Parker's best performance of the year came during the NCAA tournament. He scored career-high 22 points and grabbed 13 rebounds in UK's 80-76 setback to Southern California.

But things didn't work out for Parker, who later twice suffered knee injuries, as Hanson never saw him play another game in a Wildcat uniform. Parker was dismissed by UK in the fall of 2002 because of unspecified team rules violations.

* * *

Like Hanson, his wife, Lynelle, enjoys sports. A native of Louisiana, she is a faithful fan of the NFL's New Orleans Saints. She watches the Saints on TV as much as she can. Lynelle, a 5-7 standout, also starred in the prep ranks. "She played some high school basketball. I saw some clips," Hanson said. "She had some pretty big games – 35- or 40-point games. She showed me some pictures and stuff in the newspaper."

They met during the 1993 NCAA Final Four in her hometown of New Orleans where the Jamal Mashburn-led Cats fell to Michigan in an 81-78 overtime thriller. Pitino had invited Hanson to go with the squad as a special guest. "(During) my first year in Japan when I got back, I traveled with the team to the SEC tournament and to the Final Four in New Orleans, and that's when I met my wife," said Hanson, who received his bachelor's degree in education from UK in 1991.

The couple later married in London, Ky., in 1994. They reside in Lexington with two daughters, Sakia and Jaitesha.

* * *

While it is understandable that Hanson probably still has a soft spot in his heart for the North Carolina Tar Heels, he definitely knows the "Tar Heels" are listed as dirty words in the eyes of the Kentucky faithful. UK and UNC are major enemies, fighting for the right to be college basketball's winningest program in history. But Hanson attempts to keep his emotions in check whenever both rivals meet on the hardwood floor.

Hanson commented that he doesn't have "any more emotions than I usually have. As a player, I got to play against North Carolina during my last two years in college – one at North Carolina and one at Louisville. You know it was very exciting. We played them (in 2000) at the Dean Dome and it was exciting. So I look at it as not just another game, but another big game that I get excited about. But there won't be any extra emotions (when UNC is involved)."

Hanson may be born a Tar Heel, but he will always be a true Big Blue faithful who stayed and helped the wounded Cats lick their wounds after an ugly NCAA fight.

Chapter 6

....

Monster Mash

To his current NBA opponents, Jamal Mashburn is a 6-8, 241-pound multi-talented monster, terrorizing them with his dominating presence on the hardwood floor. The former UK All-American usually beats them with his overall game – shooting, rebounding, passing and quiet leadership. For that reason, folks still call him the "Monster Mash," a nickname that has stayed with him for years.

The "Monster Mash" label originated even before he arrived at Kentucky in 1990. It began in his hometown of New York City when he had a great game in high school. "That was a nickname given to me when I was a sophomore in high school," recalled Mashburn in an exclusive interview for this book. "We were playing in the Christmas tournament at Cardinal Hayes High School in Harlem. It was my first year starting on the varsity and I had a big game. They just started calling me "Monster Mash" the next day in the paper. You know you have (radio) announcers and it was in the (New York) *Daily News* and things like that. Then it just sort of stuck (with me). It is just one of those things."

And Mashburn doesn't mind the scary nickname and he kind of likes it. "It's alright," he said. "I mean it is something people identify with and I think other people have more fun with it than I do. It's cool."

* * *

Mashburn and Regis Philbin have something in common. *Yes, that same Regis, the famous talk show personality.* While both men are true New Yorkers, having grown up in the Big Apple area, they also went to the same high school. They are both graduates of Cardinal Hayes, which is located in the Bronx.

While Mashburn grew up as a Protestant, his mother, Helen, sent him to Cardinal Hayes, figuring the Catholic school would give her only child a supporting and caring academic atmosphere filled with discipline.

Photo Courtesy of New Orleans Hornets/NBA photos

Ex-Cat Jamal Mashburn, shown here with the NBA's New Orleans Hornets, guns for a basket against Seattle.

She wanted him to have structure while she was at work. She wanted him where the faculty and staff, including dedicated priests and nuns, care about their students. She wanted him away from the tough New York streets and the undesirables – drugs, gangs, shootings, pimps, prostitution or other crime-ridden activities. She sometimes worried about her son out in the Harlem playground where he spent long hours pretending he was Magic Johnson, his childhood idol. At any rate, in her mind, he was attending a fine school that she felt comfortable with. And he would play basketball in a good environment.

He eventually became a three-year starter for Cardinal Hayes, catching the eyes of many college recruiters with his spectacular moves on the hardwood floor. However, before coming to Cardinal Hayes, Mashburn had already established himself as a raw prospect with a promising future. Starting in his early teens, he spent summers playing for the New York Gauchos in the AAU and they traveled around the country to compete against the other powerhouses. In addition to Mashburn, the Bronx-based Gauchos over the years have produced well-known standouts such as Stephon Marbury, Kenny Anderson, Andre Riddick and Heshimu Evans. Riddick, a former UK player, and Mashburn even played as teammates for the Gauchos.

While at Cardinal Hayes, Mashburn – as a UK signee – guided his team with his senior leadership to the state Catholic High School title in 1990, defeating All Hallows, which was *USA Today's* pre-season No. 2 team, by a score of 52-46 for the school's first championship in 46 years. During his senior year, he averaged 26.3 points, 10.5 rebounds and 4.3 assists. For his superb efforts, he received many honors, earning a spot on *Parade Magazine's* second-team All-American squad. A forward, Mashburn was also named "Mr. Basketball" in the state of New York and player of the year by *Newsday*. Many recruiting gurus compared Mashburn with NBA standouts J.R. Reid and Charles Barkley. "Jamal was on everyone's list of the top five or ten players in the country at the end of the year," said then-Kentucky coach Rick Pitino.

Earlier, Mashburn, however, wasn't really listed as a super prospect. The big shots in the Class of 1990 were Grant Hill (who went to Duke), Clifford Rozier (North Carolina), Shawn Bradley (Brigham Young), Damon Bailey (Indiana), Anfernee Hardaway (Memphis), Ed O'Bannon (UCLA) and Dwayne Morton (Louisville), to name a few. Whether the player is a top dog or not has never been a major concern to Pitino. While there was talk that Mashburn had a bad reputation of being lazy on the floor, Pitino still ignored the comments, saying the player's laid-back demeanor was misunderstood and he just recruited players who can fit into his exciting run-and-shoot game.

* * *

Mashburn and his mother enjoy a very special relationship. They share their feelings about everything. They stay in touch even if they are hundreds of miles apart. Now a retired bookkeeper for the New York City Housing Authority, she lives in Fort Lee, New Jersey, located across the Hudson River from the Bronx. "We are very close and my father wasn't there (at home)," Mashburn said. "My father and mother separated when I was younger, probably about 11 years old. So I'm a mama's boy and proud to say that. She not only treated me as a kid, as a son, but she also treated me as a friend. I can talk to her about anything and she has taught me to be independent, to be self-sufficient and just rely on yourself and make your own decisions and stick with those decisions if you believe in something. She taught me a lot. She raised a good son, I should say, and I'm proud to be her son."

And she was very careful not to influence her son when he evaluated his collegiate choices. She wanted him to make his own decision. But she did tell him that he needed to be out of the Big Apple to experience the real world. "She pretty much let me make my own decision as far as schools are concerned," said Mashburn. "Her only stipulation was that I not go on to St. John's or anywhere in New York City. I didn't necessarily want to go to those schools anyway. So my choices were open." Besides Kentucky, Syracuse and Wake Forest were Mashburn's top choices.

In the fall of 1989, Mashburn inked a letter-of-intent with probation-ridden Kentucky, becoming Pitino's first UK signee, and he later joined other Wildcat newcomers Gimel Martinez of Miami, Fla., and Carlos Toomer of Corinth, Miss., for the 1990-91 campaign. Henry Thomas of Clarksville, Tenn., was also classified as a freshman but he had been redshirted in the previous season. The Wildcats, who had been punished by the NCAA for rules violations, had just come off their surprising 14-14 mark after everyone had predicted a disastrous season with only eight scholarship players on the roster, none taller than 6-7 Reggie Hanson.

"The reason I chose Kentucky was because of coach Pitino. He came (to visit me) and was very honest with me and very open and I appreciated that," Mashburn said. "Going through the recruiting process as a high school player, people think you are not intelligent enough to understand certain things and to read people. But being from New York, you learn to read people, learn to know what is truth and what isn't truth, and learn to research things. So that's one thing that I did and he was honest with me. That is one reason why I chose Kentucky." Mashburn also remembers then-UK assistant coach Herb Sendek, who played a significant role in the recruitment of the New Yorker. Sendek would often send crazy notes in the mail and he was a good recruiter, Mashburn said.

Coming to UK wasn't easy for Mashburn, but he adjusted well. Describing his personality, he said he was "pretty shy." He would be away from his familiar home surroundings. "I'm pretty much laid back," he said. "Well, people have their attention and it isn't something that I really necessarily want or play for. I play the game because I love it and that's basically it. I remember times when I was back in my yard with nobody or back in the playground with nobody. Nobody ever thought I would make it as far as being an NBA player or a top-notch Division I player. So I always kind of play for myself and play for my teammates. I have never been one to want or go after attention and I don't play for those things." Mashburn added the Kentucky culture wasn't that big of a shocker for him. Unlike the fast-paced life in New York City, he said, "Kentucky is a little bit slower so it complimented my personality a lot."

* * *

Mashburn also stays in touch with his father, Robert. Sometimes they call him Bobby. The elder Mashburn was a professional boxer primarily in the 1970s, having fought against heavyweight champions Larry Holmes and Ken Norton. Not surprisingly, since Jamal was born in 1972, he doesn't remember many of his father's bouts.

"I remember bits and pieces of his fights," said the younger Mashburn. "I don't remember all of them. I mean I was so young I can't recall who was fighting or anything like that. I remember seeing pictures of me taken with boxing great Muhammad Ali. He taught me a lot."

Even after his parents separated, Jamal visited his father frequently several blocks away from his home. The elder Mashburn retired as a sergeant from the police department after many years in law enforcement. According to Jamal, the father still lives in New York City.

* * *

While at UK, it was a well-known fact that Pitino and his assistants gave the players a psychological exam when they first arrived in

Lexington. Through testing, Pitino learned that his newcomer from New York had low self-confidence. Yes, it's true. It was hard to believe that a dominating figure with a monster body lacked self-assurance. So Pitino, using his numerous motivational tactics, began to encourage Mashburn at every opportunity.

With Pitino's never-ending encouragement, Mashburn showed promise during his freshman year. He started all of UK's 28 games, averaging 12.9 points. He had several outstanding games, including Kentucky's 96-84 win over coach Hugh Durham's Georgia club at Rupp Arena. The Monster Mash scored a then-career high 31 points, establishing a UK freshman scoring mark, and grabbed eight rebounds along with six steals and four blocked shots. Needless to say, he had an impressive campaign as the ninth-ranked Wildcats finished with a 22-6 mark, the best in the SEC.

But the first several weeks of school were pretty rough for Mashburn. Like most freshmen, he was homesick. At the time, he was actually 17 until late November. But he managed and learned to adjust to the college life away from home. "At first I did (get homesick) but that was because we didn't have practice. We had to wait until (mid-October)," admitted Mashburn.

Having a roommate from a big city certainly paid big dividends for Mashburn. "As long as I had a TV set, I was fine and my roommate, Gimel Martinez, kept me busy," he smiled. "He was from another big city, Miami, so we related to one another. We had a lot of fun together. So it wasn't one of those things where I was (real) homesick."

The Wildcat freshman began to feel more comfortable with his new life when the team launched its pre-season training camp with the annual Midnight Madness festivities. He eventually became very busy with practices, games, traveling and academics. Pitino and his assistants kept Mashburn so occupied that the youngster didn't have much free time to think about home. "We were surprised by how much work coach Pitino wanted to put us in as far as conditioning was concerned," Mashburn said. "I wasn't really homesick, but I was maybe tired, physically and mentally, going through all that stuff. But I wouldn't change a thing that I did. It was probably one of the best decisions I made in life because it's brought me closer to coach Pitino."

* * *

Mashburn's sophomore and junior years (1991-92 and 1992-93) at

Kentucky were even much better. After three consecutive years of no NCAA tournament action, his Cats finally went to the Big Dance in 1992 and '93 when they posted a 7-2 overall mark, including a 1993 Final Four trip to New Orleans. In addition, they captured the Southeastern Conference tournament titles both years, including a 101-40 demolition of the hapless Tennessee Vols at Rupp Arena in 1993.

During Mashburn's sophomore year, the 1991-92 Wildcats, led by the senior clan better known as the Unforgettables, stunned many folks when they advanced to the regional finals, losing to Duke 104-103 in that famous Philly matchup. Arguably, many observers have said it's the greatest NCAA tournament game ever played in the history of basketball. And Mashburn played well, scoring 28 points on 11 of 16 shooting, and grabbing 10 rebounds before fouling out with 14 ticks left in overtime. He even pumped in three three-pointers.

"I remember playing the game," Mashburn said. "It was a good game to play. People were playing defense, but it was such a high offensive game, too. Because of so many runs and so many stories within the game, it became a good game. Nobody expected us to be there (NCAA regional finals), especially coming off probation my freshman year."

The heartbreaking setback marked the end of Kentucky's unforgettable seniors – John Pelphrey, Deron Feldhaus, Sean Woods and Richie Farmer. "I remember Pelphrey and those guys feeling so disappointed after the game. (I was) feeling so sad for those guys as I knew they didn't have another opportunity to (play in the NCAA tournament). This was their opportunity to be in a NCAA tournament and it was a sight to be in that locker room after the game. I just remember coach Pitino had very few words to say because everybody played their hearts out and it was one of those games where everybody wanted it and it came down to the last shot by (Christian) Laettner. It actually made me want to go to the Final Four and win the championship the next year for those guys because I knew they did not have the opportunity to do it."

Had Mashburn stayed out of foul trouble, the outcome of the game might have been different. Who knows? A victory by UK would have meant a trip to the Final Four for the first time since 1984. But Mashburn didn't think too much about it. He said fouls are just a part of the game. "That is what makes basketball so much fun," he recalled. "I did all I could and I couldn't do much from the bench. Maybe we would have won (the game) and maybe we wouldn't have." Mashburn added that he is pleasantly surprised that many people still remember that classic matchup.

Said Pitino at the press conference following the Duke game, "This was one of the more special seasons I've ever been through. We ended in one of the more special games I've ever been part of. At first, it was a bittersweet ending, but after giving it some thought, it turns into a very sweet ending." Pitino explained that's because the players, especially the seniors, ended with such a great fight. Kentucky had come a long way since the 1989 *Sports Illustrated* cover story, titled "Kentucky's Shame," when the university hired the New York Knick coach to restore the tarnished Wildcat program.

Mashburn completed his sophomore season with a 21.3-point average, earning first-team All-SEC honors by the Associated Press and the coaches. He also was chosen the MVP of the SEC tournament.

After the departures of the Unforgettables, Mashburn assumed a much bigger role on the 1992-93 squad. A member of the USA Select Team that scrimmaged against the U.S. Olympic "Dream Team" during the summer of 1992, he became a quiet leader of the so-called Roman Empire of college basketball, a popular phrase coined by Pitino in describing the UK program. Shortly before the season began, the coach said the Monster Mash was possibly one of the country's top five performers and the player had a lot of pre-season All-American recognition. In its special college basketball edition (Nov. 30), *The Sporting News* did a cover story on Mashburn, calling him "A Monster Talent." Throughout the season, Mashburn continued to get national attention and it grew with the Cats gunning toward the Final Four in New Orleans.

While Mashburn had lots of national publicity at Kentucky, he didn't ask for it. If he got it, fine. If not, no big deal. That's his nature. He's a humble person. "I really don't take too much into (magazine) cover issues or press or things like that because those things come and go," commented Mashburn. "I just concentrate on being Jamal. If people want to interview me as Jamal, that is fine. I don't consider myself anything special as far as being a basketball player or anything like that. I take everything in stride and I guess that is how my mother brought me up. So, I mean, it was fine. I think the recognition was more for the University of Kentucky than it was for me. I really don't keep the clippings. Now my mother keeps most of those things and I just play basketball."

Although he was only a junior, Mashburn was on his way to pro stardom with Pitino saying the 1992-93 campaign would be Mashburn's last at Kentucky. Along with Mashburn, the Cats' other primary starters were junior Travis Ford and senior Dale Brown in the backcourt, freshman forwards Rodrick Rhodes and Jared Prickett, and center

Rodney Dent (who transferred from Odessa Junior College in Texas). It was a young, but talented team with a recruiting class hailed by many observers as the best in the nation. Long bomber Tony Delk, a rookie from Brownsville, Tenn., was also on that team, playing an average of 9.6 minutes a game.

The Wildcats got off to their best start in almost 10 years, winning their first 11 games. The hot streak propelled Kentucky to the No. 1 ranking in the Associated Press poll for the first time since 1988. Folks became very excited about the team, catching the Wildcat fever. In coffee shops around the state, they began to talk about the NCAA championship for the Cats. It was certainly a happy time for the Wildcat faithful. In Nashville, the unbeaten Wildcats, however, ran into a roadblock. Coach Eddie Fogler and his hot-shooting Commodores played the role of a spoiler, stopping Kentucky by 15 points, a 101-86 verdict. They held Mashburn to only 14 points. (Vanderbilt, led by All-American guard Billy McCaffrey, surprisingly went on to have a remarkable season, winning the SEC regular season championship with a 14-2 mark in league play and a 28-6 overall record.) And Kentucky only lost a couple more regular season games – both on the road (Arkansas and Tennessee). UK concluded its memorable season with an 81-78 overtime loss to the Fab Five of Michigan, finishing with a 30-4 worksheet.

Mashburn, the 1993 SEC Player of the Year and a first-team All-American, had trouble picking the highlight of his UK career. He had several memorable moments, to be sure. "Highlight of my UK career? I really don't have one," Mashburn said. "I have three years. I think those are my highlights. Just an enjoyable time -- I mean being with coach Pitino and going there. We were on probation in my first year and we got to the NCAA tournament my second year and did quite well, and then we went to the Final Four my junior year. So I think my whole three years were the highlight of my UK career. There is not one moment I can really pick out. It was just a lot of fun for me and just a great experience. I wish everybody could have the opportunity to go and experience Kentucky basketball on that level because it is a different level and it really prepared me for the NBA being with coach Pitino. Just the atmosphere and things like that. It just really prepared me for what I'm doing now."

* * *

There was a familiar face in the 1993 NBA draft, which was held in Auburn Hills, Mich., a suburb of Detroit. None other than the telegenic

David Stern. Before a national TV audience, the NBA commissioner was there to announce the draft picks. And Mashburn -- who had already signed a lucrative $7 million shoe endorsement pact with Italy-based Fila -- was there, too, anticipating a very high selection in the first round. He wasn't the league's No. 1 pick, but close. The Dallas Mavericks selected him as the fourth selection overall. (Chris Webber of Michigan was the NBA's top overall pick by the Orlando Magic before he was traded to Golden State.) Although Mashburn would have loved to be the league's top pick, it was nevertheless a joyous moment for him and his family. He liked the Dallas franchise and its location after visiting the organization prior to the draft. He had an enjoyable visit with the newly-hired Mavericks coach – ex-Indiana Hoosier standout Quinn Buckner. In other words, he was very satisfied with Dallas and later signed a multi-year contract, reportedly worth nearly $33 million, with the Mavericks. The pact was the largest ever in the Dallas Mavericks' history.

Mashburn, who left UK as the school's fourth-leading all-time scorer with 1,843 points, later said he definitely has no regrets in departing Kentucky after his junior year. "It was my time to leave," he recalled. "Everybody develops quicker than others and it is just time and situation. I think coach Pitino did a real good job of letting people know that I was going to leave early so they could treat me as a senior and things like that. I think that was touching class on his part. (Also) it allowed other players like Tony Delk to step in and play. (Immediate playing time) is a big time thing in these years as far as recruiting.

"And I have no regrets at all. I mean I wish I had won the national championship. But I feel that all the championships they won after me, I feel that I had something to do with that. That is just how I am. They won and I feel like I had a ring. I was just as happy when they won and happy just to see their success. I didn't necessarily want to be there to take away from their moment. I just watched it on TV and I was so proud of those guys because I know in my heart how hard they work and what we go through as a team and I know what coach Pitino put them through. I had just as much enjoyment watching them as if I would have played also."

Even though Mashburn wasn't a senior, UK still honored him in a special ceremony following the Wildcats' 80-78 win over Auburn on Senior Night at Rupp Arena as the junior star said good-bye. Before the matchup, three Kentucky seniors – Dale Brown, Junior Braddy and Todd Svoboda – participated in an emotional moment, which ended with the singing of "My Old Kentucky Home." Mashburn scored a team-high 22 points as Kentucky barely survived when Auburn star Wesley Person, who took the game's scoring honors with 24 points, missed a 28-footer at the buzzer.

His mother, by the way, attended the ceremony, cherishing a special moment for her son. Mashburn was very pleased that she was able to come. During his years at UK, mom wasn't able to watch him play very often in person. The travel was too far and costly from Harlem. "She probably came once a year," he said. "She got down (there) to see quite a few of the games as much as she could. She was still working at the time. But she was always there for me, a phone call away."

Leaving UK early meant Mashburn did not get his bachelor's degree. A communications major, he needed more credit hours. And nearly 10 years later, Mashburn said he plans to complete the degree requirements. "It will be a while coming but I plan on getting it," Mashburn said. "It's a priority in my life." He hopes to receive his communications degree by completing the courses on the Internet and through a correspondence program (independent study), saying it's tough to do the coursework on the UK campus while playing in the NBA.

* * *

There is little doubt that Mashburn was Pitino's best player in college. The Mash said he learned a lot from Pitino, as they had a good player-coach relationship. "He was a good figure for me in college," Mashburn said. "He was more one-on-one. It was something I needed at the time. Very honest guy. I'm just always in his corner because he has meant a lot to me. I mean he could have been selfish enough just to keep me as a senior, but he said, 'Jamal, it is your time to go.' So he looks out for the best interest of his players and that is the type of coach a person ought to have. He treats his players like family. You might have some differences (with Pitino) sometimes like a lot of players do because of different personalities, but he has always been a very truthful and very honest person, and you have to take the good with the bad. That is something I've always learned."

After Mashburn left UK, he and Pitino have continued to stay in touch frequently. During the basketball season, they crossed paths many times on the court with Pitino coaching the Celtics and the Mash playing for Miami and Charlotte. And they have fostered a close relationship that goes beyond basketball. Mashburn, who would like to own an NBA franchise some day, has several business interests, including partnerships, with his college coach. They both have significant shares in car dealerships in Kentucky. Mashburn sometimes was seen in local TV commercials or magazine advertisements in the Bluegrass, promoting one of his dealerships. "And we have some restaurants out in California," said Mashburn. "We do a lot together. He's a true professional. It is just one of those relationships where it is just a lot of fun being with him because he has a lot of opportunities as well as I do. He is a good business partner now and good friend. He's introduced me to people that I probably would have never met. You know he got me to this point and I owe him a lot."

In addition to his automobile dealerships in Lexington, Berea and Corbin, Mashburn got involved in the boat business in August 2003. An investment group led by Mashburn purchased Sumerset Custom Houseboats, a boat manufacturing facility located in Somerset. Ex-Wildcat star Ron Mercer was also named as one of the new investors. Steve Lochmueller, who played for UK in the early 1970s, was chosen as the new chief executive officer (CEO) and president of the Somerset firm, which had been owned by the Neckel family in recent years.

If Mashburn is not running his business ventures or playing basketball, you'll probably find him on a golf course. He began playing golf during his collegiate days in Lexington and the sport has become one of his favorite hobbies.

* * *

Approximately two weeks before he signed a rich NBA pact, Mashburn decided he wanted to be a giver rather than a taker for a change. With his newly-found wealth, including his generous shoe contract, he wanted to make a difference in other people's lives, especially the needy children in Lexington. He generously gave $500,000 to UK to establish and administer a scholarship fund for the qualified eighth-grade students, who must maintain good grades and attendance in high school to obtain free tuition later at UK. Those who knew the Monster Mash weren't really surprised with his gesture, but his action, however, stunned many folks. Then-UK president Dr. Charles T. Wethington Jr. described Mashburn's gift as precedent setting, saying he didn't know of any other pro rookies who have made such a monstrous gift in the very early stages of their pro career.

"I think it was time for somebody to help out the program as far as on the academic end," Mashburn said. "(Since I left early), I wasn't going to get my degree that year. It is for the minority kids to really get the experience that I had at the academic level at the University of Kentucky. It wasn't something that was really a whole lot for me to do. I mean I have sent a kid from my neighborhood to the University of Kentucky and you know he wasn't in a $500,000 scholarship (program). Just to get the same experience I had. I had such a great time and I think a lot of kids don't get an opportunity to go to the type of university like that and experience all the school has to offer. Even though I was in the basketball program, I'm sure I didn't explore all the options that UK had as far as academics and all the things that it had. But I did the best I could."

In 2002, the first Jamal Mashburn Excel Scholarship recipients, including Wildcat football receiver Dougie Allen, graduated from UK.

* * *

The New Yorker had some rocky moments at Dallas. During his rookie season with the weak Mavericks in 1993-94, Mashburn and his coach, Quinn Buckner, as it turned out, couldn't get along. They had several disagreements. Perhaps it was Mashburn's growing pains in the NBA. He hated to be on a losing team. Or perhaps it was a rookie coach's lack of experience. Or perhaps Mashburn wanted Buckner to be a father figure like Pitino. Or perhaps it was miscommunication between both parties. The team's continuous habit of losing certainly didn't help. The Mavericks compiled a pitiful 13-69 mark, worst in the NBA.

Despite his difficulties, Mashburn posted impressive numbers on the court, averaging 19.2 points and 4.5 rebounds a game. And he was named to the 1994 NBA All-Rookie first team, joining Chris Webber, Anfernee Hardaway, Vin Baker and Isaiah Rider. In his second year under the direction of the squad's new coach, NBA veteran Dick Motta, Mashburn improved, hitting at a 24.1-point clip, good for fifth place in NBA scoring. The Mavericks were much better, too, coming up with a 36-46 mark. In a 124-120 overtime victory against host Chicago at the brand-new United Center, Mashburn pumped in 50 points against a tough defender by the name of Scottie Pippen. He became the second youngest player in NBA history to score at least 50 in a game. No, he didn't play against Michael Jordan, who later returned to pro basketball in March 1995 after a brief fling in minor league baseball with the Chicago White Sox organization.

And Mashburn stayed in Texas until February of 1997 when the Mavericks sent him to Miami in a four-player swap. Looking for a change of scenery, Mashburn was happy to leave Dallas. He felt unwanted and lonely. Pitino even applauded the move. At Miami, he would have the chance to play for one of the game's greatest coaches ever, Pat Riley. Many observers believed the change was what Mashburn needed at the time. He needed a coach who could communicate with him on the floor. But the overriding concern was, could Mashburn and Riley work together? Only time would tell.

* * *

For the next four years, Mashburn and his Miami Heat teammates found success under Riley's rigorous control. They posted 61-21, 55-27, 33-17 (lockout-shortened 1998-99 season) and 52-20 records. Mashburn said his dealings with Riley were on a professional level and nothing else. But he had hoped to develop a personal relationship with Riley, a former collegiate All-American who played for coach Adolph Rupp at Kentucky in the mid-1960s. Oddly, they rarely shared any stories, if any, about their UK days, according to Mashburn.

"We didn't have that type of relationship where we talked about Kentucky basketball a lot," he said. "He came from a different time, played in a different era from when I played. So we didn't really discuss it all. The whole four years that I was there (in Miami) it was more of a business relationship between him and me, coach and player, and nothing more. He mentioned some story about Kentucky or something like that, but it wasn't one-on-one. He mentioned it more to the team. I only remember one story. We didn't really have any dialogue about Kentucky basketball at all."

Interestingly, both Mashburn and Riley had their UK jerseys retired in 2000 during a ceremony before the Kentucky-Mississippi contest at Rupp Arena. But only Mashburn attended the event. Mashburn didn't really want to say much about Riley's absence, but UK officials commented that the Heat coach couldn't attend because of previous commitments. The Wildcat jersey of the late Bill Spivey, a 7-foot All-American in 1951, was also retired that evening.

* * *

During the 1999-2000 season, Mashburn, in a highly-publicized feud, said the Miami organization practically made him a scapegoat after he had failed to lead the Heat to the promised land. The problem became nearly unbearable in the spring of 2000 when Miami lost to the New York

Knicks in seven games in the Eastern Conference semifinals. In 37 postseason games with the Heat, Mashburn only posted an 11.7-point average, well below his career average.

In Game 7 of the series, Mashburn made a controversial decision in passing up a potential game-winning 12-foot shot in the waning seconds. Instead, he threw the ball to Clarence Weatherspoon, who ultimately missed the shot, as Miami lost an 83-82 heartbreaker. Since then, Mashburn has been often criticized for his failure to be a clutch player. Looking back, he later admitted that he probably should've taken the field goal attempt.

One week earlier, the aggressive New York media had a field day with Mashburn's behavior in Game 4. For instance, New York's *Daily News* printed a headline "Writer's Arm Gets Mashed," referring to a halftime episode which saw Mashburn getting angry. On his way to the dressing room, he got so frustrated that he kicked a table on the press row, which hit the arm of a female New York reporter. The writer reportedly had to get x-rays. Later, shortly after New York defeated Miami 91-83, Mashburn apologized to the sportswriter, explaining that he was upset with the officials that no foul had been called at the end of the first half. But he also said that he shouldn't have gotten real upset anyway.

Nevertheless, it wasn't a very pleasant time for Mashburn, whose performance would face a lot of scrutiny in the next few months.

* * *

Mashburn, who came to the Charlotte Hornets in a major nine-player deal in August of 2000 and later signed a six-year contract extension worth nearly $54 million, has said traveling in the NBA is difficult, going from one city to another nearly every night. But because of his astronomical salary, he said he shouldn't be complaining too much about the traveling and other woes. While the big-money contracts have made his life much more comfortable, Mashburn added that his NBA green bucks haven't really changed his personality much, if any. He is still a soft-spoken individual with a friendly smile who cares about people. He doesn't forget where he came from. For instance, when he played for the Miami Heat, he bought 35 tickets to every home game for local outstanding students to sit in the "Mash Pit."

"It changes your lifestyle," said Mashburn, who is married and has one daughter, Taylor, and one son, Jamal Jr. "It changes things like where you live and how you live. What it does not change is the person. I mean you still stay the same. You still have the same values that you always had as a kid growing up.

"It is just people change from being 17 years old to 28 years old even without money. So it depends on you. It is for good or for worse. I know I've changed since being 17 years old, since leaving Kentucky and being around new environments and being around different people. I met a lot of people. That is a lot that could have influenced me, but the money hasn't changed me. It just means you can do a lot more things. Money comes and goes."

Ex-Charlotte assistant coach Lee Rose, a Kentucky native who formerly coached at Transylvania University and Purdue, among others, agreed that Mashburn is one of the more unassuming stars in the NBA. "We are talking about his personality here and he is such a friendly, outgoing, pleasant and receptive individual," Rose said. "When you have been in it as long as I have, you just feel so fortunate to have a player like this on your team because he is approachable and he is reasonable and he works hard. So he brings with it a total package."

* * *

Call Mashburn an early bird if you like. He usually arrives early for a team practice or a game. Before every contest, the Mash performs an interesting ritual in the locker room. He always puts his left sneaker on before the right and he makes sure that his shoe laces are even.

Rose liked his attitude and work ethic. "He is generally the first player here when we are getting ready to play a game," Rose said. "So this is a typical day for him. He comes in early. He'll come in a half hour early before any of the other players arrive and get his workout in and get his shooting in. He is a consummate player. He does all the things that as coaches you would want him to do in terms of staying in shape and conditioning. He has his own personal trainer who helps him in terms of stretching and he is an extensive stretcher before and after practice, which really is such a smart thing because that will extend his career considerably."

While at Miami, Mashburn suffered various injuries, missing numerous games in parts of the 1997-98 and 1998-99 seasons. The Mash thought part of his frequent injury woes came about because of tightness in his muscles. So, he later decided to use the services of a special trainer, Ed Downs, who was hired by the Heat. Mashburn figured it doesn't hurt to try something different and the new workout scheme could pay off in the long run.

After the Mash went to Charlotte, he continued to utilize the services of Downs. Since Mashburn was no longer a member of the Miami Heat, he had to hire him as a personal trainer, beginning with the 2000-01 season. So Downs, based in Miami, flew to Charlotte or wherever Mashburn and the Hornets were playing, usually every two weeks. The Hornet superstar pointed out that while people like to spend their money on vehicles, he instead spent his on a personal trainer. Mashburn acknowledged that some people may find his expensive business arrangement with his trainer rather unusual, but he just wanted to protect his lucrative professional career and play basketball.

* * *

His first year with the Hornets was a very interesting one. For the most part, the 2000-01 campaign was fun. Mashburn was having one of his best NBA seasons. He enjoyed his teammates as well as coach Paul Silas' laid-back coaching style. The 6-8 swingman played a significant role in Charlotte's success. The team's top scorer with a 20.1-point average, Mashburn led the squad to a regular season mark of 46-36. The Hornets surprised everyone when they also won a franchise-record six post-season games, sweeping the favored Miami Heat in the opening round, before dropping to Milwaukee in the seventh game of the Eastern Conference semifinals. Mashburn, who finished the season on a high note, averaging 24.9 points and 6.2 rebounds in 10 playoff games, pointed out his success at Charlotte mainly came about because he had more freedom and control with the ball in the Hornets' system.

But he had a big scare earlier in the season. In October, when his 54-year-old mother, Helen, wasn't feeling right, she decided to go to the doctor. She had bad news. It was discovered that she had cancer. It was a major setback for the Mashburn family. Helen underwent colon cancer surgery and received chemotherapy treatments. That made her weak and sick. And she had to miss her son's New York debut as a Hornet when the Knicks hosted Charlotte at Madison Square Garden in early November. With his ailing mother recovering at home, the Mash tried his best to keep the focus on the game in his hometown. He did fairly well, getting 18 points and 11 rebounds, both team-highs, but it wasn't a pretty night as the cold-shooting Hornets dropped 81-67 to coach Jeff Van Gundy's club. "She has been battling that and most of the family has been battling that," Mashburn said of her fight with cancer. "She is doing well."

Although he is generally a very private person, Mashburn had good publicity – local and national -- during his first year at Charlotte, including a four-page spread in *Sports Illustrated* magazine. Also, the magazine, in another issue, did an impressive cover story on the Hornets titled, "A Week in the Life of an NBA Playoff Team," along with several "behind the scenes" photos, including three on Mashburn. One photo had Mashburn relaxing and laughing with other teammates at a major league baseball game in Milwaukee. The media, for the most part, liked him. Unlike some NBA players, he is a gentle and humble person.

After a home game in March with the Chicago Bulls in which Mashburn scored a game-high 28 points and dished out career-high 14 assists, the author sat down with him in the team's dressing room for one of two pre-arranged book interviews. He had just finished the post-game interviews with the other members of the news media that cover the Hornets on regular basis. The author sarcastically told him that he must be pretty popular, as everybody wanted to interview him. He just grinned.

"Yeah, that's how it is," Mashburn said. "(It's) just part of being a professional basketball player and I take everything in stride and continue to work at it, never taking anything too seriously. This is just part of my life and it is just a lot of fun right now."

In the opening-round playoffs, the Hornets stunned Riley's Miami club, dominating the Heat in three games in the best-of-five series. For Mashburn, the sweep was even sweeter as it involved his former team. During the emotional series, he unveiled unflattering comments about Riley, saying the coach wasn't always sincere. According to *The Miami Herald*, the Mash also questioned Riley's worth as a super motivator.

* * *

Later, after Charlotte moved its franchise to New Orleans in 2002, Mashburn got off to a fresh start in the Big Easy. During the 2002-03 season, he stayed healthy, playing in all of the team's 82 games, and finished as the Hornets' top scorer with a 21.6-point average. The month of February 2003 was good to Mashburn. He earned his first-ever NBA All-Star Game appearance in Atlanta, pouring in 10 points on 4-of-7 shooting in the East's 155-145 victory over the West in two overtimes. About two weeks later, he hit 50 points against Memphis, matching his career high.

It was a very special time for Mashburn, who at the end of the previous season had suffered a mysterious illness that wouldn't go away.

While in Charlotte, he was sick for awhile and no one, including the doctors, knew exactly what was wrong. Mashburn said he had been diagnosed with everything. Some say it was a stomach virus. Some say it was flu. Some say it was anemia. Some say it was vitamin B-12 deficiency. Some thought it was related to a lower abdominal strain which earlier had caused him to miss the first 42 games of the 2001-02 season. It was his concerned mother, Helen, who encouraged him to find another opinion. Finally, it was determined that Mashburn had a positional vertigo and he eventually became healthy again after recovering at his off-season home in Miami. Nevertheless, it was a very scary moment for Mashburn and his family, who at one time had thought his roundball career might be ending prematurely.

* * *

In a polite manner, Mashburn refused to reveal his political views, whether he was a liberal, moderate or conservative. He would not say if he generally voted for a Republican, Democrat or another party candidate. Asked if he was a Democrat like President Clinton, who had established an office in Mashburn's hometown of Harlem after leaving the White House in January of 2001, Mashburn just smiled. "I'd rather not discuss my political status or what I believe in," he said. "I keep that personal. I think it is a little private (matter)."

But he was happy to see Clinton locate an office in Harlem for his post-presidential duties. The former President's decision to move to New York City provided a public relations boost for economically-depressed Harlem, which had already begun to attract new businesses and tourists. In the summer of 2000, retired NBA star Magic Johnson opened a movie theater, becoming a part of the new $66 million Harlem USA shopping and entertainment mall. The Starbucks Coffee Co., in a joint partnership with Johnson, also opened a Starbucks coffee retail store in Harlem.

"That means Harlem is growing," said Mashburn. "Anytime the President wants to buy real estate and be in an office up there, it means a lot to the community itself. Magic Johnson has invested in a lot of companies there. Old Navy and a lot of big corporations have invested in there and it really brings up the value of the area. It is a good location for a lot of different things. It would be one of the better things and something that you can be proud of. I'll probably end up there myself one of these days."

Call it home sweet home.

Chapter 7

Coal Miner's Son

In West Virginia, the city of Fairmont with a population of nearly 20,000 folks is the home of U.S. Olympic hero Mary Lou Retton, who captivated an international audience with her stunning gymnastic moves in 1984. After winning five medals, the 4-foot-8 beauty with a cute smile became a big celebrity, reaching the covers of many magazines, appearing on television shows, and splashing her face on a Wheaties cereal box.

While Retton, whose father, Ronnie, once played as a 5-7 guard on West Virginia's 1959 NCAA Final Four basketball team, is certainly the city's biggest sports star, Fairmont also boasts another well-known athlete. His name is Jared Prickett, a former Wildcat hoops standout who was a member of UK's three Final Four teams in the 1990s. In 1992, before coming to Kentucky, he was the state's high school player of the year, leading Fairmont West to its first undefeated regular season.

Although Prickett actually didn't live in Fairmont, he still listed the city as his hometown in UK's media guides during his college years. If you want to be technical or picky about it, his true home is actually about a couple of miles or so from Fairmont. "The town's name is Barrackville," said Prickett. "It is two or three minutes from Fairmont. It has about 1,000 people at the most. That might be pushing it. Everybody knows where Fairmont is and that's why I say I'm from Fairmont."

Located in the northern part of West Virginia, the Fairmont area is where Prickett grew up and learned the game of basketball and other sports. His father, Don, once played hoops for a local college team, coached by Mary Lou Retton's uncle. At Fairmont State College, a former NAIA powerhouse now a member of NCAA Division II, the elder Prickett was a contributor to legendary Joe Retton's head coaching career, which lasted from 1963 to 1982 with an overall record of 478-95.

"They went to two Final Fours in Kansas City and I think they ended up losing both of them, but you know they were there," said the younger

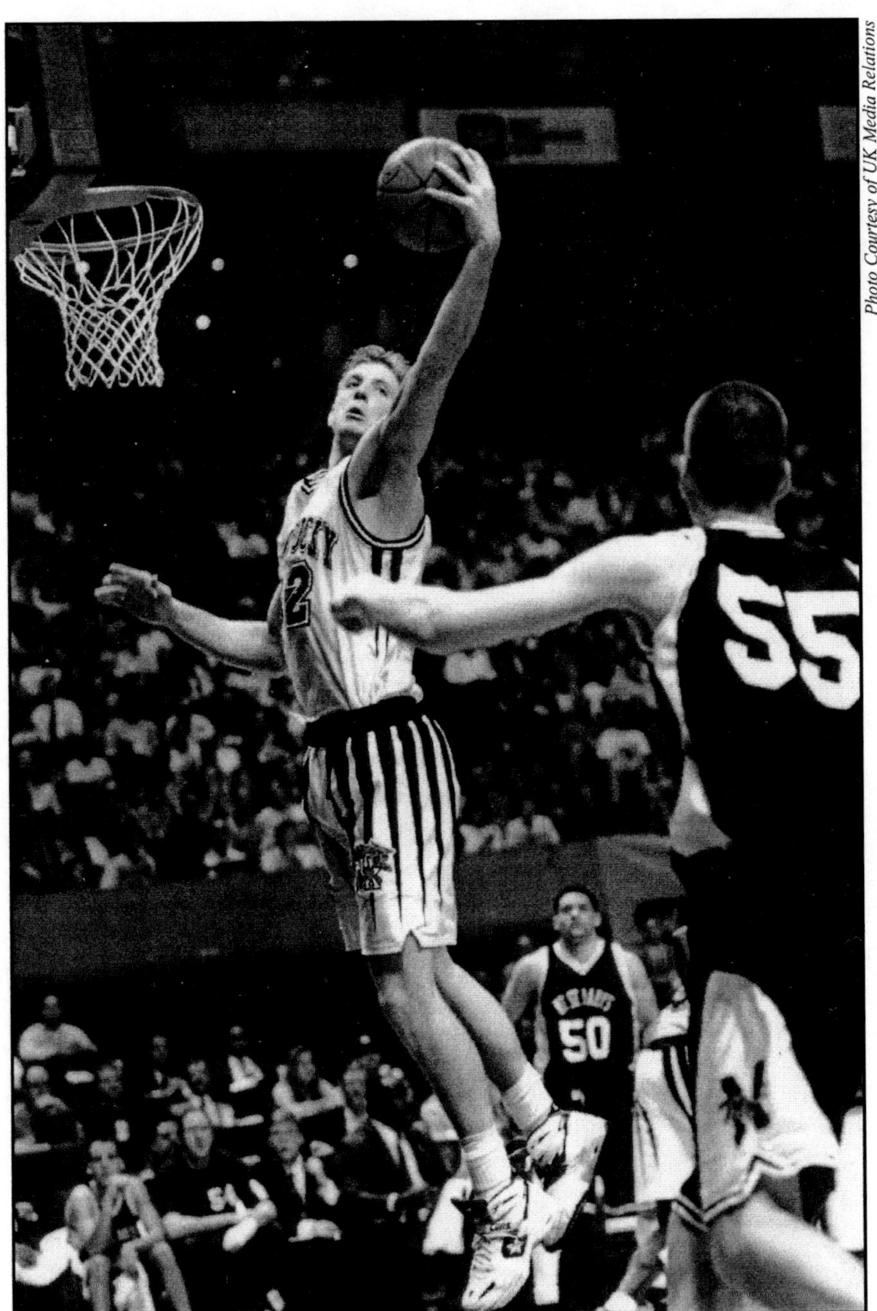

Photo Courtesy of UK Media Relations

Kentucky's Jared Prickett is shown here grabbing a rebound at Rupp Arena during the mid-1990s. Prickett comes from Fairmont, West Virginia, the hometown of U.S. Olympic hero Mary Lou Retton.

Prickett. "He was a good ball player."

Unlike Jared, who stands at 6-9, the elder Prickett didn't fight the boards. Said the younger Prickett, "My dad is 6-foot-1. He is not a very tall guy at all. He is the one who taught me how to play ball and taught me how to use both of my hands and do all the little things with the ball.

"I had a pretty typical, normal childhood. I was a young kid who liked to play all the sports – basketball, baseball and football. I had a big brother and a little sister. So I had a big brother to beat up on all the time and a couple of the neighbors. I always liked to hang out with the older guys, which was kind of good later on in life and made me tougher."

Growing up in the 1980s when Boston and Los Angeles often battled for the NBA championship, Prickett had a favorite player. "I was a big Magic (Johnson) fan and you know he was my favorite out there on the court," he said. "I used to like the Lakers. You either liked the Celtics (who had star Larry Bird) or the Lakers and I was a Lakers fan."

And when he was in the eighth grade, his parents took him to see an NBA game in Cleveland. It was a special trip that he will never forget as the family didn't attend many college or pro sporting events. "I had some relatives that lived in Cleveland and that was the closest NBA game that we could get to and I had an option to either go see the Lakers or the (Chicago) Bulls," Prickett said. "Actually I passed up (the Lakers) at this point in time and that's when Michael Jordan was playing. I chose the Bulls to go see Michael Jordan play. I think Michael had like 44 (points) that night. So it was definitely worth the trip and I had a good time."

Prickett also listed his dad as his primary inspiration in sports. Like many folks in West Virginia, Prickett's father worked in the coal mines. "He is a foreman in the coal mines so he overlooks a lot of the guys," said Jared in the summer of 2001, adding that his father, who was in his mid-50s at the time, was about to retire after over 25 years in the coal fields. Meanwhile, Prickett's mother basically stayed home as a housewife. When the younger Prickett had a problem, he went to his mom. "If there was any kind of problem, mom was taking care of it," he said. "Dad was working a lot so mom took care of all the problems."

* * *

At Fairmont West High, Prickett wasn't known as an academic scholar. But he was a good student and had no problems with the teachers. "I did my work and I made over 3.0 (GPA) in high school," he said. "I was a solid 'B' student."

By the time he was a junior, major universities actively began to recruit Prickett with basketball in mind. And he became one of the nation's top recruits as a senior. The scouts and coaches liked his potential with his 6-7, 205-pound frame. As Kentucky coach Rick Pitino would later say, Prickett was a more talented version of Deron Feldhaus.

During the fall of his senior year, Prickett fell in love with UK and Lexington during his official visit on a football/basketball weekend, which included the Big Blue Madness festivities at Memorial Coliseum. As a result, he made a verbal commitment, selecting the Wildcats over Notre Dame, and three weeks later he kept his promise, inking a national letter of intent with the school. According to Prickett, the campus visits to Notre Dame and Kentucky were the only ones he made. The other tentative visits were planned for Florida State, Wake Forest and Connecticut, but they were canceled.

Later, while he was a fifth-year senior at Kentucky, he still listed signing with the Cats as his greatest moment in sports, according to UK's 1996-97 media guide.

Prickett, though, nearly signed with the Fighting Irish, then coached by John MacLeod, who also was the former head coach of the NBA's Phoenix Suns in the 1970s and '80s. And the youngster wasn't even Catholic. He also liked Notre Dame's high academic standards. "After I went to Notre Dame, I was ready to sign," he said. "My dad told me, 'No, you have lots of time to make sure. You take your other visits and make the decision after you visit all the schools.' "

When Prickett decided that he wanted to attend UK after visiting the campus, his cautious father again had the same response, strongly suggesting that the youngster take all of the official visits arranged by the other universities. But this time the younger Prickett held firm, telling his father, "No, I don't want to take any more visits. I'm ready to sign."

At the Big Blue Madness, which was also attended by highly-ranked prep stars Rodrick Rhodes, Tony Delk and Walter McCarty, Prickett was impressed and thrilled. "I was overwhelmed how great the fans were," he recalled. "It's another whole world. They treat basketball like you are family. So once I saw that I knew there was no other choice for me. (Kentucky) was definitely where I wanted to go.

"My parents were there, but they didn't sit with me. I sat with the other players and stuff. Whenever you come to Madness, you kind of get cold chills when they start playing the songs and you know the crowd gets that loud. It is definitely a different feeling. So I got cold chills and that was another reason that I knew I wanted to come there."

According to Pitino in his 1993 paperback edition, *Full-Court Pressure*, associate coach Herb Sendek deserved a lot of credit for persuading Prickett to come to the Bluegrass by comparing Kentucky and Notre Dame in the area of academics during their visit to Prickett's home in Fairmont. While acknowledging that Prickett is a very capable student, Sendek explained that a classroom environment at Notre Dame is very competitive, like a college player going against a professional player on the floor, and it wouldn't be easy for Prickett.

"It went over well," Prickett said of the in-house visit by Pitino and Sendek with his parents. "He (Pitino) said if you want to make it to the NBA he definitely would do all the work to help me get there. He said, "I've been there." He knew what it takes to get there and he said you will be coming to the right place."

Despite Pitino's New York City background, Prickett had the feeling that the head coach was at ease at his home in a rural mountain area. "Coach Pitino is comfortable wherever he goes," he said. "It doesn't matter if he is in the city, country, wherever. You know he can handle himself in any environment. So I think he felt pretty comfortable and laid back. He was confident in what he was speaking and you know that goes a long way."

So, with his collegiate decision out of the way, Prickett was able to focus on basketball and enjoy his senior year. Indeed, it was a fun year as Fairmont West High was ranked No. 1 virtually the entire campaign, finishing with a near-perfect 28-1 mark. He led the Polar Bears in scoring (19.2 points) and in rebounding (14.6), guiding them to the state title game where Beckley Woodrow Wilson upset them in a 79-59 decision.

On losing the state tourney's championship game, Prickett commented, "It was a rough situation. None of us had a good game. The other team was ready for us. We had beaten them earlier in the year, but just by like four or five points. They were a really good team and they were second all year. They were playing really well at the time and they had a great night. We just didn't have it together that night. I felt pretty bad."

* * *

After that dreaded setback in the tourney, Prickett, who was ranked among the Top 35 in the 1992 senior class by *Hoop Scoop*, was ready to move on. He said signing with UK certainly helped him to overcome the disappointment. "I put that (setback) behind me. I came down (to UK) early in the summer time and made sure everything went well with my college career," he said.

Now a 6-9, 210-pounder, Prickett got off to a good start as a freshman, impressing Pitino in pre-season practices and scrimmages with his hustling attitude and strong rebounding. And he played in all 34 games, starting nine of the last 10 game as the 30-4 Wildcats gave Pitino his first Final Four trip as UK boss.

During the NCAA tournament, Prickett got national attention when he sparked the top-seeded Cats to a 106-81 victory over Florida State in the Southeast Regional finals in Charlotte. He led all scorers with 22 points, which later turned out to be his UK career high, and grabbed 11 rebounds along with three assists. "I remember the Florida State game," said Prickett, whose outstanding performance earned him a spot on the NCAA All-Southeast Regional team. "That was a good game for me. Actually in that game I just handled the ball a lot of the time and they were coming to me. I had a little bit smaller guy on me with (6-5) Bob Sura. He just couldn't (defend) and he was too small for me.

"We had so many good players on the team while I was there at UK that I was never really the "go to guy" where they would just give you the ball. So I had to fit into the system. It was kind of hard to play like that and expect to get 20 or 30 points per game. But that particular game (against Florida State) they came to me a couple of times and I scored. Then they came back a couple of more times and I kept scoring. So they started coming to me all the time. And I had a good game."

As a rookie playing in the NCAA Final Four for the first time, Prickett was obviously thrilled. It was something that he will never forget, going against Michigan's Fab Five and star Chris Webber, although Jamal Mashburn-led Kentucky lost 81-78 in overtime. "That's definitely a good experience to go out there and play against Webber," he commented. "Now I'd put him in the Top 10 players in the NBA, if not the Top 5. It's a good feeling to know that you played out there and competed against these guys."

Webber took the championship contest's scoring and rebounding honors with game-highs of 27 points and 13 rebounds. Prickett, meanwhile, had nine points, including 7 of 7 free throws, and a team-high seven rebounds before fouling out.

And Prickett was on his way to a very productive career at Kentucky in the next four seasons, including the one he had to sit out most of the year because of an injured knee.

* * *

Later, as a fifth-year senior when the 1996-97 campaign began, Prickett, a power forward, was UK's only big man with significant playing experience in the frontline. Kentucky had lost 6-10 Mark Pope, 6-10 Walter McCarty and 6-8 Antoine Walker (along with 6-1 Tony Delk), all NBA draft picks, from its 1996 championship squad. And that was a major concern even though the team still had plenty of talent, especially on the outside, with 6-5 swingman Derek Anderson and 6-7 forward Ron Mercer. Big men lacking experience included 6-10 freshman Jamaal Magloire, 6-10 sophomore Nazr Mohammed, 6-9 sophomore forward Scott Padgett (who was returning after sitting out the previous season for academic reasons) and 6-8 sophomore forward Oliver Simmons. Magloire and Mohammed were the team's only centers.

But during the pre-season workouts, Pitino wasn't real sure about the West Virginian's contribution to the team. Pitino had commented that Prickett could have done better in the seasons after his rookie campaign. Said Pitino, "The jury is still out on Jared. If he can regain the ferociousness he showed as a freshman, and keep working hard, he'll be a good ball player."

Prickett didn't really argue Pitino's viewpoint that the player hadn't reached his potential. "It's possible," he said, "but you know with the talented players that came in, it was hard to get the time to do anything well underneath Pitino. So I was happy to get 20 minutes a game. We just had so much talent. It was hard to fit people in there. I felt that if I had more playing time and got the ball a little bit more, my stats definitely would have been higher. It's just a matter of being out there a little bit more on the court, but whenever I'm splitting time 50-50 with Scott Padgett or Walter McCarty and those guys, it's hard for me to get playing time."

With him being the squad's only experienced big guy, Prickett claimed he wasn't under a great deal of pressure to produce. Perhaps he was right. The defending national champion Cats managed to cruise to a 35-5 mark with a runner-up finish in the NCAA tourney. "There wasn't really any extra pressure," said Prickett, who was a co-captain that season. "By then I was just so used to it by playing. There isn't really any pressure. But at the same time if there was pressure, it's a good pressure to have when you are out there on the court. As long as I'm playing basketball, I'm pretty comfortable out there. So that kind of takes the pressure away. You don't have time to think out there because you are doing the coach Pitino system. By then I knew it backwards and forwards. It's pretty easy to go through it, just go out there and play hard."

During Kentucky's run for the NCAA title, it was Prickett who helped the foul-plagued Wildcats stay alive in the Big Dance. He and Cameron Mills combined to hit 26 of Kentucky's 35 points in the first half in leading the team to a 75-69 second-round victory over Iowa. All of Prickett's 15 points, ironically, came in the opening half.

But Prickett couldn't do enough in the title game against a quick Arizona squad in Indianapolis. Like three other teammates, he fouled out, finishing with six points as Arizona prevailed 84-79 in overtime. According to Prickett, that was his most disappointing moment at Kentucky. "The absolute most frustrating moment was when I fouled out in the final game," he said. "I wish I could have stayed on the court just to help the team win. Probably the most frustrating (part) is that we had it. We could have won it and we didn't."

Despite the loss, Pitino told the squad at the hotel not to feel ashamed for their performance, according to Prickett. "Coach P sat us down and said, 'We played our hearts out and gave it a great effort.' So we held our heads high and went on about our business.

"You have to accept a loss. You've got to accept it whether you win or lose. We played hard and it was the game of the season. We were one of the last two teams in the nation to be there and we went into overtime. So that is not a bad run at it. It was a great season."

Like Prickett, it also was Pitino's last game at UK. Less than two months later, Pitino accepted a challenge to rebuild the storied Celtics franchise in Boston.

The hard-nosed Prickett, who at the time broke a 48-year-old school record for most games played with 143, completed his UK career with 998 points, just two points shy of the 1,000-point club.

* * *

On the academic side, when Prickett first came to UK as a freshman, he wasn't sure what he wanted to study. But that wasn't a problem as the freshmen and sophomores had to take the basic courses anyway. General education courses such as history, mathematics, English and psychology courses were required at UK. So he had time to decide on his field of study.

And there were several classes that Prickett really liked. The Wildcat standout especially enjoyed the courses taught by history professor Dr.

Randolph Daniel. Prickett was motivated and liked listening to what Dr. Daniel had to say about various historical events. "I had about four different history classes under Dr. Daniel," he said. "Those were definitely my favorite classes.

"There were usually a lot of athletes in there that you could talk to and meet before class and stuff like that. (There were) baseball, basketball, football and some tennis players in there. You know you get to talk to them a little bit. I had a few other (courses) – marketing classes and a couple of communication classes – which I really enjoyed as well. But if one had to stand out, I would say Dr. Daniel's history (classes)."

In mid-March of 1996, just before the Cats began the NCAA tourney action, Prickett, who had missed most of the campaign because of a bad knee, apparently didn't study or do his homework. When Pitino found out about Prickett's poor academics, he got very furious with him. So the coach suspended Prickett from the team.

But it was just a temporary setback for the upperclassman, who had finally picked his major. Later, according to Prickett, he received his bachelor's degree in communications. "I got my degree and I'm proud of it," he added.

* * *

Throughout his UK career, Prickett, whose nickname is JP, had different roommates at the Wildcat Lodge. "The first year I lived with (Jeff) Brassow, my second year with Gimel Martinez, my third year with Jeff Sheppard, my fourth year with Nazr Mohammed and my fifth year was again, I think, with Sheppard," recalled Prickett.

But Prickett, like his other teammates, had different roommates when the team traveled on the road. "The thing is you never knew who you were going to room with," he said. "You didn't have a particular roommate. You just show up (in the room) and you might be rooming with Ron Mercer one day, the next time Anthony (Epps) and the next time Wayne Turner."

According to Prickett, the players were comfortable with Pitino's traveling policy on roommates despite their different backgrounds. "Nobody had any problems with that," he said. "You know it brought everybody (closer). It made everybody like everybody. Some guys are from the country and other guys from the city and you put them both in one room. If you have to room with them, you get to know other people."

His closest friend on the team? "I didn't really have one particular close friend," Prickett said. "I was pretty close friends with all of the guys. I hung out with Jeff Sheppard and (Scott) Padgett quite a bit. But I'm pretty good friends with Nazr Mohammed, Allen Edwards and Antoine Walker. I'm a pretty easy-going guy and pretty much friends with all the guys on the team. But you know I think everybody was pretty much the same way."

* * *

During his Wildcat tenure, Prickett has seen many interesting happenings. For instance, he saw his teammates beat LSU 99-95 in a stunning come-from-behind victory in 1994. He saw a copy of the *Sports Illustrated* magazine, featuring Pitino as "A Man Possessed" in an unflattering cover story. He heard annual rumors about Pitino leaving the Wildcat program for big bucks in the NBA. Here are Prickett's comments on various topics:

On Kentucky's nationally-televised victory at LSU which saw the Cats fall behind by a big margin in the second half before getting hot: "I'd say the most surprising moment and game that we had was the one at LSU when we came back. To be down 31 points and come back like that, like we did, is just amazing. You don't see teams down 31 points with 15 minutes to go in the game and come back and win. But we did and it was an unbelievable game.

"(Earlier in the game) they were on fire and we weren't. We were playing (decent basketball). It wasn't that we were playing horrible. We were getting good shots, but our shots weren't going in and they were hitting everything that they shot up. We just couldn't do anything, but we came back actually with most of the guys off the bench -- Chris Harrison and Jeff Brassow -- coming in and having a big game. You know that was an interesting moment."

On LSU players and coaches after that game: "I don't think they were too happy."

On Pitino's comments to the team in regard to Sports Illustrated's 1996 article on the coach: "He was on the cover. I don't really remember but he probably said, 'Don't pay any attention to this. You know we are here to take care of our business and you just put that to the side.' That's the type of guy he would be. He would just say, 'Don't pay any attention to all this. This hype doesn't mean anything if you don't get it done on the court.' "

On Pitino's thoughts about his players reading the newspaper articles: "Coach P told us to stay away from the newspapers. He told the players, 'Don't even look at the newspapers, good or bad.' So that is pretty much what I did. I didn't look at the newspapers a whole lot. We just played basketball and concentrated on our books. And that was it." (But Prickett now keeps up with current events on a regular basis. "I read the newspaper and keep up on the news and stuff of that nature," he said.)

On never-ending rumors about Pitino departing the Bluegrass for the NBA: "That didn't make me nervous. If he would have left, another coach would have had to come in and it would have been a big difference to switch coaches. But I'm thankful that he didn't (leave) at the time. Our style and system were good. But Tubby (Smith) came in (1997) and has done a great job with them. I possibly could have played on one of his teams. I think I'd enjoy playing for Tubby just one year to see a different style of basketball. But I really don't know any other style but coach Pitino's. I had a blast running his style. I have no regrets."

On Pitino's comments about wanting Prickett to rebound like Dennis Rodman: "That made me feel great. I guess I just have a knack for the ball, knowing where the ball is going. I can see which way it is going to come when they are shooting and just be around the basket at the right time. That is what it is about."

His favorite story about Pitino: "My favorite story? (He laughed.) There are so many stories. Coach Pitino was definitely a disciplinarian and a strict person. But at the same time you had a lot of respect for him just because you knew what he could do. How he could motivate you to get you to win and I have the utmost respect for him when it comes to that type of situation. But no one thing really stands out. I could tell you story after story after story, but it was a good time to go through the UK system and to be under him – just to learn responsibility, making sure you go to class, respect him as a coach and treat everybody else the same way that you would like to be treated. You know he ran a first-class program and I definitely benefited from it."

Asked if Pitino ever played a practical joke on him: "Did he play a practical joke on me? Not really. He called me quite a few names if you can count that as a practical joke along my stretch of career. I don't think you can print the names. He said it was all for a reason and you know he tried to get the best out of everybody."

* * *

One of Prickett's basketball shortcomings, according to NBA scouts, was his lack of shooting consistency. That was a big reason he wasn't selected in the 1997 NBA Draft. However, that didn't prevent him from chasing his dream, making money while playing basketball. He became a free agent and tried out for the Atlanta Hawks.

According to Prickett, he performed well in the league's rookie camp during that summer. "I was one of three players out of 20 to get invited back (to the Hawks' training camp)," he said. "So that made me feel good. I went down there and played well, actually, for Atlanta but the coach released me. He said he wanted to keep a veteran.

"I was disappointed. I definitely wanted to make it. I went to the CBA for a year and tried to make it through there. The money just wasn't good enough for me to stay in the states another year and try to make it so I had to go (overseas) to make some money."

He since has played pro basketball in France, Italy and Argentina. "They take care of you (financially)," said Prickett, pointing out that some of his pay is already tax-free. "They give you free housing, free food, and a car. You get two round-trip tickets. They give you everything that you need and then they pay you on top of that. So they treat you good over there. No problem."

But staying in a foreign country has drawbacks as well. "I'm away from home too long, away from friends and family, you know, nine months at a time, and that gets to be old. Other than that, everything else was great," said Prickett, who also tried out for the NBA's Philadelphia 76ers. "It is a whole different culture and it is a whole different world over there so it is nice to come back here (in Kentucky) and see what (we have). I think we take for granted what we have here because everything here is so nice. But once you get over there and realize how nice we really have it, it is good to know."

Well, no matter where Prickett is today, playing basketball or working as an entrepreneur, he will always be a Wildcat at heart.

Chapter 8

Nashville Star

In 1997, not long after he left Kentucky, Ron Mercer gave his mother, Birdie Mercer, a very memorable Mother's Day gift – a very big and expensive present. Since he could afford just about anything with his forthcoming guaranteed rich contract with the Boston Celtics, it was a thoughtful way of showing his appreciation for all she had done for him.

"The first thing I did was grab my mom a car for Mother's Day," said Mercer, who purchased a brand new Cadillac for her. He commented that's his biggest thrill.

Even though he has been away from his hometown of Nashville during the basketball season since his high school days, Mercer and his mother have maintained a very close relationship. "I talk to her three or four times a week," he said in an interview before an NBA game. Mercer, who lives in Nashville during the off-season, also has three siblings – Monia, Mario and Michael.

* * *

Mercer said he has no regrets about leaving the Bluegrass early in 1997 for the NBA. During his sophomore year at Kentucky, he showed everybody, including coach Rick Pitino, that he was ready to move on to bigger things. Indeed, he was. He was named consensus first-team All-American and SEC Player of the Year. He also led the league in scoring, averaging 18.1 points. In UK's 101-87 victory over Purdue at Chicago, Mercer pumped in his career-high 30 points, hitting 13 of 16 shots from the field.

"I think I made a good choice," Mercer said several years later. "You always look back and think about what could have been if I had stayed. Would we have won three (NCAA titles) out of four (years), maybe? You wonder about those things."

In Mercer's last season in a Wildcat uniform, Kentucky nearly won

Photo Courtesy of Indiana Pacers (Ron Hoskins/NBAE/Getty Images)

Wearing a white headband, NBA standout Ron Mercer, a former Indiana Pacer who is now with the 2003 league champion San Antonio Spurs, dribbles against Philadelphia's Allen Iverson (3) during a 2003 contest. Mercer played only two years at UK before leaving for the NBA.

the national crown for the second straight year. But coach Lute Olson's surprising Arizona Wildcats were just a better team – barely -- as they defeated foul-plagued UK 84-79 in overtime. Before fouling out, Mercer – who announced earlier in the season that he was turning pro – had scored his last points for the 35-5 Wildcats and it was in the NCAA championship game. He finished with 13 points, nine rebounds and six assists.

By skipping his junior and senior years at Kentucky, Mercer became Pitino's third underclassman bound for the NBA to leave the Wildcat program. Jamal Mashburn and Antoine Walker were the other stars who went to the pros early.

Joining Mercer in the 1997 NBA Draft was his friend and teammate, Derek Anderson. They were both lottery picks with the Boston Celtics (who had just lured Pitino away from Kentucky) getting Mercer as the league's No. 6 selection overall and Cleveland selecting Anderson as the 13th pick overall.

That would mean Mercer would get to play for his college coach in the NBA after all. Not many players can say that. Mercer is one lucky player. And that made his transition from Kentucky blue to Celtic green a lot easier. Mercer pointed out that Pitino also brought in a couple of his Wildcat assistants – Jim O'Brien and Winston Bennett – and other UK staffers to Boston. As a result, the Celtics had a lot of Kentucky flavor and the coaches pretty much ran the same plays at Boston as they did at Kentucky.

Mercer was asked if he was then excited about playing for Pitino again at a new place. He commented, "I think it helped me out for my first year to go to a coach that I already knew, trainers that I already knew and plays that I already knew so I kind of had a step up on everybody coming into a whole other level." Also helping Mercer adjust at Boston were 6-10 forward Walter McCarty, a former Kentucky teammate who was beginning his first year as a Celtic after spending his rookie year with the New York Knicks, and second-year 6-9 forward Antoine Walker.

* * *

May 18, 1976.

That will always be a very special day in the ML and Birdie Mercer household. A bouncing baby boy, named Ronald Eugene Mercer, came into the world in Nashville. And it wouldn't be too long before Mercer became exposed to athletics. Like many other typical kids, he had a childhood hero. Not surprisingly, his favorite sports figure was Magic Johnson, the NBA superstar back in the 1980s. Mercer, who was usually the tallest player on the playgrounds, liked him because Magic was very tall for a guard and it gave the youngster hope that he could do other things besides playing center.

But the very shy kid also excelled in other sports – football, golf and baseball. It looked as if he would be a big star in baseball. Mercer had natural talent for the summer pastime. He had a strong arm. When he was 12 years old, he pitched for the 13-and-under team, helping the squad advance to the semifinals of the Continental Amateur Baseball World tournament in Nebraska.

And he became a household name in the prep ranks where he starred at Goodpasture Christian School in Madison, Tenn., located about eight miles from Nashville. As an eighth-grader, he was throwing strikes for coach Jeff Forehand's Cougars' varsity squad and folks began to notice. A year later, he threw a no-hitter through six innings during the regional tournament as a freshman. The major league scouts, including the ones from the Pittsburgh Pirates and the Cleveland Indians, started to follow his career. While he also participated actively in basketball, he showed more promise as a baseball player.

Mercer, however, decided to give up the summer sport for basketball after his sophomore year. While admitting he was a better player in baseball, he decided that he liked basketball more and started to devote more time in hoops. As a sophomore he had already captured a prestigious honor, winning Tennessee's Mr. Basketball honors in 1993. His hoops coach at Goodpasture was 6-foot-9 Steve Reece, a former Vanderbilt standout for coach C.M. Newton in the mid-1980s. (Reece later resigned from his coaching post in April 2000 after 10 years at the helm, compiling an overall mark of 246-81, including four state tourney appearances.)

While at Goodpasture, Mercer had a strong supporting cast. One of his close friends and teammates was 6-4 Drew Maddux, a highly regarded recruit. In the 1994 Class A state tournament, the Cougars, led by the duo of Mercer and Maddux, nearly won the title before losing 65-62 to top-ranked and defending champion Battle Ground Academy in overtime. As it turned out, it was their last game together at Goodpasture with Mercer moving to Oak Hill Academy for his senior year and Maddux heading for Vanderbilt. With Mercer getting his second straight Mr. Basketball honor in the state, Goodpasture finished its campaign with a 32-6 mark.

Several months earlier, Mercer got himself involved in an unwanted controversy. It was a very unsettling moment for him. In October 1993, Mercer received word that he would miss his entire junior year because of the state rules violations involving prepsters. Mercer and another Tennessee player, 6-10 Lorenzen Wright of Memphis, received one-year suspensions by the Tennessee Secondary Schools Athletic Association (TSSAA) for accepting $100 gift certificates and sportswear from Nike for participating in its all-star basketball camp. Their schools, however, appealed the TSSAA's decision, resulting in a much lesser penalty. After hearing the arguments, the state athletics board reduced the suspension to the season's first seven games. Nike officials claimed responsibility for the mess, saying they should have done more in assuring that the players stay eligible by contacting the high school governing bodies. In addition to Mercer and Wright, many high school stars throughout the country also had their eligibility status questioned because of their participation at a Nike-sponsored event.

* * *

Things began to get very hectic for the Mercer family which had to deal with zealous college recruiters who sought the services of the talented Mercer, who was preparing for his last year in high school. He participated in several summer camps, including the Nike Festival in Deerfield, Illinois, where he was named the top player. Like he did in the previous years, Mercer also played for the Tennessee Travelers AAU squad that summer of 1994, facing teams primarily from the southeastern states. UT coach Kevin O'Neill, recognized as one of the nation's top recruiters, was among several coaches who made frequent trips to the AAU games. Like Kentucky's Rick Pitino, Vanderbilt's Jan van Breda Kolff and other coaches, O'Neill wanted Mercer badly. Mercer was that good, they said. And Mercer took a serious look at three schools – Kentucky, Tennessee and Vanderbilt – as all three were within easy driving distance of his home. He also considered Florida, North Carolina, and Miami (Fla.), among others.

At the start of the school year, Mercer transferred to Oak Hill Academy, a school located in the middle of nowhere in southwestern Virginia's Blue Ridge Mountains. The Baptist boarding school was a 6-hour drive from his hometown. And its closest fast-food restaurant was almost 20 miles away. With distractions on the small campus very few, he helped coach Steve Smith's Oak Hill team become the nation's top prep squad by averaging 26.3 points and 6.3 rebounds.

Many recruiters, in the meantime, kept a close eye on Mercer. The heated recruitment of Mercer continued as UT and UK engaged in a war of words. When several Wildcat players visited Mercer in Louisville after an Oak Hill game in the dressing room, it raised a red flag for a possible NCAA violation. O'Neill reportedly contacted the NCAA about it, but he commented that wasn't true. Interestingly, several UT players earlier saw Mercer perform in Johnson City, Tenn., where Oak Hill was playing. Published reports later indicated the whistle blower was Florida.

After the season ended, Mercer garnered several top awards. He was named first-team Parade and McDonald's All-American. He also received the Naismith National Prep Player of the Year honors. But in early April Mercer was still undecided about his collegiate choice.

So Pitino and his assistant, Delray Brooks, made a last-minute trip to Mouth of Wilson where the academy was located. In a face-to-face meeting, they personally informed Mercer that Kentucky was definitely the place for him to display his basketball skills before he went to the NBA. Mercer remembers their visit. "I was trying to decide between Tennessee and Kentucky at the time," said Mercer, a 6-7 swingman. "We got down to the basketball aspect of it and I knew what to expect because of the tradition of the school and the basketball program. I was just trying to decide what position I would be in once I got there."

Pitino used his final recruiting pitch, using the name of the Vols' all-time leading scorer, in getting Mercer to come to Kentucky. "He knew I liked Allan Houston and I was considering going to Tennessee," said Mercer. "He always told me that Allan Houston really didn't have good games every time (UT) played Kentucky because they (the Wildcats) always double-teamed him and triple-teamed him. (He explained that) on Kentucky's team you have so many good players around you, it was hard for other teams to double team you if you were the (main) guy on the team.

"I looked at Tony Delk. He had a great career and you never could double-team him because he had other guys like Anthony Epps and Walter McCarty and those guys were behind him. And you couldn't double team one of them because the other guys would kill you in the end. So I looked and decided that (UK) was the place for me.

"The coach knew everything – the ins and outs of the basketball game. But he's going to do it his way, which has been a success at everything they (Pitino and his staff) have done at every level. So I knew I was in a win-win situation when I chose to go with Kentucky."

It certainly didn't hurt when Pitino brought Brooks, a former Indiana

Mr. Basketball, along on that recruiting trip. A first-team McDonald's All-American in 1984, Brooks played at Indiana before transferring to Providence where Pitino was the head coach.

"Delray was one of those guys I could identify with more because he was in a similar situation," Mercer said. "He was one of the top high school recruits coming out. So I had a lot in common with him and he is one of those guys who during my short career at Kentucky helped me out a lot with everything. (He helped me) especially on the basketball floor because he knew exactly what I was doing wrong. We kind of had similar games (or styles) a little bit so we got along very well."

UK's Derek Anderson, the 6-5 guard from Louisville Doss High School who was sitting out the 1994-95 season due to NCAA transfer rules, also played a part in Mercer's collegiate decision. And over the years, they have become very close friends. "I just think he is one of the reasons that I came to Kentucky," Mercer said. "There are a couple of reasons that I went there, but he is one of the main reasons because he took me out on my visit. I had a good time with him. He is a funny guy. He is a caring guy and I think if you ask him anything, he is willing to do anything for anybody at any given time." The media and the fans later labeled the dynamic duo of Mercer and Anderson as "Air Pair" in reference to their frequent flying and soaring tactics all over the floor.

If Mercer hadn't come to UK, he very likely would have been a member of the Vol family in Knoxville. UT was his second choice. Mercer was very familiar with the UT campus where he made frequent visits, playing basketball in summer camps and AAU competition. Tennessee was his home state school. Of course, it didn't hurt that coach O'Neill recruited him vigorously.

"They had a lot of guys that I played AAU basketball with," said Mercer. "Those are guys that I kind of grew up with and played with along with the AAU program. So I had a feeling they were going to go to Tennessee and it was just a matter of whether I was going to go (there) and join those guys because we spent most of our childhood together. And the basketball program was on the rise."

When Mercer was still pondering his future, he also looked at Vanderbilt very closely. But the Commodores got knocked out of the Mercer recruiting sweepstakes. The now-defunct *Nashville Banner* reported that Vanderbilt, known for its very high academic standards comparable to the Ivy League schools, denied Mercer's admission to the university because of insufficient grades and ACT entrance scores.

What did his mother think of Pitino? Mercer said he does not believe they met before he inked with the Wildcats. "I don't think so. Not that I know of," he said. It was a rather unusual situation as the parents of the recruits generally meet the head coach and the staff before their child decides on his or her collegiate future. But Pitino somehow got the Nashville kid to come to his Wildcat empire without even personally meeting his mom, who obviously had heard a lot about the coach and trusted her son's judgment.

* * *

In Wildcat country, the winter of 1995-96 began with lots of expectations and excitement. The UK faithful were buzzing at a fever pitch. Will Pitino win his first national championship at Kentucky? Entering his seventh year at the university, Pitino's stable was loaded with talent and experience. Many pre-season polls had selected Kentucky as the heavy favorite to win the NCAA crown. Coming off a 28-5 campaign which ended with a 74-61 loss to North Carolina in the NCAA Southeast Regional finals, UK had several key players coming back, including four experienced seniors in Tony Delk, Jared Prickett (who later received a medical hardship because of an injury), Walter McCarty and Mark Pope.

Also on the roster were Anderson, a talented transfer from Ohio State, and sophomore Antoine Walker, who won the MVP honors in the 1995 SEC tournament as a rookie. Walker had just completed a remarkable summer in the U.S. Olympic Festival, averaging 20.5 points and 7.3 rebounds. In addition, Pitino had very talented freshman guard Wayne Turner, a first-team Parade and McDonald's All-American, to supplement Mercer.

But Pitino was very comfortable with Mercer. The coach felt the youngster already had the maturity to step in and play right away. As a result, Mercer became the third true freshman at UK under Pitino to start his first collegiate game – the Hall of Fame Tip-Off Classic when top-ranked UK defeated Maryland with a 12-point victory. Mercer wasn't all that impressive in the season opener, hitting two of seven shots for six points and snatching five rebounds. But he was a rookie and things would get better.

Over two months later, Mercer set his hometown on fire with his superb performance against Vanderbilt at Nashville, hitting 15 points and grabbing four rebounds in 22 minutes as hot-shooting UK dominated the Commodores 120-81. Even though a crowd of 15,311 saw Vandy take its worst setback in Memorial Gym's 45-year history, the appreciative fans welcomed Mercer with open arms as he entertained them with several brilliant moves. Mercer's high school teammate, Drew Maddux, gunned in 18 points for Vanderbilt. The victory improved UK's record to 19-1.

It was a night Mercer certainly would never forget. But on April 1 Mercer had the game of his life, playing a key role for the national championship against Syracuse in East Rutherford, N.J. Earlier, he had been very nervous all afternoon before the tip-off. He had butterflies. He couldn't relax. He couldn't wait for the game to start.

"Once I got in the game I was fine," said Mercer, who came off the bench and scored a then career-high 20 points, including three of four three-pointers, in UK's 76-67 victory. "Everything (distractions) kind of goes away and you just focus on what is going on at that particular time and everyone had the same focus and goal, and that was to win a national championship.

"It was a great experience. Going into the game I probably wasn't going to be a major factor at the time but unfortunately some of the other guys got in foul trouble. So they kind of brought me off the bench. I went in and tried to play my game and stay calm. I didn't have any pressure on me like those guys – Tony Delk and McCarty – had. I just went out and helped my team win the national championship which was just great for every one of us."

Mercer joined Delk, who scored 24 points with seven of 12 three-pointers in the victory, on the NCAA Final Four's all-tournament squad. A member of the SEC's all-freshman team, Mercer finished the year on a very high note with an 8.0-point average.

With Kentucky's amazing 34-2 mark (including an unbeaten SEC record of 16-0) and several lopsided victories over decent teams, some folks called the Wildcats one of the strongest and deepest teams in college basketball history. Mercer was glad to be a part of the "Untouchables," a nickname Pitino used to describe his powerful squad just minutes after UK's NCAA title.

* * *

Even though he stayed at Kentucky for only two years, Mercer managed to realize how huge Kentucky's program was. The Wildcats were more popular than he had previously thought. He has had some bizarre moments with the Wildcat fans and he recalls one very interesting encounter.

"One thing, I do remember that I was using the restroom and a guy came and asked for an autograph," he smiled. "I guess he was so excited he couldn't wait until I finished. So he asked me while I was using the restroom." The incident, said Mercer, "was more of a shock than anything else because you don't expect people to follow you around, especially to follow you in the men's room.

"I had never seen a team or been on a team where you can go to the local mall and get treated like celebrities everywhere you went whether you are the first guy on the team or you are the last guy who doesn't play that much. They get treated like NBA players. You know you always had to look good because everyone was watching you and everybody knew who you were. We had guys who hardly played and they were just as popular as the top guy. I had never seen that before and that was always good where everybody was looked at as the same."

His days at UK were fun, Mercer said. "I would say so because of the national championship, college experience, the first time being away from home – all of those things combined. Those were probably my happiest years," he said.

* * *

While Mercer obviously enjoys a huge salary in the NBA with a reported four-year, $27 million pact he signed with Chicago in 2000, he once said in another interview with the author that the college players should be given some form of compensation while in school. Under current NCAA rules, those on athletic scholarships are allowed to receive free room, board, books, tuition and fees – but nothing else. If players want to make money, they can only work during school vacations. But many players don't have summer jobs, as they need to take two or three classes to catch up on their academics and to hold daily workouts at the gym. And most players, for practical purposes, don't have the money to pay for expenses such as clothes, laundry and entertainment.

"Yes," Mercer told the author in the Middlesboro's *Daily News* in 1996, responding to a question whether or not college athletes should be paid. "The schools are making a lot of money over the jerseys and stuff like that. The players don't get anything besides their education, which is good.

"But I think (we) deserve a little bit more. As a result you see a lot of people leaving school early to get money. Somewhere down the road, they'll (NCAA) have to draw a line so college players get a little money from somewhere."

Added NBA player Jamaal Magloire, a Wildcat freshman at the time, "Yes, I feel even though the school offers tuition and board (free), a young student still needs other things. You have other personal things that you might need like clothes, furniture. There are a lot of little things (that you'll need)."

* * *

Mercer spent his first two NBA years at Boston with the intense Pitino constantly barking all over the hardwood floor. As anyone can imagine, with Pitino nosing around, it wasn't easy to find emotional peace in the Celtics' territory. While Boston failed to make the playoffs both seasons, Mercer had some good times. However, he did encounter some difficult moments, including his coach's high expectations.

"He was real tough," commented Mercer, who was selected to the NBA All-Rookie first team in 1998 after averaging 15.3 points. "He was real demanding. We knew what to expect once we stepped out on that floor. He had us prepared not only for basketball, but also for life, period. In every aspect he had us prepared for life." The player also added that Pitino is a superb teacher and motivator.

Interestingly, Mercer's first NBA game came against Michael Jordan and the defending champion Bulls in which the young Celtics won 92-85 at Boston. In his pro debut, Mercer scored 11 points and had five rebounds. It was a night he will always remember. In fact, the ex-Wildcat said he was so anxious that he couldn't sleep for a couple of nights with MJ as his first pro opponent. For the record, Jordan pumped in 30 points in that game at Fleet Center.

Even though Mercer improved in his second year, with a 17.0-point average, the second highest on the Celtics in scoring, Pitino dealt him off to Denver in a major 1999 trade because the coach, who also served as the team's president, knew his franchise couldn't afford Mercer's salary. That meant Mercer would be going to another squad that was coached by someone who also has strong Kentucky ties. That person is the UK's men's all-time leading scorer with 2,138 points. Dan Issel would be Mercer's new boss. It was a gamble for the Nuggets as Mercer had one year left on his contract. He would be a free agent soon – after the 1999-2000 season.

Like Boston, Denver was a struggling franchise searching for better days. With their new 19,099-seat Pepsi Center ready to open, the Nuggets, who had a horrible 11-71 record just a couple of years before

(1997-98), hoped that Mercer would propel them to the land of respectability. Issel was optimistic with Mercer's potential to be an NBA all-star. Their Kentucky connections certainly helped them to get to know each other fairly well.

"I think the greatest thing was that he (Issel) was a hard-nosed player, just like he is as a coach," Mercer said. "So I kind of learned a little bit. I didn't know he was such a great player, great shooter. I think he obtained some kind of scoring records or something like that. I really didn't know all that until I got there and had a chance to meet him."

At the beginning, Mercer was pretty enthused about playing for Denver, which featured stars Antonio McDyess and Nick Van Exel. But his excitement didn't last long as Denver informed him that the club had no plans to sign him to a new long-term pact before the season started. The Nuggets wanted to make sure if Mercer could fit in the team's long-range plans.

After averaging 18.3 points and 4.1 rebounds in 37 games with Denver, Mercer was sent to Orlando in a Feb. 1 trade. According to published reports, the Nuggets said money was the stumbling block, saying they couldn't afford Mercer's new contractual demands of approximately $9 million a year. Issel told the *Denver Post* that Andy Miller, Mercer's new agent, came to his office before the season and suggested the player be traded if the club couldn't guarantee a maximum contract. (Mercer hired Miller after dismissing rap star Master P as his agent.) But Mercer told the newspaper that wasn't the case, saying he had never asked for that amount of money. The player said the ownership and the team's instability were two of the reasons why he didn't mind going to Orlando, where he led the Magic in scoring eight times, including two 27-point outings, in 31 games.

In the summer of 2000, Mercer became a free agent. He seriously considered the possibility of returning to Boston where he would be reunited with Pitino, who had advised Mercer that if the player had a better deal from another team, then he should accept it. However, if the contractual offers weren't satisfying to Mercer, Pitino would have a spot for him on the roster with a reported $2.25 million for one season.

But Mercer ended up a Chicago Bull. On August 2, he signed a multi-year contract with the rebuilding Bulls franchise, which had failed to obtain other marquee free agents such as Grant Hill, Tim Duncan and Tracy McGrady. Even though the Bulls had the league's worst record at 15-67, Mercer finished his first year with Chicago on a positive note despite an injured ankle, which forced him to miss the season's last 10 games. While playing in a leadership role as a tri-captain, he placed second in team scoring behind Elton Brand with a 19.7-point average and ranked fourth in the NBA in minutes per game (41.6). In a 104-100 loss to Portland, Mercer gunned in a career-high 39 points.

Then, in February 2002, Mercer was traded to the Indiana Pacers, his fifth NBA team. While he understood the deal would probably lead him to a reduced playing role, Mercer nevertheless was very pleased. Joining Indiana meant that he would basically get to play for a winning team for the first time in his pro career. It would be just like his early days at Kentucky when he helped the victorious Cats to a two-year record of 69-7. While Mercer only started three games in his first full year with the 48-34 Pacers in 2002-03, he played in 72 games, the most since his rookie season at Boston, and averaged 7.7 points.

The well-traveled Mercer, however, didn't stay very long with the Pacers. In a three-team, five-player deal in July 2003, he was shipped to the defending champion San Antonio Spurs. San Antonio is Mercer's sixth NBA squad. Mercer didn't seem to mind the trade since it gave him an opportunity to play for another winning franchise.

* * *

Mercer wasn't the most outgoing person at UK, but he got the job done, helping the Wildcats advance all the way to the NCAA title game for two consecutive seasons. If he had a choice, he would try to stay out of the spotlight, avoiding the news media. He doesn't want attention. However, at a high-profile basketball program like Kentucky, he had no choice but to cooperate.

"Ron was a very private person," explained Brooks Downing, the former director of media relations for UK sports. "It's not that he didn't trust the media. He was a young man who just kept to himself. He never felt comfortable in front of a microphone or a reporter, but would accommodate most of the (media) requests I had. But if he could find a way out, he would."

During his years at Kentucky, Mercer wasn't known as a great interview. In a poll of SEC writers, they voted Mercer the worst interview. Unlike Tennessee's Ron Slay, he wasn't a real colorful copy. He just provided his comments in very general terms, disappointing many sportswriters or television reporters looking for one-liners or good quotes. Nothing exciting, but he did his job. Mercer's low-key personality was one reason why he didn't rank real high on reporters' interview lists. He was just a private and shy person who has learned to deal with the spotlight over the years.

Mercer, who majored in psychology while at UK, claimed that he doesn't pay much attention to the press and he also couldn't really recall a negative article that he didn't like. "I tried not to read those (newspaper stories)," he commented. "I don't know because really when we were at Kentucky, Rick Pitino had us not to read the newspapers and that has kind of stuck with me now. I don't read the newspapers. He always kind of kept us away from that and told us to focus on what was going on and not what people read."

But he later admitted that he reads a newspaper occasionally. "I pick up *USA Today* maybe every now and then," Mercer said. He also enjoys watching ESPN. "You have to watch something to keep up (with the news)."

While he may not read the magazines like *The Sporting News*, Mercer has been recognized by the St. Louis-based publication in 2002 and 2003 for his efforts in various community projects. *The Sporting News* recognized the ex-Cat as one of the NBA's "good guys," especially for feeding the needy children and adults at holidays like Easter and Thanksgiving, and giving away backpacks and supplies to hundreds of disadvantaged children.

While Mercer is not an easy guy to know, Jamal Crawford, his ex-teammate at Chicago, commented Mercer is a very helpful person who cares about friends and family. "He doesn't trust people easily, but once he trusts you, he'll do the world for you," said Crawford, who played one year of college basketball at Michigan, in an *Indianapolis Star* story by Mark Montieth. "He's funny and outgoing, but people would never know that because he's laid back and sits back and looks at a situation before he enters it."

Mercer was questioned if there is anything about him that a lot of people don't know about. "I will keep that to myself until they come and find out," he replied. But he also revealed a personal tidbit. At his home, he has two rottweilers named Kato and Gotti (after celebrities Kato Kaelin and John Gotti).

Asked if he'd like to make any concluding comments for the book, he just smiled and said, "Go UK! Go Big Blue!" So, even though he stayed in college for only a couple of years, Mercer still has a soft spot for the Wildcats.

Chapter 9

Gentle Giant

A couple of months after the terrorist attacks of Sept.11, 2001, Nazr Mohammed sat down in an interview with the author in Atlanta and reflected on the tragic events that changed America forever. Like everyone else on that September morning, Mohammed was very shocked and was staying in his hometown of Chicago with his close friend and ex-college teammate at UK, Antoine Walker, when he learned of the stunning news. So, needless to say, he and Walker were glued to TV all day, watching the rapidly-developing news.

"It was extremely scary," the 6-10 Mohammed said of the tragedy. "I was in Chicago at Antoine's house and we were getting ready to go and play (pickup basketball). He woke me up and told me what happened. We just sat there and watched the news, trying to figure out what was going on. You just sit there (watching the news) and you felt that it couldn't be real.

"I was supposed to be leaving later on that day, but the airports were shut down. I just stayed home for a couple of days."

A practicing Muslim, Mohammed said his faith has nothing to do with the attacks, explaining that it doesn't preach the killing of another human being. He commented the terrorist attacks on the U.S. were based on their political beliefs, not religion.

Interestingly, Mohammed was fasting when he discussed the 9/11 attacks in an interview for this book. He was observing the holy month of Ramadan, a season of prayer, fasting and self-reflection. Ramadan is "going on right now and it is very important," Mohammed said. "But I don't want to make a big deal about it. It is part of my life. It helps me stay at peace with myself. It helps me learn discipline. You know it is not just about yourself all the time and (it's) sometimes a sacrifice."

For Mohammed, observing the fast is a way of life. Like other practicing Muslims, he doesn't eat or drink during the daylight hours. So he avoids a lot of activities during the day, conserving his body energy.

Photo Courtesy of UK Media Relations

Playing against Vanderbilt at Rupp Arena is Nazr Mohammed (13), who left Kentucky for NBA after his junior year.

About a couple of hours before he and his Atlanta Hawks teammates faced the Boston Celtics in a November matchup at Philips Arena, Mohammed was busy getting all his nourishment, including a light pre-game meal, in the dressing room as the evening arrived.

For the record, Mohammed played 33 minutes in Atlanta's 112-103 victory over Boston, hitting a perfect 6 of 6 field goal shooting for 14 points, and grabbing nine rebounds. During fasting, Mohammed said there is no drop-off in his game performance because of his mental attitude, staying focused on his game plan.

His Muslim teammate, Shareef Abdur-Rahim, by the way, led the Hawks with 29 points on 11 of 17 shooting and 12 rebounds in an entertaining game, which saw both teams hit 24 out of 49 three-pointers.

* * *

Mohammed comes from a large family, growing up in the Windy City. "There were 10 brothers and sisters," he said. "It was good. You know you always have some type of family support. You always have somebody to play with."

But he didn't play organized basketball until his freshman year in high school despite his massive physical build. "I played in the neighborhood," said Mohammed, who starred at Kenwood Academy. "You know there just wasn't any organized basketball team in my grammar school. I didn't get a chance to go out to the Y and all the things like that. So when I got to high school I met my junior varsity coach and he taught me how to play ball and everything went from there."

And that's where Andre Peavy, his junior varsity mentor, enters Mohammed's life. Peavy is even mentioned in the Hawks' media guide as Mohammed's most-admired person. In 1995, he was the one who even announced that Mohammed was making a verbal commitment to attend Kentucky. "He saw me in eighth grade and he saw me playing in the gym. He just took me under his wing," Mohammed said. "You know he just told me how to play. He told me the right things to do. I mean he just loved kids. He is still helping kids to this day. So I've got a lot of respect for him."

And they still stay in touch. "I talk to him all the time. He is still in Chicago. He is actually at a different high school." Peavy once served as an assistant coach at Northern Illinois.

At Kenwood, Mohammed wasn't a Parade All-American, but he was good enough to play at UK. During his senior year, he earned All-State honors from the *Chicago Sun-Times* and the Associated Press, averaging 20 points and 15 rebounds. Then-Kentucky mentor Rick Pitino, still looking for his first NCAA championship at the time, however, warned him that he needed to lose weight if he was going to play a future role in the UK program. Many folks, including Pitino, labeled Mohammed as a long-term project.

But Mohammed said Pitino "never told me that I was a project. He told me that he liked the way I played. He liked the skills that I had and he wanted to get me in shape and improve those skills."

Even though Pitino never visited Mohammed's Chicago home, the youngster nevertheless decided on UK after a pleasant visit to Lexington. "They got into the (recruiting) scene late so they didn't make the home visit. But I made an official visit down there (in January)," said Mohammed, who selected UK over coach John Thompson and his Georgetown program, among others. "I always liked coach P when I was in high school. And Andre Peavy liked coach (Pitino) and his system. I saw how hard they work. He told me that if 'you come here, you are going to be in the best shape of your life and be the best ball player you can be. It is up to you.' I like the way he came at me straightforward, and I wanted to go there and play for him."

Mohammed's father, Alhaji Tahiru Mohammed, took an active role in sorting out the recruiting interest by various schools. Was that good or bad? "He helped a lot," said the son. "Every step of the way he was right there with me. It was funny – at one point he wanted me to go to Georgetown. He loved John Thompson and it was a great situation, but they wanted me to sign early (in November) and I didn't want to sign early. But he helped me a lot in the whole recruiting process."

Pitino didn't promise the Chicago standout any playing time. "He told me we would have a great team that year and if I came in, worked hard and outplayed somebody, I would play. He said he just wanted me to concentrate on getting in shape and he was going to have a jayvee squad. He was planning on having a jayvee squad for me, Oliver Simmons, Jason Lathrem and Cameron Mills. He wanted us to develop skills out there and be ready to play."

The coach established the school's junior varsity program for the first time in 20 years and the baby Wildcats finished the 1995-96 season with a 9-4 mark. Mills and Mohammed led the jayvee squad with 23.7 and 23.1-point averages, respectively. It was during the record-setting year of the "Untouchables" with the 34-2 Cats winning the school's sixth national championship.

* * *

Despite his lack of playing time on the varsity, Mohammed said winning the 1996 NCAA title was an "unbelievable experience." He had fun. He had a great time with the squad and the fans. It was an enjoyable time in the Wildcat program. While playing a total of only 88 minutes in 16 varsity games as a rookie, he said he never considered dropping off of the team.

"I never thought about quitting the team," commented Mohammed. "It was tough because you wanted to get out there on the varsity and you wanted to play more," he said. "But we were so good and had so many good guys ahead of me that there was no chance of me doing that (playing). I wanted to play because I saw my other peers playing at their respective schools and I wanted to get out there and play, too. But the chance wasn't there yet."

Nevertheless, he got to wear his NCAA championship ring. But his enjoyment of wearing this special jewelry with pride temporarily ended. The ring had disappeared from his Wildcat Lodge dormitory room in April. "It was stolen out of my room," said Mohammed. "We went on a trip and when I got back my window was open. They came in and stole my championship hats, my ring. Just little things. But the ring was the big thing."

But Mohammed later received good news. He got his ring back. The juveniles had stolen Mohammed's possessions. "We found out later that some kids saw my window and came in through my window and took it. One kid was wearing it on a bus at his school with my name on it. So the bus driver reported it (to the authorities) and I got it back."

* * *

By the time his sophomore season rolled around, Mohammed became a different person. And Pitino was happy, too. The mentor was definitely pleased to see Mohammed's efforts in lowering his playing weight. Said Pitino, "Nazr has shed a person. He's gone from 315 to 240 pounds. He's turned a lot of fat into muscle and he'll only get quicker and better each year he's in our program."

Shedding pounds wasn't easy, said Mohammed, who worked with UK strength and conditioning coach Shaun Brown. "It was extremely hard," he commented. "I worked with Shaun Brown and he told me exactly what to do in order to get down. I had to work out every day. Burn off over 1,000 calories every day. I just stayed on the StairMaster and had to watch my eating. I had to change them (eating habits) dramatically. I couldn't eat after 7:00 p.m. I couldn't eat a lot of creamy stuff and had to cut out the fried foods. But it all worked out."

Indeed, his efforts paid off. Mohammed earned his first collegiate start in the second game of the 1996-97 campaign against Syracuse in the Great Alaska Shootout, a pre-season tournament. He didn't do much, however, seeing only nine minutes of action and scoring two points. He lost his job in the starting lineup in the next game as freshman center Jamaal Magloire, who had tallied 16 points and snatched eight rebounds against the Orangemen in a reserve role, took over.

Several games later, Mohammed reclaimed his starting spot in a New Year's Eve matchup with Louisville and finished with 10 points as third-ranked UK won 74-54 at Freedom Hall. Four other Wildcat players, led by Derek Anderson's 19 points, also scored in double figures.

Mohammed had 10 more starts before losing his job to Magloire again in a late season run which saw the Cats nearly capture their second straight national crown. But the business management major played well in several games as a backup. He posted his seventh double-double in the NCAA title game against Arizona, hitting 12 points and grabbing 11 rebounds in 25 minutes. He also finished fifth in the SEC in blocks.

Still he had yet to play his best overall game at UK.

* * *

During the 1997-98 national championship season, under the fierce-looking eyes of new Kentucky coach Tubby Smith, Mohammed posted impressive numbers in several matchups. In addition to several double-double performances, he scored his UK career-high 22 points against Alabama in Louisville. In another game, facing UCLA in the NCAA tournament, he and Magloire each blocked six shots in UK's 94-68 victory at Tampa, Fla., helping Kentucky establish an NCAA tourney record for blocks in a contest with 14.

According to Mohammed, his best Wildcat game, though, came in a six-point victory against Tennessee in Lexington. "My best performance was probably against Tennessee," he said of the 1998 game. "I remember I had 22 (actually 21), 16 rebounds and five blocks." His teammate, Scott Padgett, also recorded a double-double with a 17-point, 10-rebound performance against the Vols.

But the Wildcat fans will always remember "The Shot" Mohammed made in the Music City, helping the seventh-ranked Cats to an exciting 63-61 win over Vanderbilt after catching a long pass across the hardwood floor in the waning seconds. With the game deadlocked at 61-61, he banked an improbable 10-foot basket at the buzzer, stunning a pro-Vandy crowd of 15,311.

Added Mohammed, "Actually when I caught the ball, I was thinking, 'Oh, my goodness, why did you throw it to me way out there.' I think Shep (Jeff Sheppard) threw it to me. So I looked around at the basket and I just started (to run toward the goal). I wanted to at least get an attempt up. If I miss it at least we go into overtime. So I was going toward the basket and looking at the clock, and I just threw it up at the last second and it went in."

And when Kentucky advanced to the 1998 Final Four, Mohammed, a first-team All-SEC selection, saw himself on the front cover of *Sports Illustrated* magazine.

"I cherished that and I got a couple of them framed," said Mohammed. "And I still have a stack of them in my house now. It was just amazing because that is something that you dream about as a little kid being on the cover of *Sports Illustrated*. I was fortunate enough to be on the cover of *Sports Illustrated*."

Mohammed is very appreciative that he was able to complete his UK career on a winning note, beating Utah 78-69 for the NCAA title.

"That was a great experience, you know, that my last game was winning the national championship," he commented. "The first one (1996 title), you know, I didn't help as much as I wanted to and the second one we lost to Arizona (in the 1997 finals)."

Mohammed's father, a successful entrepreneur in Chicago, didn't attend the title game in San Antonio, Texas. "It was too far of a trip for my father. He was still trying to run his businesses," he said. "But he watched it (on television) and he talked to me right after the game."

* * *

Weeks after the Comeback Cats' dramatic performance in the NCAA tournament, Mohammed announced his decision to turn pro before his senior year. He made the move after discussing his promising future with his father and coach Tubby Smith. But many observers, including NBA scouting director Marty Blake, thought Mohammed should stay in college for another year. They said he wasn't ready for NBA.

Said Mohammed, "A lot of people said I wasn't ready for Kentucky basketball. I think I came here and did a good job. The university has done a lot for me, and in turn I think I have done a lot for the university."

It was an agonizing decision for Mohammed. But he said Kentucky's three Final Four appearances made it easier for him to leave Lexington. "It was a tough decision because it is a dream to go to the NBA." he added. "I had such a great college career that you know I didn't want to leave. But it also made it easier that I was fortunate enough to win two championships and get a runner-up.

"So I wanted actually to have a chance to help my family, instead of being sort of a burden. I have so many brothers and sisters that I wanted to get out there and have a chance to help."

As the NBA Draft approached, Mohammed was getting anxious. He had been told he would be a first-round pick and some scouts even predicted a lottery pick status for the Wildcat star. For Mohammed, making the first round (with a total of 29 players) would mean financial security with a guaranteed three-year contract. He was hopeful about his chances.

However, the night of the nationally-televised NBA Draft in Vancouver was getting to be a very long one. The clubs continued to bypass Mohammed, who attended the affair along with his family members and friends, and he was getting very restless and disappointed. Things were not going well.

Finally, when the 29th overall pick came around, Mohammed heard his name called by NBA Commissioner David Stern and became the choice of the Utah Jazz. Instead of being chosen as a lottery pick, his low first-round draft performance had cost the future NBA player between $2 and $3 million.

"I was extremely nervous because that was the last pick of the first round," he recalled. "If you're not in the first round, you don't have a guaranteed three-year (contract). But I was extremely nervous because they had invited me to the draft and I had pretty good workouts with all the teams that I worked out for. It was just one of those situations where Jason Williams (from Florida) sneaked up into the draft and was the seventh (pick). Paul Pierce (Kansas) slipped down and was 10th. He was projected as a No. 2 pick. The draft just jumped around a little bit, but it all worked out."

Mohammed didn't remain a Jazz very long. On the draft night, he was shipped to the Philadelphia 76ers for a future first-round pick. And the 76ers, coached by Larry Brown, signed the rookie to a contract reportedly worth a total of $1.8 million for three years.

* * *

Since Mohammed didn't see much action in his first three years in the NBA, some people thought he had made a big mistake in leaving Kentucky early. Instead of sitting on the bench in the NBA, many argued Mohammed could have spent a productive senior year at UK where he could've improved his game as well as gaining maturity.

During his early NBA days, Mohammed admitted he had some reservations about his pro decision. But now he has no regrets. "There were times when I had doubts when I was at Philadelphia and not playing. But that comes with not playing, you know, when you start out," said Mohammed, who was traded to Atlanta in a six-player deal during the 2000-01 season. "But it all worked out (for me) and I'm happy where I am now and you know hard work pays off."

Mohammed became the biggest surprise of the Hawks' acquisitions. He earned 19 starts, averaging 12.3 points and nine rebounds in 28 games, for Atlanta and then became a free agent after the season. The Hawks, however, liked his potential and re-signed him to a lucrative five-year contract reportedly worth $25 million in July 2001.

* * *

While Mohammed understands that having financial security is nice, he says he is not the type of person who craves or values materialistic things. He is using his NBA paychecks to help his large family and others.

"I'm still the same guy," Mohammed said. "I don't feel different at all. Most people don't believe the size of money I make. I'm still cheap. I'm not a miser, but you know there is nothing much that I want for myself. Everything I want is basically for my family, my brothers, sisters and now my wife. You know I want things for them more than I do for myself."

Mohammed's wife is the former Mandi Phelps, whom he married in Lexington during the summer of 2001. The wedding, attended by several teammates at UK and in the NBA, took place at the Lexington Opera House. The Rev. Ed Bradley, who has served as the hoops squad's chaplain at UK for many years, officiated the wedding.

The couple met at UK when she was a junior and he was a freshman, according to Mohammed. Mrs. Mohammed once worked as a teacher at an elementary school in Louisville for several years. "It has been great," Mohammed said of his marriage. "It is all that I dreamed of. I mean having a great marriage. My wife is very supportive."

* * *

Unlike the memorable summer of 2001, Mohammed went through the worst moments of his life during the summer of 2000. Not just once, but twice. It was a horrible summer. A summer he would like to forget.

The first incident involved Mohammed, who had just completed his second year with the 76ers in the NBA, and Antoine Walker when they were robbed at gunpoint during the early morning hours in Chicago. The loot included cash and jewelry worth over thousands of dollars.

Mohammed described the robbery as "very scary. (I lost) just a little cash, and a watch. Antoine lost his bracelet, a watch and some cash. I don't think about it (the incident) very much now because we are safe and we lost material things, which you know are nothing. We both have our lives and you know are just living every day one at a time."

However, the second incident wasn't as fortunate as it involved a death in his family. Mohammed's father, 55, was beaten to death at his auto parts store in Chicago. The city police ruled the death a homicide.

"They caught the guy," Mohammed said. "He got caught and he pled guilty. But (the case) has been solved so we got to put that behind us." A Chicago jury later convicted the killer in 2003 after deliberating for three hours. The convict was sentenced to 42 years in prison.

It was a very difficult time for the Mohammed family members, who came to the U.S. many years ago from the African nation of Ghana. "We were extremely close," said Mohammed of his relationship with the father. "We talked all the time and he was an important part of my life because he taught me how to be strong, to work hard, and get whatever I wanted. If I worked hard, I'd eventually get it.

"He came over here from Ghana and he established himself as a businessman and he worked extremely hard to do it. So he instilled that (work ethic) in me."

As for his mother, she remained in her home country until she moved to the U.S. in 2001, months after his father died. "She just moved to Chicago," Mohammed said. "She wasn't with us when I grew up."

* * *

In the spring of 2001, when coach Rick Pitino returned to the Bluegrass state to guide the Louisville Cardinals basketball program,

Mohammed was seeing red. He didn't know what to think about the stunning news that Pitino has become a new member of the Cardinal family. He wasn't too thrilled about it but he reluctantly accepted the news. Mohammed said he will always think of Pitino as a Kentucky coach.

Interestingly, Mohammed's younger brother, Alhaji Mohammed Jr, ended up at Louisville a few months later as a non-scholarship player after transferring from Ventura College in California. As a favor to Nazr, Pitino gave Alhaji a chance to make the squad. And, as it turned out, the 6-3 guard was good enough to help the Cardinals, earning a spot in the starting lineup several times during the 2001-02 campaign.

* * *

When away from basketball, Mohammed enjoys bowling and playing volleyball. "I go bowling with friends every chance I get," he said. In addition, he likes to watch the popular TV program, "Seinfeld."

He also follows college and UK football games. This book interview, by the way, was interrupted briefly in the Hawks' dressing room when Mohammed noticed the college football game highlights on a giant TV screen, featuring the upset-minded Wildcats in a fierce battle with Tennessee. UK led the game in the fourth quarter before dropping to the Vols 38-35 in Lexington. "I love watching Kentucky football," smiled Mohammed, who frequently returns to Lexington during the summer months.

Call him a soft-spoken Gentle Giant who still has a very warm spot for UK.

Chapter 10

Fearless Canadian

Jamaal Magloire's family is originally from Trinidad, a small Caribbean island located off the eastern coast of Venezuela. While he enjoys some of their Caribbean culture and the West Indian food, he calls Canada his home country. Born in 1978, Magloire grew up in Toronto where ice hockey was (and still is) the most popular sport and he didn't even follow hockey closely. For many folks in Toronto, watching basketball will put them to sleep even though the interest in the sport has grown dramatically in recent years and there is the NBA's Toronto Raptors. Basketball, for the most part, is just simply not very big in Canada as compared to hockey, Magloire explained. With his huge size, his folks nevertheless steered him to basketball when he a very young kid. The younger Magloire really enjoyed playing basketball and it kept him busy as a child.

"I think my first love is basketball," said the former UK standout. "I played a lot of sports (including soccer) but being able to play the game of basketball is something that I started playing and stuck with."

* * *

Magloire, who was not rated among the pre-season Top 100 prepsters by *The Sporting News* in 1995, has never forgotten then-Kentucky coach Rick Pitino's recruiting pitch at his parents' home in Toronto. "He was very professional," he said. "I had confidence in him right away. He displayed himself and he talked about the program very well and I was impressed. Before Pitino came to the house, we knew a lot about him. Making a decision for the school would have to include the fact that he was a great coach."

With the 6-10, 236-pound Magloire in Canada, it was somewhat difficult for him to get a lot of recognition in the U.S. during the recruiting race. Of course, it didn't help that his first two years in high

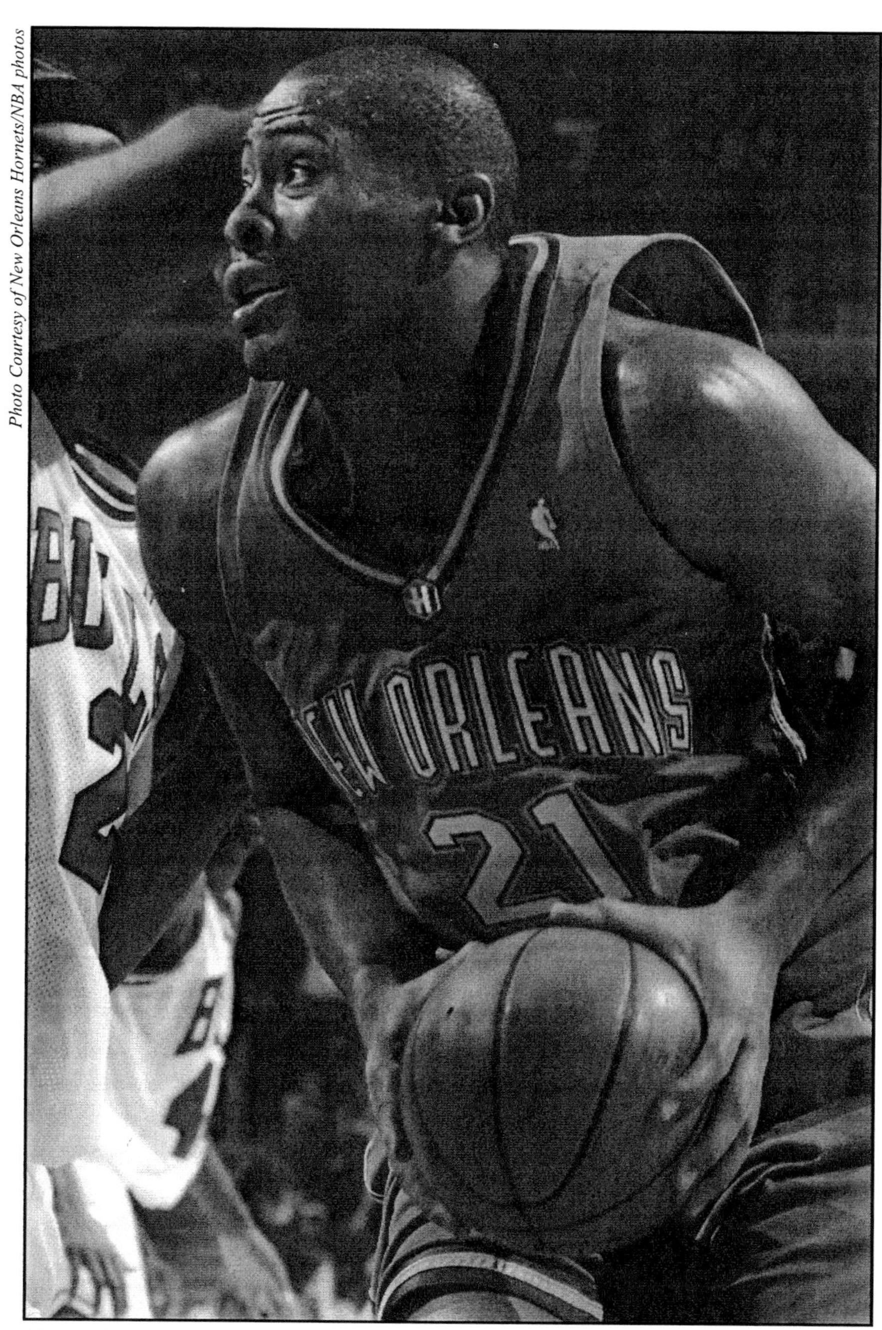

Photo Courtesy of New Orleans Hornets/NBA photos

New Orleans' Jamaal Magloire, a former Kentucky intimidator, goes up for a shot against the Chicago Bulls.

school were spent at Wexford Collegiate Institute which didn't take basketball too seriously. The Toronto school was known for its strong emphasis on fine arts. After his sophomore year, he transferred to Eastern School of Commerce where he began to develop and polish his raw basketball skills. After participating in one of the highly publicized summer camps and the National Kingdom Tournament in Florida (where he was named MVP), Magloire gradually got more attention and many colleges sought his services.

During his senior season at Eastern School of Commerce, he averaged nearly 24 points, 15 rebounds and seven blocks, guiding his squad to its second straight Ontario Golden Ball title, a provincial title that is equivalent to a state crown in the U.S. Coached by future UK administrative assistant Simeon Mars, Commerce was nearly unbeatable, finishing with a 39-3 mark. Magloire was also named to Toronto's Dream Team, an honor for the Top Five players in the metropolitan area.

Before he announced his decision to attend Kentucky on his 18th birthday during a ceremony at the high school, Magloire considered Syracuse, Pittsburgh and Purdue. He wanted to play at a school where he could start immediately. At Kentucky, Pitino was losing a couple of big men from the 1996 NCAA championship team – 6-10 standouts Mark Pope and Walter McCarty – which opened up a spot for the giant Canadian. (Pitino also lost 6-8 Antoine Walker, another frontline standout, who left early for the pros.) That played a key role in Magloire's decision to attend Kentucky and Pitino promised him significant playing time as a Wildcat rookie. His primary competition for playing time would be 6-10 sophomore Nazr Mohammed. As it turned out, Magloire was Pitino's lone scholarship freshman in 1996-97.

On leaving his parents, Marion and Garth Magloire, for UK, "It was hard for me to leave them," said Magloire, who also has a younger basketball-playing brother (Karlon). His mother and father both work in the insurance business.

* * *

Magloire was not the only person from Toronto to join the Wildcat program. His high school coach, Simeon Mars, joined Pitino's staff as administrative assistant. Mars, who served as head coach for four years at Eastern School of Commerce, replaced George Barber who had taken a job as an assistant coach at Bradley. However, Mars' arrival at UK, which came a little over three months after Magloire revealed his collegiate decision, created some buzz in the college basketball world. Some speculated the hiring of Mars had sealed a package deal that was used to lure Magloire to UK.

When Magloire was asked if he encouraged Mars to come to Lexington, he didn't provide a direct answer. Instead, he said, "I think coach Pitino spoke with him and really valued what he had to bring and what he had to offer to the game and they went from there."

Before coming to Kentucky, Mars had compiled a head coaching record of 140-21 at Eastern School of Commerce, including a perfect 44-0 campaign in 1994-95, Magloire's junior year.

Interestingly, Mars left UK in 2000 by the time Magloire's collegiate eligibility expired.

* * *

During Magloire's freshman year at Kentucky, the Wildcats, coming off their memorable national championship year, attempted to be the second team to repeat a national crown since the days of coach John Wooden's UCLA teams of the early 1970s. (Duke was the other team, winning the NCAA title in 1991 and '92.) But could the Cats do it again without the four standouts who moved on to the NBA? Tony Delk was gone. Walter McCarty was gone. Mark Pope was gone. Antoine Walker was gone. Losing their top three scorers and top three rebounders, the Cats had big shoes to fill. But Pitino, who had turned down a lucrative coaching job offer from the NBA's New Jersey Nets, had just enough experienced bodies returning along with sophomore star Ron Mercer to be a serious threat in college basketball.

Kentucky's first game that season took place in Indianapolis' RCA Dome in mid-November, facing a good Clemson squad in the Black Coaches Association classic. It wasn't a game to remember for the Wildcat fans, who were plentiful among a crowd of 32,250. Ranked No. 3 in the pre-season, Kentucky jumped out to a 37-31 halftime lead before dropping 79-71 in overtime. And Magloire spent most of his time on the bench. He missed his only field goal attempt. Of course, Magloire wasn't real happy with his performance along with the loss. As for the playing time, he tried to be patient and knew his time would come.

Nearly two weeks later, UK went to Alaska and won three games to capture the Great Alaska Shootout where Magloire blossomed. In an 87-53 victory over Syracuse in a rematch of the 1996 NCAA title game, Magloire came off the bench and played a key role, getting 16 points, eight rebounds and two blocked shots. That performance earned Magloire his first starting assignment as a Wildcat in the next game – a second-round matchup with host Alaska Anchorage. Against Alaska, the UK center notched the first double-double of his collegiate career with 10 points and 10 rebounds.

And the rest is history as Magloire and 6-10 teammate Nazr Mohammed both shared the starting spot at center the remainder of the 35-5 campaign. Magloire, who was named to the SEC's All-Freshman team, started 22 of the team's 40 games, including five of the six in the NCAA tournament. He also led the conference in blocked shots with 79 despite playing only 15.7 minutes a game. (Mohammed also placed fifth in that category.)

* * *

For Magloire, things were going well. But it didn't last long. He lost his coach to the Boston Celtics in the spring of 1997. There would be no Pitino around the UK camp. And he even casually considered the possibility of transferring. Anyhow, Magloire was very unhappy with Pitino's decision. "I was disappointed because he is the one who recruited me and he only coached me for a year," explained Magloire. "I had expectations of him coaching me throughout my college career."

UK radio broadcaster Sam Bowie, a former Wildcat All-American, had a talk with Magloire. He advised the player to stay in the Kentucky program. "I think he thought it was in my best interest and I really trusted in his opinion," said Magloire, adding that Bowie was the "most interesting person I met in college." And they have become friends. Said Magloire, "He made a great impression and he taught me a lot as far as a person."

Like many of his teammates, Magloire wasn't so sure about Pitino's successor, Tubby Smith. The player would have to build a new relationship with the new Wildcat coach. He didn't know how things would work out. "I was concerned because I didn't know much about coach Smith," Magloire said. "He coached at Georgia, an SEC school, and I didn't know too much about him. When a new coach comes in as far as discipline, I think you have to develop a new relationship and get used to the change."

* * *

Away from the basketball court, you can call Magloire a gentleman. He is very polite when it comes to media interviews, including for this book. However, he is a different story on the hardwood floor. He is a hard-nosed competitor who wants to win. While at UK, some of his opponents have characterized his physical play as rough and dirty. Tubby Smith admired Magloire's competitiveness, calling the defensive specialist a warrior. But the coach tried to get the player to control his emotions.

"Jamaal is our most aggressive post player," said Smith at the beginning of the 1997-98 campaign. The new mentor also said the 6-10, 240-pound sophomore needed to improve his offensive production and stay out of foul trouble for the Wildcats to be a threat. His fiercely competitive nature, however, got him in trouble occasionally. While he started the first 12 games of the season before losing his job to Mohammed during UK's incredible run to the 1998 national title with a sparkling 35-4 mark, Magloire improved in the "foul trouble" category. Unlike his freshman year, which saw him foul out five times, he did not foul out a single time during the "Comeback Cats" season.

Magloire fondly remembers Kentucky's 78-69 national championship victory over Utah in San Antonio, Texas. It was the third straight game that Kentucky had bounced back for a win after trailing in double figures. In a backup role, Magloire had seven points despite four fouls. "I think the national championship game was the most memorable (of his UK career) because we ended up winning the national championship," Magloire said. "It was special. I think the whole season was special because we came back and regained credibility."

Nicknamed "Jam," Magloire can be very outspoken. His mouth sometimes made Smith and his assistants cringe. A couple of months before Kentucky's NCAA title, Magloire had predicted the squad would win the crown. "I talked to the press and said we were going to win the national championship," he recalled. "I said that we refused to lose and that's what ended up happening. After we lost in 1997, I vowed we were going to come back the next year and win. So I really believed that we had a chance and a shot at winning everything."

Ex-UK publicist Brooks Downing agreed that Magloire's big mouth was a concern in the UK camp. "Jamaal Magloire made me nervous because he could be very boastful and, at times, used his own statements for motivation," he said.

* * *

Nearly three months after UK's NCAA championship, Magloire got himself in hot water with Smith for at least the second time. Earlier, he had served a one-game suspension for a team rules violation, sitting out UK's 82-71 win over Alabama in the SEC tournament. The latest incident had him riding with two men, including his high school teammate at Toronto, who were arrested on drug-possession charges in the Louisville area. Even though Magloire was not charged, Smith commented he was still very disappointed in the player's judgment. Therefore, the coach punished Magloire by suspending him for four contests, including two exhibition games, at the beginning of the 1998-99 campaign.

However, that was not the last time Magloire made the headlines off the court. In January of 1999, Smith suspended the junior again, this time for breaking a curfew. Also, Magloire encountered problems on the hardwood floor with his physical play. In the Ole Miss game won by Kentucky 63-57 at Oxford, he received a technical foul and Smith suspended him for one game for that and for violating a curfew policy. Later, on Senior Night, honoring Scott Padgett, Wayne Turner and Heshimu Evans at Rupp Arena, Magloire had to leave early in Kentucky's 88-63 win over Vanderbilt as he was automatically ejected for two technical fouls.

It was Magloire's never-ending intensity to be the top player that put him at odds with opponents and others. "I think people don't know my desire to be great," explained Magloire. "I'm not a complacent person and I'll stop at nothing in order to become great. I want to be one of those known as being the best at what they do."

Because of his strong physical play, many observers at the time said the NBA would be a better place for Magloire. He agreed with their viewpoint and thought about jumping to the pros after his junior year. After entering his name on the NBA draft eligibility list, Magloire attended several camps and had private workouts with a number of NBA teams. He changed his mind, deciding he wasn't completely ready. So he came back to Kentucky for his senior year.

* * *

Coach Tubby Smith then had high expectations for Magloire. "I think he has learned a lot from his experience prior to the NBA draft," reasoned Smith at the start of the 1999-2000 season. Magloire would be Kentucky's only returning senior with experience, having already started

40 games during his Wildcat tenure. After the stunning loss of two players who left the school, Michael Bradley and Ryan Hogan, the team needed him more than ever. The coach said, "His leadership will be critical. I think he will have to carry a bigger offensive role and a much bigger rebounding role than he has in the past. He will be a focal point of our team."

And Magloire had his best year as a Kentucky senior. His NBA experience along with his growing maturity helped him tremendously. While the short-handed Wildcats finished with a 23-10 mark after a second-round 52-50 loss to Syracuse in the NCAA tournament, Magloire, who had a few rough moments such as Dick Vitale's criticism, performed well individually. A first-team All-SEC pick, he had 15 double-doubles, completing the season with averages of 13.2 points (behind sophomore Tayshaun Prince's team-leading 13.3 points) and an SEC-best 9.1 rebounds.

Despite several difficult moments with Smith, Magloire still praised his former coach. "I think our relationship was very, very good," he said. "I think he gave me opportunities to play and he is one of the more personable coaches that I have had in my career. I think we all did (feel close to him) as players. He was a good coach and he built relationships with his players because he is one of a big family. I think he really values family and treated us like his. I was blessed with having coach Smith."

Smith and his wife, Donna, frequently invited the team members to their Lexington home. They also had cookouts. It was their way of getting to know them outside of basketball. "All the players went to his house for special occasions and had fun," Magloire said. What did the coach serve? "He had food catered," added Magloire.

After spending four years in the Wildcat camp, Magloire now knows what's like to be in a fish bowl. "It definitely is a special program, I think," he said. "It's the most exciting program in the country. The fans give so much life to it and you have so much support that you have no choice but to win. I think it is like a religion down there for the Kentucky fans and there is no place like it in the country. The fans are great in Kentucky and there is no place like it as far as the amount of people that are involved with the game. Everybody is so die-hard down there." He encountered some of the most unusual autograph requests from the Kentucky fans. "I'd say the most unusual one was signing on their arm or on their shoulder (at the team's hotel)," said Magloire, who majored in business. "I think it was after we won the national championship (in 1998)."

* * *

On the evening of June 28, 2000, Magloire was back in his hometown of Toronto, watching the NBA draft on television. He had booked a room at the luxurious Fairmont Royal York Hotel, a downtown landmark in Canada's largest city, so that a large crowd of relatives and friends could celebrate his new pro career. And he anxiously waited for the Toronto Raptors, who had the No. 21 pick overall, to select him. They were his favorite pro team. About a week earlier, with new Raptors coach Lenny Wilkens and the front office staff looking on, Magloire had a good individual workout. They had plans to select him.

"I don't think I was nervous," Magloire said of that draft night. "I think I was more excited. I had a good workout in quite a few places. I was excited to find out where I was going to be."

But when the No. 19 selection came, the Charlotte (now New Orleans) Hornets made Magloire their first-round pick. Shortly afterwards, he had a phone conversation with Charlotte coach Paul Silas, promising his new boss that he would not be a disappointment. He became the third Wildcat player to be drafted by Charlotte. The other two were Rex Chapman, who was drafted in 1988, and Tony Delk, in 1996. While he preferred the Raptors, Magloire was nevertheless happy to be given an opportunity to play in the NBA. His dream finally had come true. Needless to say, it was an exciting time for the Magloire family.

And he didn't have much sleep as he had to travel to Charlotte for the next day's press conference where the team officials introduced him. Less than a month later, Magloire reportedly signed a three-year contract for about $3 million.

"I do think the NBA is a better fit for me not only because of the physical play but because of the demands and the expectations," he said. "I've always strived to be the best and to achieve the best and there is no better level. There is no better place to do it than the NBA."

As a first-year pro who averaged almost 15 minutes a game with 4.6 points and four rebounds, Magloire nearly made the 2000-01 Schick NBA All-Rookie team. He came up one vote short of earning second-team honors. During the season, Magloire, interestingly, had a very memorable night when he helped the Hornets whip his hometown Raptors 100-64 in Toronto. He scored a season-high 16 points, while grabbing eight rebounds and blocking three shots in 22 minutes. And Magloire got to see his former coach, Rick Pitino, when their teams clashed in mid-December at the Charlotte Coliseum. Magloire, however, was sidelined with a sore left foot. "Unfortunately, I didn't get to play that game," he said. "I was hurt. But it is always a pleasure to see him and I think we played well and we ended up winning that game and that is what it is all about." Behind Jamal Mashburn's team-highs of 20 points and 12 rebounds, Charlotte defeated Boston 99-87.

Later, in the 2002-03 season, Magloire had his most productive NBA campaign for the Hornets, who by then had moved to New Orleans. He started all of the team's 82 games, averaging 10.3 points and 8.8 rebounds. Against Indiana in February 2003, he grabbed a pro career-high 20 rebounds. He also matched his NBA career-high in scoring, gunning in 22 points against Phoenix about a month earlier.

* * *

It wasn't too long after Magloire had completed his pro rookie year when a tragedy hit him hard. He lost his younger brother – actually his half-brother. A promising 6-4 power forward, Justin Sheppard, 19, was shot in the head during the early morning hours while crossing a pedestrian bridge in a Toronto neighborhood. And a very shaken Magloire asked for help from the public as police attempted to solve the mystery case.

Just hours before he was killed, Sheppard, who was several days away from his graduation at Eastern School of Commerce, reportedly had played pickup basketball with friends. A member of the school's highly-rated basketball squad, Sheppard had planned to attend a prep school in Maryland on a basketball scholarship in the fall of 2001.

While at Eastern, Sheppard wore No. 21 on his jersey, which was the same number Magloire wore in high school and now wears in the NBA. According to the *Toronto Star*, Eastern's vice-principal Lou Sialtsis said the jersey No. 21 had been retired but Magloire wanted his younger brother have the number.

Needless to say, it was a very sad chapter in Magloire's life.

* * *

In the spring of 2001, when the rumors were churning at full speed during U of L's courtship of Pitino for the school's coaching post, Magloire was asked by the author what would be his reaction if Pitino takes the job. "That is a tough question," he said. It didn't help that the Kentucky and Louisville have one of the country's hottest basketball rivalries. The ex-Wildcat found the stunning romance of U of L and Pitino amusing. He didn't know what to think. To him, it didn't look quite right to see Pitino wearing Cardinal red, instead of Kentucky blue.

However, he supported the coach's dramatic return to the state of Kentucky when Pitino accepted a fabulous offer from U of L to replace Denny Crum. "I think coach has to look out for his best interest," said Magloire. "He knows best. I think he has proven that over and over again. It will be tough because of the rivalry between Louisville and Kentucky. But you know in this business you have to make decisions and live with them."

While his former college coach may be at a rival school, looking for ways to upstage UK, the fearless Canadian will always be a Kentucky Wildcat.

Chapter 11

Mr. Comeback

Scott Padgett's life transformation story is something that the Hollywood bigwigs would shoot for. They would love to have his story in their movie. It would include just about everything -- glamour in boyish-looking coach Rick Pitino, Kentucky's high-profile basketball program, campus parties, Padgett's academic suspension, his college sweetheart and his comfortable lifestyle in pro basketball.

Before he became a success, Scott Padgett saw himself in troubled times. He was a college dropout who flunked out of UK and found low-paying jobs, working around the yards, among others, in his hometown.

While he loved basketball and campus parties, he didn't want to study. So he failed his classes and went back home to Louisville, missing the entire 1995-96 basketball season, which was the year Kentucky won its first national title since 1978.

In the book interview held at a downtown Lexington hotel, Padgett discussed his troubled times and his dramatic comeback in becoming an academic and a basketball standout. "I was frustrated from not playing (much during his freshman year)," he said. "College is tougher. I never had to study in high school to get good grades. So I just thought I would come to college and show up for class, (thinking) the work would be easy and I'd do it and I'd get the grades. Well, it is tougher in college. And then I partied too much. I'll be honest with you. I went out and had a lot of fun and ended up not taking care of business in the classroom."

As a Wildcat rookie from St. Xavier High School, Padgett saw action in only 14 games, averaging 4.1 minutes and two points as Rick Pitino's talented club posted a 28-5 mark and a final No. 2 national ranking. Kentucky finished the 1994-95 campaign with a disappointing NCAA tourney setback to North Carolina 74-61 in the regional finals.

Pitino was pretty ticked off when he learned of Padgett's academic woes. "I think (he was seething) because with my academic background that I had from high school I don't think he expected to have to worry

Under the watchful eyes of the Utah Jazz head coach Jerry Sloan, Scott Padgett, a former Wildcat standout from Louisville St. Xavier High School, drives during an NBA game.

about academics with me. I was a good student in high school," Padgett said.

Before he flunked out, Padgett admitted the coaching staff had warned him about his grades. He told them not to worry and that he would "take care of business." He added, "They were on me pretty much my whole freshman year. They tried to stay on top of me. It was one of those things if I wasn't going to do the work, they can't do it for me. They definitely posted the warning signs."

His parents, Wilbur and Linda Padgett, not surprisingly, weren't very happy with their only child's attitude, especially in the classroom. "They were definitely upset," said the younger Padgett, who stayed with his parents during the suspension. "But I think once they got over initially being upset, they were really supportive and helped me get back to school. During that time of sitting out, I thought about transferring several times. My dad was the one who said, 'No, this was your dream. Don't let your screwing up your freshman year keep you from your dream.' He basically got me to go back to Kentucky."

Also during that time, Padgett and his girlfriend, Cynthia Dozier, (who would later be his wife) had broken up. Things weren't too rosy for Padgett. So he stayed busy with two jobs, including selling fertilizers and mowing grass.

"It was a good experience," said Padgett of his jobs. "I wouldn't want to do it again. Definitely, it helped me in my growth and maturity. It helped me see where I might be if I didn't go back -- take care of academics, graduate and get my education. And at that time I wasn't even thinking about the NBA or anything like that. I was worrying about just going back and getting my education so that I wouldn't have to work those kind of jobs."

So, with his father's encouragement, Padgett came back to UK for the spring semester of 1996. Pitino had left the door open for the player to return. But, Padgett said, "I don't think he really expected me to come back." By becoming a Wildcat for the second time, Padgett sought another chance to prove people wrong about his intelligence, basketball skills, attitude and potential. He wanted to show them that he could study and play as well. He was highly motivated. "I consider myself a fairly smart, intelligent guy," Padgett said. "I wanted to prove to people that I wasn't an idiot and let people know that I wasn't as dumb as they thought when I flunked."

However, just a few days before his Lexington arrival in early January, Padgett nearly created a firestorm. He almost became a member of Louisville coach Denny Crum's squad. The Cardinals had recruited him hard while Padgett was in high school. "Two days before I was supposed to come back, I had decided I was going transfer to Louisville," commented Padgett. "I actually went through an orientation, had filled out my class schedule and was going to be enrolled (at U of L). The guy I played summer basketball with knew Crum very well and he was actually kind of a go-between because I didn't have a release (from UK) or anything so I couldn't actually go and talk to them. So I kind of had him as a go-between. But I had basically worked it out to where I was going to be able to make the team (at U of L). I was going to have to sit out the rest of that year."

A phone call from then-UK assistant coach Winston Bennett changed Padgett's plans. It was the first time that Padgett had heard from the basketball staff in several months. He had thought the coaches didn't give a hoot about him. "I talked to coach Pitino at the end of August and that (Bennett's call) was the first time I had talked to anybody from Kentucky as far as the staff until Jan. 6 or 7 that year," Padgett said. "So I went five months without talking to anybody on the staff. And when nobody called to even keep up with me, I just assumed they could care less if I came back or not.

"When coach Bennett called he told me they wanted me back. That changed everything. I was like, 'Well, I'm not going back to Louisville. I'm going to Kentucky. I'm going to try and work this thing out.' When I first came back, coach Pitino told me I had to have a 3.0 (GPA) to get back on the team. I really don't think he thought I would get it, but I made sure I did."

* * *

As the 1995-96 Wildcats caught the nation's attention with their awesome display of talent and domination, Padgett said he was not depressed during the year he sat out. But he really wanted to be a part of that winning team. "No, it was frustrating, especially as well as the team played that year," he commented. "I mean that was one of the best teams in the history of college basketball as far as one through 10 (depth). The talent on that team was ridiculous and to see how they just rolled through the season and won the championship – it (sitting out) was tough. But I also think that whole experience probably made me a lot better player and also made me grow up a lot."

After enrolling at UK for the spring semester, he decided to visit his old girlfriend, who also played volleyball at Kentucky. They hadn't been in touch for several months.

"When I came back to school, I just showed up at her door one day," Padgett said of his visit to Miss Dozier, who is a native of Colorado. "So we got back together and we have been together since."

And they got to watch the NCAA title game together with friends when the Wildcats beat Syracuse on red-hot Tony Delk's seven three-pointers. Padgett said he had a funny feeling watching the game. After all, if he had kept his grades in order, he knew he would've been with the team, participating in college basketball's biggest event of the year.

"I definitely had mixed feelings," he said. "I was so happy for the guys that they got everything that they had worked for. But at the same time I was missing out on being part of a national championship. So it was definitely tough for me. But I think that is another thing that helped the next year in becoming a better player to (get) where I wanted to get back (to the Final Four). I wanted to be part of a national championship."

After the big victory, the young couple went outside and saw the wild massive celebration on the streets. "We went out to Woodland and Euclid for a little while and watched all the people get crazy and tear up the streets and everything for a little while," said Padgett.

Padgett and his girlfriend first met when they were both freshmen in 1994. They had seen each other a couple of times before, but they actually chatted for the first time in Memorial Coliseum's training room, rehabbing their bothersome shoulder injuries. "We were both in there getting treatment on our arms," commented Padgett. "I had separated my shoulder in high school and she had also separated her shoulder in high school. (The shoulders) kind of flared up – a little sore. We actually sat there and talked to each other for a while. That is how we met and I think the next day or two I asked her out on a date and we've been together pretty much ever since except for the time I was out (on academic suspension)."

* * *

His suspension from UK wasn't the only time he had gotten himself in trouble.

While at St. Xavier, where he was a three-year starter who averaged 19 points, 13 rebounds and five assists as a senior, Padgett had to miss some playing time as well. The all-stater drew a suspension for an incident at the junior prom.

"I got suspended for the first two games in my senior year because in my junior year we got in trouble at the dance," Padgett recalled. "The two guys I went with played baseball and were suspended because they were in the season. The athletic director didn't feel that it was fair for them to get suspended and I wasn't. Since I was already out of season, I had to carry mine over to my senior year. So basically I got suspended for something I did six months earlier. I had to sit out the first two games and it kind of hurt because we ended up losing two games to the teams that we had beaten by 30 points when I played. So that was difficult."

In mid-December, Padgett also had to sit out a month because of an injury. He suffered a broken wrist in a win against Newport Central Catholic when he was hit and fouled at the game-ending buzzer.

* * *

Then Padgett, who also played football as a freshman and sophomore, was on his way to his boyhood favorite team, Kentucky, picking the Wildcats over Florida, Florida State, Louisville, Ohio State and Purdue. While some Wildcat fans weren't too excited about Padgett's arrival at UK, Wildcat boss Rick Pitino said that the player should have an excellent career. "Scott reminds me of a bigger version of John Pelphrey," added Pitino.

Doing most of the recruiting for the Wildcats was assistant coach Billy Donovan, now the head coach at Florida. But Donovan wasn't around when Padgett arrived on the UK campus in 1994.

"I loved Billy from the first time I talked to him on the phone," recalled Padgett, who has a nickname called the 'L-Train.' "I was in like my freshman year (in high school). I really, really like him a lot. I was kind of sad to see him go when he got the Marshall job because he actually did all the recruiting of me and then he ended up leaving right before I got there (at UK). I was kind of hoping to get to play under him a little."

Padgett half-jokingly said that he himself was probably the easiest recruit Pitino has ever had. After all, Padgett was a die-hard fan who bled blue.

* * *

Padgett's first exposure to the Wildcats?

It was around 1979 or 1980 when Padgett saw his first basketball game on TV with his father, and 7-1 high school sensation Sam Bowie was playing for the Wildcats as the team's newest star. Padgett was three years old at the time.

"He was the only guy I could say," Padgett said of Bowie. "I couldn't really say his name. I would say just 'Bo,' instead of Bowie. I would say, 'Go Bo,' because he was my favorite player at the time. I think the first game I ever watched was the Kentucky versus Georgia game. I can't tell you who won or lost. My dad was always a huge Kentucky fan. I would kind of watch the game and kind of watch him and learn how to react to the game from how he reacted."

His mom, however, didn't care too much for the Wildcats when Padgett was growing up. Before she changed her team affiliation to UK, she cheered for the hometown university, U of L. "Until I was probably about 10 years old, my mom was a Louisville fan," said the son. "Eventually my dad and I wore her down and she became a Kentucky fan. Now she is a huge Kentucky fan and keeps up with it all the time. But we had to wear her down a little at first.

"I've got one uncle who is a big Louisville fan and other than that everybody else in the family are Kentucky fans. So he usually took a lot of ribbing and stuff from everybody else in the family. He was fighting an uphill battle."

In the early 1980s, Padgett had another thrill. He saw basketball legends Joe B. Hall of Kentucky and Denny Crum of Louisville signing autographs at a store. "I was five or six years old and there was an autograph signing that Denny Crum and Joe B. Hall did together and they had a poster," Padgett said. "It was a Converse poster. It was split down the middle with Joe B. Hall and his Kentucky stuff (on one side) and the other (side) was Denny Crum with all his Louisville stuff. I got both of their autographs."

As Padgett got older, he used to pretend he was Rex Chapman on the playgrounds and then Jamal Mashburn. "Those were the two that I really liked. They were my two favorites," said Padgett, who saw his first Rupp Arena game in person when the Eddie Sutton-coached Cats defeated North Carolina-Charlotte 84-81 for the 1987 UKIT championship.

* * *

Remember the fiery Kevin O'Neill, the one-time Marquette head coach who later moved on and took similar jobs at Tennessee and now with the NBA's Toronto Raptors?

Padgett has a story about him. O'Neill wrote a letter, saying the player wasn't of high enough quality for him. Interestingly, O'Neill's statements came about a week after Padgett had already made a verbal commitment to UK. "I don't know if it was one of those things where it was a bitterness thing or whatever, but it just seemed like a bitter letter when he wrote it. So that (recruiting experience) kind of stood out in my mind," said Padgett. "He writes me a letter, saying that we no longer feel that you are the type of player that we would like at Marquette and we are no longer recruiting you." Padgett added that he thought it was rather odd that O'Neill was telling him that he wasn't good enough, since he was good enough to play at Kentucky.

While on the NBA circuit in recent years, Padgett and O'Neill have casually met each other a few times. "I haven't told him that story where I remember the letter," Padgett said.

* * *

When Padgett was a high school freshman, he got to meet Pitino for the first time. No, they didn't meet at a gym or a summer camp to discuss basketball. Instead, they briefly met by chance at a major horse racing event. They were at Churchill Downs in Louisville, where Padgett worked at the Kentucky Derby. On the first Saturday in May, the youngster was doing some ushering work, taking people to their seats in the skyboxes.

"I sat coach Pitino (along with his wife and family) at his table," said Padgett. "At the time I was only about 6-2 and I told him that one day I was going to play for him. And you know, he kind of laughed. When he (later) came on his recruiting visit to my house, I told him that story again and we had a little laugh. He didn't remember it."

* * *

At Kentucky, Padgett also had to miss the fall semester of the 1996-97 campaign in order to regain eligibility. He still had to work on his academics. And it paid off as the sophomore made the Dean's List both semesters. Despite sitting out several early games, he finished the year as the squad's third-leading scorer with an average of nearly 10 points, starting the last 22 games after a season-ending injury to Derek Anderson.

Padgett concluded his remarkable comeback in the NCAA title game, pumping in a team-high 17 points in UK's 84-79 overtime loss to

Arizona. However, the game, as it turned out, would mark the last time Padgett played for Pitino, who later departed Kentucky for the NBA's Boston Celtics.

And Padgett's new boss would be Tubby Smith, the one-time UK associate coach under Pitino. After two years of playing under Pitino, the adjustments of the coaching change weren't too difficult, according to Padgett.

"As far as their demeanors, I don't think it was that tough," he said. "You know coach Pitino yells a lot. When he gets upset, coach Smith yells a lot. I think, for us as a team in 1998, the biggest adjustment was defensive styles. Defensively, with Pitino, it was 40 minutes; we're going to press, and run up and down. With coach Smith, I think he picked his points. If the (other) team's back-up point guard was in, we pressed or if they didn't have a very good ball-handling team, other than their point guard, we would press them. But I think the biggest change for us was the half-court defense."

With Smith in charge, Padgett, who was now a maturing junior, started 37 of the national championship team's 39 games in 1997-98. In the South Regional finals against top-seeded Duke, he gunned in what would be one of the school's most famous baskets, leading the Cats, who trailed by 18 at one point, to a stunning 86-84 win and a third straight Final Four spot. Padgett, whose three-point field goal had broken a tie with 39.4 seconds left, finished the game with 12 points. Jeff Sheppard led the Cats in the scoring and rebounding departments with 18 points and 11 rebounds.

Padgett gives Smith a lot of credit for the team's big turnaround after giving a halftime pep talk to the players when UK was down by 10 at the intermission. The coach expressed confidence that his team would prevail over the Blue Devil club.

"I think it was his demeanor and how he came in there (the dressing room)," Padgett said. "He was so confident that we were going to win the game. It was how he put it across to us. I think that was very good mental coaching for us. And everybody on that team said, 'You know, you are right. We are going to win this game. We are the better team.' We hung in there (at the end).

"If he had come in there, yelling and screaming about how bad we were playing, there's a chance they could've beaten us by 20."

The Wildcat victory, witnessed by a Tampa, Fla., crowd of 40,589, was one of the sweetest in UK's storied hoops history. Kentucky had just avenged its 1992 NCAA regional championship loss to the Blue Devils, who won on a miracle shot by Christian Laettner. (That 1992 classic also marked Cawood Ledford's last appearance as the "Voice of the Wildcats.")

The following week at San Antonio, Texas, was another exciting time for the Wildcats. Like many of the other players' families, the Padgett clan took part in the festive Final Four atmosphere along with his girlfriend, Cynthia. "She went to the game with my mom and dad," said Padgett. "I have an aunt and uncle (his dad's brother) who live in Texas. So they came to the game, too. My parents went down and stayed at their place in Dallas and then they drove from Dallas to San Antonio for the game."

Padgett and his teammates made the 1998 Final Four games memorable for them as well as the fans. After UK came up with another come-from-behind win in edging Stanford 86-85 in overtime, the Wildcats, who were now popularly called the "Comeback Cats," became the second team since the 1973 UCLA team to play in three consecutive NCAA title games. (The other school was Duke, which played in three straight championship games in the early 1990s.)

In college basketball's biggest matchup of the season, Padgett gunned in a game-high 17 points against Utah in leading Kentucky to another comeback victory. Using its valuable depth of eight players who performed at least 10 minutes each, UK overcame its 10-point halftime deficit.

* * *

While in college, Padgett spent much of his free time with wrestling, fishing and golf. "I remember in my junior year everybody used to come into my room and Shep (Jeff Sheppard) was my roommate at the time. Everybody would be in there watching wrestling (on TV) and wrestling each other," Padgett said.

Asked if he still follows wrestling today, Padgett laughed and said, "Not as much. I don't have much time now plus my wife doesn't like it."

With his friendly personality, he practically got along with everyone. "We had a very close-knit team. Everybody was close," said Padgett. But his closest teammates were actually Sheppard, Jared Prickett and Steve Masiello.

Padgett has many stories about his teammates. "I remember Mark Pope and Shep were driving one of their cars and it broke down in the snow," he said. "They just pushed (the car). They didn't call anybody.

They just pushed. It is funny to me just picturing Jeff Sheppard and Mark Pope pushing this car through downtown Lexington on Main Street or something. They told us about it and it is funny when you try to picture (them doing it) in your head."

* * *

Coming off Kentucky's surprising 1998 NCAA championship performance, the Wildcats had a challenge for the 1998-99 campaign. They had to replace three seniors from the previous team – Sheppard, Allen Edwards and Cameron Mills – and Nazr Mohammed, who left early for NBA.

Despite the loss of four key performers, the Cats, with coach Tubby Smith beginning his second year at the Wildcat helm, nevertheless were expected to do well. In the AP pre-season poll, they were ranked No. 4. The senior leadership responsibilities went to tri-captains Padgett, Wayne Turner and Heshimu Evans.

Padgett, who appeared on almost every list of pre-season All-American honors, was ready to go. Now a senior, he would be wearing the proud Wildcat uniform for the last time that winter.

After Padgett helped the Cats capture another SEC tournament title in Atlanta, scoring a game-high 20 points in a 76-63 victory over Arkansas and winning the tourney MVP honors, he excitedly looked ahead to the Big Dance. Could the Cats advance to the NCAA championship game for the fourth straight year?

No, Padgett and his 28-9 Cats couldn't make it that far. But they almost did, advancing all the way to the Midwest Regional finals before dropping to second-ranked Michigan State 73-66 in St. Louis.

But the power forward had the best game of his career a week earlier in New Orleans where UK faced Kansas in a post-season matchup of two of the country's all-time winningest teams. It was the second time both schools had met on the floor that season with Kentucky winning the first encounter by a lowly score of 63-45 in Chicago.

In the second contest with the 22nd-rated Jayhawks, the Wildcats relied on two seniors – Padgett and Turner – to carry the dramatic show. With Kentucky winning 92-88 in overtime, Padgett hit his UK career-high 29 points, including 4 of 8 three-point field goals, and Turner got 19 points. They not only scored, the duo went to the boards hard. Padgett and Turner grabbed 10 and six rebounds, respectively. Turner also passed out seven assists.

"That is definitely one of my favorite games because that's Kansas-Kentucky," commented Padgett, who as a senior was named honorable mention All-American and earned All-SEC honors. "(It's) the first time both schools have ever met in the NCAA tournament. The whole game was a battle. You know, we would make a big play, and then they would make a big play. (We'd) hit a three, they would make a three-point play at the other end. It was just back and forth the whole game (as both teams hit 23 three-pointers).

"Another thing I remember about the game was the time that Wayne became the all-time leader in games played. He set the record for most games played in college basketball. So it was a special game. It was a great game."

With Kentucky down by three with less than 20 seconds remaining in regulation, Padgett poured in one of the two biggest shots of his Wildcat career – a critical three-point downtown jumper at the top of the key – which tied the game at 79. The long basket came just moments after an offensive rebound by reserve center Jamaal Magloire gave the Cats another life when Turner missed a field goal.

Padgett said Turner "made a nice move and the ball just came off the front of the rim and Jamaal made a nice rebound. I remember him kicking it to me and when I first caught the ball, I remember Kenny Gregory (of Kansas) running at me. (He) jumped about 45 inches off the ground. He's got a huge vertical leap on him. So I shot faked and I took the dribble in. And about that time, I remembered we needed a three. So, as I started to take the dribble in, I took a step back (behind the three-point line). It seemed like there was nobody in line with me. It was like I had never been that open in my life all of a sudden. And as soon as I shot it, I knew it was good. It was definitely an exciting moment to be able to hit a shot in a big situation where the team needed it and then for us to go on and win it in overtime."

* * *

Outside of basketball, Padgett majored in social work with a minor in business.

With his slow start in academics, it took him awhile to raise his grade-point-average to a very respectable level. According to Padgett, he finally finished with a GPA of 3.0 (out of possible 4.0) at UK before getting his bachelor's degree.

"This was how bad my freshman year was," he said. "My last three and a half years at Kentucky, I had a 3.65. That's not bad. One (bad) year dropped me to a 3.0 (overall)."

During his Wildcat career, Padgett twice earned Academic All-SEC honors (1998 and '99).

* * *

Serving as the team's unofficial chaplain, the Rev. Ed Bradley was a familiar sight on the UK bench and Padgett enjoyed his spiritual presence. In addition to his UK duties, Bradley kept busy in Henderson where he served as pastor of Holy Name, a Catholic church.

"I've really grown closer (to him) since I came back (to UK after sitting out due to poor grades)," said Padgett, who is a Catholic. "I didn't really know him as well when I was a freshman. But when I came back I got to really know him and I have been down to see him in Henderson. He is a great guy."

Bradley also played a part in the Padgett-Dozier wedding at St. Paul in Lexington. "Father Bradley actually did our wedding when we got married," said the ex-Cat.

Bradley, by the way, baptized their first child, Logan, at Padgett's home church, St. Gabriel, in Louisville even though the Padgetts made their home in Utah where he played for the NBA's Utah Jazz.

Padgett and his wife had another son, Lucas, who was born in 2003 during the NBA playoffs. The proud father said he had to sleep on a cot in his wife's hospital room to be with her and the new baby.

* * *

Just days before the NBA teams opened their pre-season training camps in 2002, Scott Padgett was getting somewhat uneasy.

Coming off his best NBA campaign in 2001-02 when he averaged nearly seven points in 17.3 minutes of action in a reserve role, the former UK hoops star didn't have a contract.

Where was he going to play? The NBA? Perhaps overseas? What was he going to do? His three-year rookie pact with the Utah Jazz had expired after he was chosen as the team's top pick -- the league's 28th pick overall -- in the 1999 NBA Draft.

"To be honest, I was a little concerned about not having a deal done before the camp started but not about being in the NBA this year," Padgett said in another interview with the author. "I had three or four other teams besides the Jazz showing interest in me so I was pretty confident that something would work out."

As it turned out, things did work out for Padgett as the Jazz signed the forward to a one-year contract in late September 2002, just four days before the pre-season camp began. According to *USA Today*, Padgett's 2002-03 salary was $612,435, the NBA minimum for a three-year veteran.

Padgett was very pleased. Playing for the same team meant that he wouldn't have to make any new major adjustments. Had he gone to a different NBA squad or even to a foreign country, Padgett would have had to learn a new system all over again like when he first joined the Jazz in 1999.

Like the previous year, he had another productive year in 2002-03, playing in all of the team's 82 games with an average of 16.1 minutes. Scoring-wise, he averaged 5.7 points a game. He also started two games.

Padgett admitted his first two years in the NBA weren't easy. After starting 96 of the final 98 games of his collegiate career at Kentucky, it was very difficult for Padgett to sit on the bench. He wanted to play so bad and got frustrated at times.

As a pro rookie, the former All-SEC performer managed to play in 47 games, including nine as a starter, averaging over nine minutes a game. In the second year, he saw his playing time decrease significantly. He began that season on the injured list, sitting out the first 40 games supposedly because of tendinitis in his right knee. As a result, he played in only 27 games with an average of 4.7 minutes.

But Padgett said he really wasn't injured. "We made a trade and brought in (6-9 forward) Donyell Marshall, who played the same position that I did, and I kind of got bumped down a notch behind him because he played a lot and played well for us," Padgett commented. "There weren't a lot of minutes there (for both of us).

"My injuries were non-existent, but in the NBA they have to make up an injury for you. So I wasn't hurt. I had a couple of little minor things but nothing that would have kept me from playing. But it is one of those things you kind of have to do when you are one of the younger guys in the league."

His third and fourth NBA seasons, however, were different stories. He found playing time and became a more productive player. Against Denver in 2002, he poured in an NBA career-high 21 points.

During his early pro career, Padgett commented that his Utah teammates were helpful to him, especially standout guard Jeff Hornacek (who has since retired) and 6-9, 256-pound star Karl Malone (who later joined the Los Angeles Lakers).

"One of the guys that I tried to ask questions a lot was Jeff Hornacek," Padgett said. "He was in the last year of his career. He was a guy I felt like was kind of similar to my situation. He came out of Iowa State. He originally was a walk-on (at Iowa State). Nobody expected him to ever make it in the NBA and he went on to have a 12-year (actually 14-year) career.

"I thought he was somebody similar to (my situation). I don't think a lot of people expected me to be able to make it to the NBA. I tried to learn little things from him – where I could get a shot off somebody or things on defense that would help me out.

"Another guy I talked to a lot was Karl Malone. But it is different with Karl. Karl is a different kind of guy. I think it was more of a friendship thing with Karl, and Karl helped me get through tough times. He would tell me to hang in there and things like that.

"Karl has his own way of saying things. I don't know if he necessarily talks a lot, but whatever is on his mind, Karl tells you. You know he doesn't hold anything back and I think that is what most people (in the media) like in an interview."

* * *

Like Malone, Padgett has his own way of talking, too. While at UK, the Louisville native was one of the most cooperative players as far as interviews are concerned. The news media loved his outgoing demeanor. "You always knew where you stood with Scott Padgett," said former UK basketball publicist Brooks Downing. "You always knew what was on his mind, whether you wanted to know or not. Scott just liked to talk.

"When he left (Kentucky), he ranked up there with Derek Anderson among the former Cats whom the local press hated to see leave. Both Derek and Scott had media members thanking them for their honesty and candor following their respective Senior Days."

Downing doesn't really have a favorite story about Padgett, but added, "I just enjoyed every day working with him. He made my life much easier."

* * *

Bret Bearup, a former UK player during the coach Joe B. Hall regime in the early 1980s, serves as Padgett's financial advisor. Based in Atlanta, Bearup also serves an advisor for many athletes, including the NBA, NFL and Major League Baseball, and entertainers.

"Bret has like 37 percent of the guys in the NBA as clients," Padgett said. "He has NBA owners. The guy (Stan Kroenke) who owns the Denver Nuggets is his client. So he is doing very well for himself right now."

Bearup, who is also an attorney, shares a lot of his UK stories with Padgett when they get together or talk on the phone. Padgett has one Bearup story that sticks out in his mind.

"He said that he should get credit as the (school's) all-time leading scorer because he set so many screens for Kenny Walker that if you add his points and all of the points that Kenny Walker got off his screens that he would be the all-time leading scorer," Padgett said. "That was just one of his favorite ones and he definitely will talk your ear off about his college days all day."

Before coming to UK, the 6-9 Bearup was a consensus prep All-American at Greenlawn, N.Y. Upon his arrival at Kentucky in 1980, he joined other prized recruits – Melvin Turpin, Jim Master and Dicky Beal. Some say the group formed the nation's best recruiting crop at that time.

* * *

Taxi Driver.
Raging Bull.
Goodfellas.

Those were some of the movies that Padgett enjoyed. "I'm a big-time movie buff," he said. "I've got a big, huge TV screen at my house (in Utah). So I watch movies a lot. I'm one of those guys who probably annoy you because I can tell you lines from the movie before they come up. I'm really into like gangster-type movies and stuff. I like a lot of Robert DeNiro movies."

What about the Ashley Judd movies? "I've seen most of them," said Padgett.

* * *

When his playing days are finished, Padgett said he wouldn't mind coaching basketball. "I'm definitely very serious about a future career in coaching," he said. "Being the coach at Kentucky is another dream of mine. Having said this I hope to play another 7 to 10 years before I would get into coaching."

Padgett, who once bought a piece of an old Rupp Arena floor for $6,000 at an auction, said he hasn't talked about his future with his college coaches, Rick Pitino and Tubby Smith. "I have not discussed a possible coaching career with either coach Pitino or coach Smith. But when the time comes that I do decide I want to pursue a coaching career I would definitely seek advice from both."

And it wouldn't be too surprising if the players someday call the ex-Wildcat "Coach Padgett."

Chapter 12

Coal Miner's Grandson

When Herb Sendek graduated with honors from Pittsburgh's Carnegie Mellon University in 1985, Dean Smith and Mike Krzyzewski were still busy coaching basketball for the Tar Heels and the Blue Devils, respectively.

By 1996, when North Carolina State University lured Sendek away from Miami of Ohio, both Smith and Coach K already had won a combined four NCAA titles, not to mention several other Final Four trips. Talk about experience. Talk about legendary status. They were the bigwigs of college basketball as well as the deans of the Atlantic Coast Conference.

Sendek, by taking the N.C. State coaching post, would have to challenge them if he was going to make some noise in ACC country. No problem. He was ready for the challenge and the biggest job of his career. A perfectionist and quiet by nature, he was a serious student of basketball who worked long hours on the hardwood floor. He had the background and enough experience. His father coached on both the high school and junior college levels. Sendek worked for one of college basketball's biggest names in Rick Pitino at a couple of places for several years. He served as associate coach at Kentucky, a basketball powerhouse, before getting the head coaching experience at Miami.

And Pitino advised Sendek, who was 33 at the time, to take the N.C. State job in the middle of the wild ACC country, suggesting that he was ready for big-time college basketball. So Smith and Coach K became Sendek's new coaching rivals and neighbors as well. With Sendek now based in Raleigh, the state capital, the campuses of Duke and North Carolina are just several miles away. Because of such close proximity, the coaches, like it or not, share the spotlight, unlike the Kentucky counterpart who practically rules the Bluegrass. Needless to say, the heated rivalry between the schools is fierce.

"That is a tough neighborhood," said Sendek from his office on the

Photo by Jamie H. Vaught

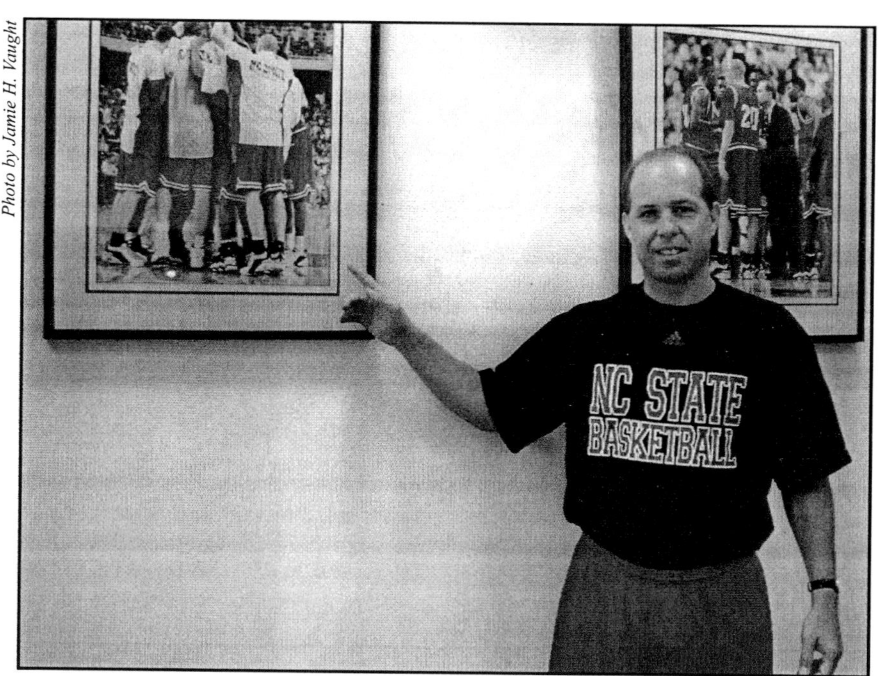

North Carolina State head coach and former Cat assistant Herb Sendek is shown here in his Raleigh office. He is a native of Pittsburgh.

N.C. State campus. "The three triangle schools – Duke, North Carolina and N.C. State – are within a 30-mile radius of each other. This is a tough street corner when you share the same newspaper and airport as Duke and North Carolina. I think it brings out the best in us at times and at other times the worst. It is a competitive environment.

"It's amazing the interest level is so spectacular that we could play a game at home the same night that Duke or North Carolina does. You know each school has their own following and both arenas can still be sold out. So I don't think we hurt for coverage, exposure or spotlight. It is just a different kind of interest because the schools are so close together whereas in Kentucky you had the University of Kentucky. It's the school of the Commonwealth so to speak.

"I have been very fortunate to enjoy two of the greatest college basketball environments that exist. Certainly, the Kentucky environment is storied and legendary, and likewise here on Tobacco Road – the two unique landscapes in college basketball, arguably the two best (in the country). They are different, but in their own way they are unique and very special."

For the record, Sendek, like most other coaches, hasn't had much luck in face-to-face battles with Smith and Coach K. During his first year at N.C. State, Sendek faced them six times, including two ACC tournament games. His 1996-97 record against the bigwigs? Not too good with a mark of 1-5. The lone victory came when his Wolfpack team upset Coach K's top-seeded Blue Devils 66-60, knocking them out of the conference tourney. But it was Smith who spoiled N.C. State's ACC tourney title hopes in the championship game by winning 64-54. It marked the Wolfpack's third straight setback to the Tar Heels during the season after two close calls – 59-56 and 45-44 decisions – earlier in the campaign. North Carolina, led by All-American Antawn Jamison and All-ACC Vince Carter, went on to advance to the NCAA Final Four.

Unfortunately for Sendek, he would never have another chance to beat the legendary Smith, who retired in 1997 as college basketball's winningest coach of all time with 879 victories, replacing UK's Adolph Rupp who had 876.

* * *

Before coming to Raleigh, Sendek found coaching success at Miami of Ohio despite the school's limited financial resources. In his first head coaching job, he guided the Oxford school, which is a one-hour drive northwest from Cincinnati, to three straight postseason appearances with an overall record of 63-26. During the 1994-95 campaign, his second year at Miami, the Redskins captured the Mid-American Conference title and earned an at-large bid to the NCAA tournament as the No. 12 seed. He made noise in the Big Dance when Miami upset No. 5 seed Arizona 71-62, before dropping to 13th-ranked and fourth-seeded Virginia in overtime.

Many schools began to take notice of Sendek's success. His close connections with Pitino didn't hurt, either. He was an attractive candidate. In the spring of 1995, shortly after his team's surprising performance in the NCAA tourney, Sendek was mentioned in connection with job openings at Georgia, Nevada-Las Vegas and Duquesne. He interviewed with the UNLV officials, but he had to withdraw his candidacy because the school wanted him to make a quick decision. A very cautious person, Sendek didn't want to rush, needing more time to think things over with his family and friends. One N.C. State official later said, "He's careful."

A year later, N.C. State came calling. After coaches such as Kelvin Sampson of Oklahoma, Bob Bender (Washington), Dave Odom (Wake Forest) and Roy Williams (Kansas) declined offers from Wolfpack athletic director Todd Turner, he contacted Sendek. For the Pittsburgh native, the N.C. State job looked very promising. Although it had fallen on hard times with five consecutive losing seasons during the coach Les Robinson era, the once-proud program had potential and resources of returning to its glorious past. Previous coaches Everett Case, Press Maravich, Norm Sloan and Jim Valvano all guided N.C. State to success. The school won national titles in 1974 (with Sloan and All-American David Thompson) and in 1983 (with a stunned Valvano who moments after winning the crown ran all over the floor, trying to find someone to hug).

So Sendek asked his friend and former boss, Pitino, about the Wolfpack program. Pitino, still at Kentucky at the time, thought it was an excellent opportunity, encouraging Sendek to pursue it, and said that he himself would call Turner. "I asked him to call the athletic director on my behalf which he did," Sendek recalled. "He has always been such a great advocate for his assistant coaches in helping them get jobs. I know he did a masterful job on the phone on my behalf and probably was very instrumental in persuading Todd Turner to hire me."

In April of 1996, Sendek became the youngest coach in the ACC and received a multi-year contract that reportedly paid him at least $300,000 annually. On his first full day on the new job, he encountered a mini-controversy when one of the players, freshman Marco Harrison, collapsed in a pre-dawn workout and had to be transported to a hospital. Not too happy with some of the players' tardiness in their first team meeting, which was held the previous day, Sendek took disciplinary steps, trying to keep the squad in the right direction by holding a very early workout.

Also, in another early coaching move, Sendek removed the players' names from the backs of their uniform jerseys to display a team concept, reflecting the coach's philosophy that no one individual is greater than the whole. He explained, "It was just one of several subtle ways that we wanted to emphasize how important it was to be together, to be 'One Heartbeat' (the slogan popularized by Sendek), to recognize how interdependent we are on each other with basketball being the ultimate team game."

However, some of the Wolfpack fans didn't applaud the new coach's decision. So, in 2000, Sendek allowed the players' names on be sewed on their jerseys on a limited basis. "The fans have continually expressed how they would like the names on the back for identification purposes," he said. "We've compromised and we do have them at home for our fans, for our players' families, and they certainly like that. Right now, we do not have our names on the back of the uniforms when we go on the road for that same stated purpose."

In his first winter at the Wolfpack helm, Sendek got off to a roaring start, guiding the team to its first winning campaign in six years. N.C. State, with two impressive wins over Duke and Maryland in the ACC tournament and a berth in the NIT, finished with a 17-15 mark. So, N.C. State's future was bright and things were looking good. The fans hoped for a return of the happy days of Jim Valvano. While Sendek may not be as charismatic as Valvano, the hard-to-please folks at Tobacco Road were certainly glad that their first-year boss had chosen to become a Wolfpack.

* * *

In the next four years, Sendek, though, struggled somewhat with overall records of 17-15, 19-14, 20-14 and 13-16 from 1997-98 to 2000-01. While he was doing much better than his predecessor, Les Robinson, it was nothing like the amazing success his friend and former colleague, Florida coach Billy Donovan, enjoyed. It didn't take Donovan very long to direct the Gators to the coveted NCAA Final Four. It took him four years, to be exact. What about Sendek? Well, it has taken him longer just to reach the NCAA tourney's opening round. His sixth Wolfpack team finally made it to the Big Dance in 2002, its first since 1991.

But before that NCAA tourney appearance, Sendek dealt with unhappy fans, who were not all that pleased with the team's several NIT trips. Some wanted him fired, saying it's taking the coach too long to rebuild the program. They didn't care for the NIT appearances. They wanted the NCAA tourney, just like the old days.

And Sendek certainly didn't help himself when he created an additional firestorm in a controversial incident in 2000. He failed to play one of his two seniors – 6-7 swingman Tim Wells – in the last home game of the regular season during the team's 66-63 loss to Clemson at Raleigh's new 19,722-seat Entertainment and Sports Arena. One of Wells' professors at N.C. State even protested Sendek's decision by writing a letter to the local newspaper.

The coach, however, defended his action, commenting a token appearance by Wells might have served no one and embarrassed the player himself. Wells, who earlier had missed most of the season with injuries, said his feelings were hurt, but didn't blame the coaches. He also added that he didn't want to play if it's only for charity. Interestingly, Wells, who started 22 games as a junior, later made his first start of the season against Tulane during the NIT.

After that contest against the Green Wave, Sendek had second thoughts, admitting his error. "I should have started him against Clemson (on Senior Night)," the coach was quoted as saying on N.C. State's official athletics Web site. "That was a mistake I made and this was a good chance to redeem myself tonight. Tim has picked his game up 100 percent. He's playing with a lot more confidence and I think he feels good about himself."

But while the anti-Sendek talk was reaching a feverish point, the coach received support from Raleigh's *The News and Observer*. "What Sendek lacks in charm, he makes up for with integrity," wrote sports columnist Ned Barnett. "He wants to win, but he wants to win the right way. He won't break rules. He won't break players.

"In that, he's reminiscent of two other coaches many fans wanted to toss out after their first few years. Dean Smith and Mike Krzyzewski. Those guys worked out pretty well. Sendek will, too."

* * *

The following season of 2000-01 was even worse. Sendek had his first losing season as the Wolfpack boss. N.C. State posted a 13-16 record, including 5-11 in conference action. While injuries played a significant role in the team's poor showing, Sendek, nevertheless, was given a warning -- win immediately in 2001-02 or else. His already-hot seat was getting hotter than ever before.

Fortunately for Sendek, under tremendous pressure, the program bounced back under his remarkable leadership in 2001-02. N.C. State finally did its job, finishing with the school's first trip to the NCAA tourney in 11 years and a 23-11 record. It was a pleasant campaign, which saw the Wolfpack upset eventual national champion Maryland in the ACC tournament and defeat the hated rival North Carolina Tar Heels twice during the regular season. *The Sporting News* also named Sendek as the ACC Coach of the Year.

And to many observers, it was a nice surprise that N.C. State was able to go that far with a No. 7 seed in the Big Dance. After all, a preseason poll had the Wolfpack at No. 7 in the nine-team ACC. No one had expected Sendek to set the world on fire. So he survived and got a contract extension to 2006-07, which reportedly saw his total annual pay increase to close to $800,000 at the time.

Sendek said the pressure to win that winter was nearly unbearable, if not impossible. "It was a difficult experience," he said. "I think if you would have told me ahead of time what I would have had to go through I would have really doubted my ability to go through it."

A devout Catholic who met Pope John Paul while on a two-week summer tour in Italy in 1999 with his team, Sendek said his faith helped him to go through the ordeal. Sendek's faith is also evident in his office as he has a large framed photo of him and the Pope on the wall.

"When you are actually in the fire, sometimes you're blessed with certain graces you previously may not have been equipped with or realize that you would have at the time," he added. "In retrospect, although none of us volunteer for difficult times, that experience has not been without fruit. It has helped me grow as a person, as a coach. It has helped me continue to grow spiritually. It has been beneficial for me to be on that road. My faith is very important to me. You know I am very much on the journey trying to grow spiritually all the time. It is something that is important to me."

He is also philosophical about Mother Teresa. "I like what Mother Teresa said, 'In the end we're not going to be judged so much by our works but by the amount of love we have in our work,'" Sendek said.

In 2002-03, N.C. State also had another winning campaign. The

Wolfpack, led by All-ACC swingman Julius Hodge, finished at 18-13 with a trip to the Big Dance. Sendek's squad also made it to the ACC Tournament finals in consecutive years for the first time since the 1973-74 and 1974-75 seasons. After the season ended, there was talk that Sendek may return to his hometown of Pittsburgh, but that didn't happen. He had been one of the top candidates mentioned for the University of Pittsburgh head coaching job when Ben Howland departed the Panthers for UCLA.

* * *

Born in Pittsburgh, Pa., a blue-collar city known for its numerous smokestacks in the steel industry from the old days, Sendek entered this world on Feb. 22, 1963. He joined his parents, Mr. And Mrs. Herb Sendek Sr., and eventually became involved in athletics, both as a spectator and a participant. His parents provided guidance that he needed with middle-class upbringing and values. They were not rich or poor.

"We didn't have an abundance of material things," recalled Sendek, who also has a younger sister, Mary Beth. "My dad was a teacher. My mother was a nurse, but stopped working when she had children. I was very blessed to have a wonderful childhood – a storybook childhood. I can't imagine anybody enjoying a better one than I did. I was blessed in every way. I have a very special family. I was fortunate to have friends that have lasted now a lifetime and perhaps as important as anything I always had leaders, whether they were teachers or coaches, in my life who really cared and made a real difference in my life. I always had people around who took a special interest in me."

With his father's strong athletic and coaching background, it was obvious the younger Sendek would develop an early interest in sports. By the time the son enrolled in the first grade, he began to hang around with his father, who was coaching basketball at Penn Hills High School, at a gym where the team practiced and held games. While the kids his age were playing with toys, the younger Sendek was learning to diagram his first X's and O's.

And he was a very big fan of Pittsburgh's professional teams, especially the Pirates. Only a 15- or 20-minute drive from their home, the father often took the kid to the Pirates' home games, mostly at Three Rivers Stadium. "We could go and sit in right field for $2.50 and that is what we used to do," said the N.C. State coach. "We would sometimes go at the spur of the moment. It would be six o'clock and we would say, 'Let's go to the Pirates game,' and it would start at 7:05 (p.m.). It wasn't very far (from home). It was pretty easy access."

Before the Pirates moved to Three Rivers Stadium in 1970, they played at the old Forbes Field. Sendek remembers at least one game at the old park when he was less than eight years old. "I believe I went to one game at Forbes and I was so young that the memory is sketchy, but I think my dad took me to see the Pirates play against the St. Louis Cardinals when Bob Gibson pitched," recalled Sendek. "I was just a young fellow at the time and most of that has been filled to inform me rather than my own recollection. But I was a regular at Three Rivers Stadium."

Baseball Hall of Famer Roberto Clemente was his favorite player, according to Sendek. "I was an avid Pirate fan," he said. "I used to have an AM/FM little transistor radio and I can remember going to bed at night with the radio underneath the pillow, listening to (broadcaster) Bob Prince, when they played the (Los Angeles) Dodgers on the west coast."

The Pirates weren't Sendek's only interest. He also followed the football Steelers, as well as local colleges – the University of Pittsburgh and Duquesne University. "I just love all kinds of sports," he said. "And you know through my dad, I had an avenue into sports. But whatever was in season – baseball, football, basketball – I followed with great interest and had a lot of fun and that's what I did. That made up my childhood. That was my way of having fun.

"I never went to a Steeler game. Those tickets were hard to come by, but I watched their games on Sunday afternoons. I was growing up during their real profitable run when they won all those Super Bowls (in the 1970s)."

Sendek says he still pulls for the Pennsylvania teams, adding that Steeler coach Bill Cowher formerly played at N.C. State.

* * *

Looking back, Sendek is thankful for the time his father gave him. In addition to high school, the elder Sendek also coached at Community College of Allegheny County. "I think what I remember and appreciate now is that he was never too busy for me," said the younger Sendek. "But whether he was going recruiting or scouting or going on the road with his team, he always included me. He wasn't going to be with somebody too important to have me alongside. He wasn't going to be doing something too grandiose to have gone along with him. He went to great pains to include me.

"And I remember even when I was in elementary school, he would teach class all day and then when he was done teaching he would drive home to where I went to school. It was probably a 20-minute drive for him to pick me up at school and then drive back to where he worked for practice so that I could be there. So that amounted to 40 minutes of round trip for him to do something like that. He went out of his way so that I would be included at practice. I loved every minute of it."

Sendek said his parents "still live together in Pittsburgh in the same house we grew up in." He also had a brother, Michael, who died shortly after birth.

* * *

Although the coal industry has declined economically, Pennsylvania, like the state of Kentucky, is well known for its coal production. And Sendek's family had a key role in the coal mining business. During their younger days, both of his grandfathers worked hard in the coal mines. Unfortunately, they later suffered and had problems with black lung disease.

"Coal mining is a real part of our family background," Sendek said. "I can remember staying at my grandfathers' houses and hearing the alarm go off at midnight when they would go to work for the night shift. (I remember) coming home and only being able to see the whites of their eyes and later in their lives watching them struggle with black lung. You know they had health issues that probably were directly traceable to what they had to do every day in the mines."

Being exposed to his grandfathers' coal mining experience along with his family's respect for hard work and values helped Sendek in later years. While he was an active participant in athletics, earning all-city notice as the team captain and a standout guard at Penn Hills High, he excelled in the classroom. Sendek was the valedictorian of the 1981 class, making a perfect grade-point-average of 4.0. He was better known as an academic star than for his participation in sports. Several individuals influenced Sendek's success in the classroom.

"I think it started in my family and extended to any number of teachers and coaches," Sendek said. "I was so fortunate in every level – grade school, junior high school and high school – to have great teachers, to have people who really cared. People provided tremendous examples for me. I can't imagine somebody being surrounded with the kind of leaders that I was surrounded with.

"I was always motivated to do well in school. I watched how my mother and father made sacrifices and I think it has always been a part of my character to want to do my best. My mother and father never pushed me in a certain direction. They weren't overly demanding, but there was almost an unspoken expectation that you do your best and you wanted to do your best. You wanted to please coaches, teachers and parents."

But academics didn't come easily for Sendek, who put in long hours of studying time. He learned to manage or balance time between sports and homework. He was motivated to do well in both areas. His teachers "probably thought I was a pain in the a--," said Sendek with a laugh. "You know it's not something that necessarily came easy for me. I really worked hard at doing well in school. I was persistent and I spent a lot of time studying. I wasn't somebody who just had it come instantaneously. It was important for me to do well and I worked hard to do well.

"I think to combine sports and academics always requires a certain measure of self-discipline. You know probably some nights lasted a little longer than I ideally would have liked. There wasn't much time for television and those sorts of things. After I was done with sports and school work, that pretty much accounted for most of the day."

* * *

His efforts in academics paid off when he received a prestigious Carnegie Merit Scholarship at Carnegie Mellon University, a private institution in Pittsburgh. In addition, Sendek played basketball for coach Dave Maloney as well. He wasn't a star on the hardwood floor, but was a solid contributor during his first three years of college. "I wasn't a starter all the time, but I started a few games," said Sendek, who majored in industrial management. "I was a spot player."

Sendek was asked if his 3.95 GPA was higher than his scoring average. "Well, that's kind of been a long standing joke that might have some truth to it," he said. "In college I spent a lot of time studying. It was an extension of my high school time. You know I didn't have a very successful playing career in college."

However, in the fall of his senior year, he received bad news. After going through the pre-season conditioning program and the first week of practice, the school's new coach no longer wanted Sendek and a couple of other teammates on the basketball team. So Sendek was taken off the squad and went through an identity crises of his own. He was terribly crushed and hurt.

The new mentor "told us that he was going in a different direction and really trying to focus on some guys he had recruited," explained Sendek. "So much of my identity at that time was a function of basketball. That's who I was. That's who I was to my friends. That's who I was in town. So that was a real ego crusher. That was a blow for me to deal with at that point."

But Sendek had support and found a couple of opportunities to stay involved in basketball while finishing his studies in college. "I was so fortunate just to have a strong community and every time I was in trouble or needed help there were people there to help me," said Sendek, who accepted an offer to become a volunteer assistant hoops coach at Central Catholic High under the guidance of Chuck Crummie. The other opportunity was at Community College of Allegheny County on the northern side of Pittsburgh. But Sendek declined coach Bill Shay's offer primarily because of the distance between the community college and Carnegie Mellon.

Central Catholic was an ideal location for Sendek since it was within walking distance of the university. After his classes ended, he would walk over to the high school and help Crummie. "That was a wonderful experience and it kind of got my foot in the door so to speak," said Sendek, who graduated from the university with summa cum laude honors.

* * *

Now a new college graduate with a bachelor's degree in industrial management, Sendek could have found work in the business world and made a good living. With his good attitude and strong academic background, he could have worked at an entry-level job to become a future CEO of a major corporation. Or he could have gone to a graduate school and studied dentistry. But instead, he wanted to try his hand in coaching, just like his dad, after getting his feet wet as an assistant at Central Catholic High.

Herb Sr., however, warned him of the dangers in coaching, one of the more unstable professions around. "My father was very honest with me and he gave me the advantages and the disadvantages, the pluses and the minuses," said the younger Sendek. "I think in the back of his mind, he thought it was a really hard profession to pursue. But when it came time to make decisions, he's never made them for me. Maybe at that time (he) might have been more comfortable if I would've gone into dentistry or a more stable profession. So we had some frank conversations about it. But he has always been supportive and never made decisions for me."

And the rest is history. In 1985, Sendek began his college coaching career at Providence College, joining coach Rick Pitino's staff as a graduate assistant coach. But the way he got the Providence job makes for an interesting story. While he was eating breakfast and reading the newspaper on a Good Friday during his senior year in college, Sendek recognized a person's name in an article. He couldn't believe that person whom he had met once before was named the head coach. And it's Pitino whom he was reading about in the newspaper. So Sendek, figuring Pitino didn't really know enough about him, immediately contacted a colleague, who knew Pitino, for a favor. He enlisted the help of recruiting analyst Howard Garfinkel, who owned and operated the Five Star basketball camp. The camp director had known Pitino very well when the latter spent many summers at the Pennsylvania camp in the 1970s and the 1980s. Pitino described Garfinkel as "Woody Allen with slicked-back hair" in the coach's 1988 book, *Born To Coach*.

"I asked him (Garfinkel) if he could please help me to get an interview to get on board with coach Pitino at Providence in any capacity, most specifically and most hopefully graduate assistant," Sendek said. "Through Howard's recommendation, coach Pitino hired me without even an interview. He knew of me through camp."

Providence practically got Sendek for nothing for his role as a graduate assistant. "I didn't draw my salary," he said. "They gave me room, board, books and tuition to go to graduate school. I made a few hundred dollars working at camps in the summer time. I didn't have a car my first year out of college.

"I had better offers in the business world. I could have gone to work at Westinghouse and made more money and had a car. You know I had some material things (available) right away. But I've never done anything for money. That hasn't been my primary source of motivation."

On his N.C. State financial compensation package deal, Sendek said he never dreamed that he would be getting a very generous paycheck. "Obviously, I'm very fortunate and blessed to demand the kind of salary that I do and it certainly exceeds any expectation or dream that I ever had," he said. "I never thought that I'd make the kind of money I do now. Now that I am responsible for a family (of three children and wife Melanie), I want to take care of them well. But that is not why I got into coaching."

According to Sendek, his first encounter with Pitino dated back to

1980 at the Five Star camp during the summer between his junior and senior years in high school. Pitino, the head coach at Boston University at the time, was working at the camp. "He later claimed that he remembered me as a player, but I don't really believe he did," Sendek commented. "I wasn't that much of a player. I didn't stand out. But whether he did or didn't (remember), he said he did remember me as playing hard and not being a very good player and he liked to kid me."

Then a couple of years later, going into his sophomore year at Carnegie Mellon, Sendek returned to Five Star and worked at the camp for several summers thereafter. And he got to know Pitino a little bit. "I didn't really know him at any level of depth," he said. "(Just) hi, coach Pitino – that type of thing."

At Providence, Sendek, who advanced to assistant coach, remained there until 1989 even though Pitino had already left the Friars in 1987 to become the head coach of the NBA's New York Knicks. One of Sendek's players at Providence included a scrappy guy who was only two years younger than him. That guy's name was Billy Donovan, who led the Friars in scoring (20.6 points) and assists (7.1), leading them to a surprising run to the NCAA Final Four in 1987.

* * *

In 1989, when Kentucky snatched Pitino away from the Big Apple, Sendek arrived in the Bluegrass to begin the difficult task of helping his boss rebuild the once-proud basketball program, in shambles after a near-death penalty imposed by the NCAA. Despite UK's troubles, Sendek had no reservations in taking the Wildcat job as an assistant even though he had no previous ties to the state or the university except for a couple of recruiting trips.

"I was well aware of their storied program and when coach Pitino asked me to join him at Kentucky, I was extremely excited and you know I couldn't wait to get there," said Sendek, who was still single at the time. "We knew that (NCAA probation) would be a hurdle that we had to overcome in recruiting. There were a couple of players when we first started recruiting who didn't come with us probably because of the probation. We couldn't go to the (NCAA) tournament. That was a big (negative) thing. But I had no reservations whatsoever. I knew it was only a matter of time with coach Pitino in charge that the program would flourish. We had some early turbulence to get through, but had no doubt whatsoever that success would happen."

Sendek will always remember his first year at UK. That was when the hustling and undersized Wildcats, with only eight scholarship players, stunned everyone by overachieving with a final 14-14 mark in the 1989-90 campaign, avoiding an expected losing season.

"The one thing that group had, though, was skill and they knew how to play," Sendek said. "There were maybe teams in the future that were more athletic and more talented, but that team could shoot and that team knew how to play. Although we didn't have a great deal of size or depth, we were able to win more games than some people expected because of coach Pitino's masterful job of coaching and maybe an unappreciated skill level in basketball IQ by that group of players."

* * *

A detail-oriented person, Sendek approaches his job in a very business-like fashion. He is very intense and cares about his job. He wants to help his players to become a success story in basketball as well as life in general. But don't let his serious personality fool you. He can be very personable and funny in comfortable surroundings. With that in mind, he can recruit. While at UK, he was Pitino's best recruiter. In fact, *Sports Illustrated* named him one of the nation's top 10 recruiters in its 1992-93 pre-season college basketball issue. But he certainly didn't feel that way sometimes.

He once thought he and Pitino had blown a great opportunity to obtain highly-regarded recruit Jamal Mashburn when they both visited the youngster and his mother in a New York City gym on a sweltering September day. They chatted, sitting on the bleachers, while the kids were playing an organized game on the hardwood floor. They had trouble hearing each other since there was a guy doing play-by-play on the microphone, and people were cheering, making a lot of noise. Needless to say, it was a very loud gym with the public address announcer's voice radiating throughout the building. Because of the noise background, the coaches, Mashburn and his mom had to scream back and forth to hear each other. "We had shirts and ties on and it was so uncomfortable (with heat) and this guy was screaming play-by-play in the microphone," Sendek said. "It was so hard to hear and very distracting."

With Sendek nearby and listening his boss' recruiting presentation, Pitino – perspiring heavily from the hot weather – made a stunning comment, criticizing Mashburn that he was a lazy player and wondering why would he come to Kentucky and play for a structured, demanding coach like Pitino. "There are other programs that seem to maybe fit your personality better than ours," Pitino told Mashburn.

And Sendek, visibly upset, was thinking to himself, "Oh, no. Coach, what are you doing? What are you saying?"

But to their surprise, Mashburn looked at Pitino and said that was all right, commenting that discipline is what he needed to become a great player. Said Mashburn to the Wildcat mentor, "I know that about myself and that's why I'm interested in Kentucky because I know if I'm going to make it I need to be with somebody like you." Of course, Mashburn went on to become a popular All-American at Kentucky and an NBA superstar.

Sendek has many other recruiting stories. "I think everybody has some war stories to tell and along the way we all do crazy things," he said. "I remember being a young assistant at Providence and driving from Providence to Atlantic City to watch the Sea Gull Classic one day and that night after the game I drove all the way back to Providence, having watched the tournament all afternoon and evening.

"I remember being in Tennessee recruiting Tony Delk with Billy Donovan and driving back through the night so coach Pitino and I could catch a flight the next morning to go see Rodrick Rhodes in New Jersey."

* * *

The 1991-92 season was one of Kentucky's most exciting times in its long, rich basketball history. Coming off its ugly NCAA probation, UK became eligible for the Big Dance for the first time in the Rick Pitino era. And the hungry Wildcats, led by "The Unforgettables" with seniors John Pelphrey, Sean Woods, Deron Feldhaus and Richie Farmer, took advantage of Pitino's superb coaching and guidance with a final record of 29-7. They won the SEC tournament title and captured three NCAA tourney matchups, before dropping 104-103 to top-ranked Duke on Christian Laettner's famous, or infamous, desperation basket. Sendek, who had been promoted to associate coach, played an integral part in the program's success that year and did a lot of scouting work along with assistants Billy Donovan and Bernadette Locke-Mattox.

But a couple of nights before the Duke contest, Sendek worried sick about the Blue Devils' talent and size after watching the Duke stop Seton Hall 81-69 in a regional semifinal. Even though Kentucky had beaten Massachusetts 87-77 in the other semifinal contest earlier that night, Sendek couldn't help but think about the ways his team could overcome Duke.

"I watched that Duke-Seton Hall game in amazement because I realized how terrific Duke was," recalled Sendek. "I mean they had Grant Hill, Bobby Hurley, Christian Laettner and a guy like Cherokee Parks coming off the bench. They were loaded and they played just a great game against Seton Hall."

Even though the Wildcats had advanced to the Elite Eight and everybody was in a very festive mood, Sendek nevertheless was still very uneasy about Coach K's team. On the team's bus heading back to a Philadelphia hotel, Pitino noticed Sendek looking very subdued.

"Coach Pitino looked over at me and I'm sitting in my seat just stoic and he started to give me a hard time," Sendek commented. "My mind was turning and (thinking) how are we going to possibly beat these guys. To this day (he) makes fun of me because of the way I was on that bus."

Anyhow, after Sendek and the assistants got off the bus, they went straight to work in a hotel room. "Billy, Bernadette and I stayed up all night. We watched film on Duke trying to get some thoughts together for the coach at breakfast the next morning," recalled Sendek.

"We went to the (Duke) game knowing we'd have to play almost a perfect game to beat them and we almost did play a perfect game. Offensively, we were really good that game. One great play after another."

The overtime setback, however, was hard for Kentucky to take after coming so close to reaching the Final Four for the first time since 1984. "There was a lot of emotion in the locker room," Sendek said. "But I think there was a real sense of pride, too. Any time guys pour their hearts out the way they did, you can derive a certain amount of peace not only from that game, but all season. I think we had that resource.

"But I remember when the finals occurred a week later, I didn't watch the games (on TV). I purposely went to the movies when they were on. For me, the season was over at the end of the Duke game. You know it (the loss) was still there. You still could taste it and I didn't even want to get caught channel surfing and happen to cruise by one of the Final Four games. So, when they came on, I said, 'Come on, Melanie, let's go to the movies.'"

For the record, Duke won its second straight national title, defeating Michigan 71-51, in the 1992 championship game.

But shortly before Sendek left UK for his first head coaching job (at Miami), he was able to assist the Cats in the 1993 Final Four in New Orleans.

* * *

Sendek has many other memories during his stay in the Bluegrass and that's where he met his future wife, the former Melanie Scheuer, who is from Danville. She once played basketball at Cumberland College in Williamsburg, Ky.

"I think probably my favorite story about coach Pitino is the way he served as matchmaker for my wife and I," Sendek said with a smile. "When I was in Kentucky with him, I wasn't dating a great deal and I was just in that office working and plugging away for the Wildcats, loving every minute of it."

Pitino had noticed Melanie, a young woman working at the restaurant section of a health club in Lexington, where he worked out frequently while the facilities at Memorial Coliseum were being redone. He got acquainted with the woman and thought she would be a good prospect for his quiet assistant.

Sendek said Pitino had "asked her about who she was dating and one thing led to another. He arranged one day for our team to go down there to work out. I guess he didn't have any confidence in me doing it on my own either calling her or going down there by myself. So he knew if he said the team had to go down there to work out, I would accompany them and that is where I met her and asked her out. Our facilities (at UK) were being redone. He had something in the back of his mind. He sort of organized the whole thing."

Sendek and his wife have three daughters – Kristin, Catherine and Kelly.

* * *

During Sendek's early years at N.C. State, there have been criticisms about his team's playing style. Some say it was too slow and boring. They wanted to see the Wolfpack exhibit a faster, wide-open game of run and shoot. So the author asked Sendek if he still likes the fast-paced game advocated by Pitino and his friend, Florida coach Billy Donovan. The coach explained that he didn't have the right or enough players who can keep up with the running game.

"Well, we like to run and shoot as well," said Sendek. "This past year (2001-02) we employed our full-court press. We played a wide-open style on offense. We took a lot of threes and you know we certainly plan on continuing to do that.

"Our style of play here has kind of been an evolution because some of the early teams we had (didn't have the personnel to run and press) to be more competitive. But now I think we really have firmly established that we are an up-tempo, pressing, three-point shooting team."

Regardless of the playing style, Sendek will always be a Pitino disciple who has always worked hard, trying to do his job in the right way. Just like his parents and teachers during his younger days in Pittsburgh.

Chapter 13

Tubby and First Lady

Since 1997, when her husband, Orlando "Tubby" Smith, took the head coaching job at Kentucky, Donna Smith has been playing a very special role in the Wildcat basketball program.

At home games, you'll find her sitting several rows behind the Wildcat bench, shaking her pompon and yelling. People sitting close to her will say she is the loudest fan. Some folks like to call her the First Lady of UK Basketball. Veteran sports columnist Earl Cox once wrote that a fan told him that Mrs. Smith is "just like Barbara Bush – everybody loves her."

In addition to her family responsibilities as the mother of three basketball-playing sons, she stays busy by supporting the Wildcats and various community-oriented projects in the Bluegrass area. The couple is active with the Tubby Smith Foundation, which the coach started to assist underprivileged children. In 2001, the United Way of the Bluegrass, which serves eight counties in central Kentucky, established a new award – the Donna and Tubby Smith Community Spirit Award -- for their generous support.

With her husband often gone on the road, visiting recruits, conducting coaching clinics, attending camps, among other things, Smith looks for the things to do. "I do a lot of volunteer work," she told the author in an interview for this book. "If you are the wife of a college coach or pro coach or whoever, you can't be a weak person. You've got to have interests of your own and you've got to have a strong constitution. You can't raise your kids, telling them, 'Oh, you just wait until dad comes home.' You can forget that. You throw all that kind of crap out of the window. I stay pretty busy. I do have a life."

* * *

In the 1950s and '60s, she grew up as Donna Walls in Richmond, Va., the state capital. Her parents had decent jobs with her mother working at DuPont, and her father in the military and at a major telephone company. In her eyes, she was comfortable long before her husband started to make big money.

"I thought we were rich when in reality we were not, you know, monetarily," said the UK coach's wife, who has two brothers and two sisters. "But growing up I guess they made us feel as though we were rich. We had everything we ever needed. We didn't have a whole lot but in our minds we thought we were rich."

After the racial integration had begun in the 1960s, she attended predominately-white George Wythe High School, also located in Richmond. "I started high school right after the integration process," she said. "But those three years of high school were the best three years of my life. I had a great time. I just loved it. Most of the teachers liked me. Like I said, I had fun in high school."

Smith, who was raised a Baptist, said she had no racial problems in school whatsoever, saying she "blended right in."

A pretty teenager, Smith participated in gymnastics, reaching the state competition. She also ran some for the track team. Smith also believed she was a member of the Spanish club, but she isn't sure. "Gosh, that's a way back there," Smith said. "I'd have to look back at my yearbook. I just can't remember right now."

While she was a popular girl, she didn't make the top grades. "I was pretty average," she recalled. "I did not make straight A's, but never flunked anything, either."

* * *

Upon graduation from high school, Smith went to North Carolina's Piedmont Triad Region of Greensboro, Winston-Salem and High Point where she enrolled at a small private Methodist school named High Point College (now High Point University).

Because of her grandmother, Smith went there to get her college education. "My grandmother paid for my education and she would have final say so as to where I would go," she said. "Even though I applied to a lot of other schools around the country and got into some other schools, I had an aunt who lived in High Point whom I had never met before. She was elderly. Her husband was elderly. They didn't have any children. Because my grandmother was paying for it (college education), I had to go down there."

Photo by Jamie H. Vaught

Mr. and Mrs. Tubby Smith at a press conference in 1997 when UK hired Smith as the new basketball coach.

Smith became active in college, becoming a cheerleader, a role she never had in high school. She cheered the teams for three years. Despite her minority status on campus as there weren't many black students, she had a wonderful time. "I loved it," she said. "(I) didn't have any problems. We had about somewhere between 1,100 and 1,500 students on campus. There weren't that many kids at all from the state of North Carolina that were enrolled there on full-time basis. The majority of kids were from New Jersey, Pennsylvania and Maryland. I remember just meeting two students from High Point. But it was a liberal arts school and so, like I said, the majority of people came from out of state.

"(Not having many black students around) was not hard for me because I'm from a very mixed family. All of us were raised that it didn't matter whatsoever what your nationality or what your color was. You were always welcome into our family. You were always welcome into our home. If I was to bring someone of a different race from college home and said, 'We are dating,' my family would embrace you because my word was good enough or was okay enough that they would say, 'Well, if you are a friend of Donna's or if Donna loves you, then we embrace you, too.' That is just how we were always raised."

With her friendly personality, Smith was able to make new friends at High Point easily. "We had a lot in common," she commented. "Even though it was in the early '70s, I didn't have any problems. In fact, I was their very first black homecoming queen of the school and I enjoyed that. That was so much fun and I had a great time."

And it was at High Point where she met her future husband, a senior basketball player who later was named to the All-Carolina Conference team. But Tubby, who was also the team captain, didn't make a very good impression on her in the beginning. "When we first met each other the first semester, we didn't like each other," she said. According to Tubby on their first date, "I took her to dinner where she worked, at Sir Pizza or something like that. We really didn't get to know each other until Christmas."

Tubby had Donna's attention when he proudly drove around the campus in his 1964 two-tone Impala. "Later on, he was one of the few guys that had a car and I wanted to catch a ride home," she said. "And one time I did ask him for a ride home and we got to know each other like that and then later became friends and then dated."

Said the UK coach, who grew up in a large family of 17 children, "I gave her a ride and that was her way of getting to know me, I guess. I was BMOC, you know, Big Man on Campus, and she wanted to get to know me. So it worked. I'm glad we met and that we dated."

The couple was able to work out the holiday traveling arrangements as they both were from the north with Donna going to Virginia and Tubby to Maryland. He would drive straight up on I-85 before going on I-95 to Richmond to drop her off at her parents' house. Then Tubby drove to the rural town of Scotland in southern Maryland where his folks lived on a tenant farm.

But since Tubby finished college in 1973, leaving Donna behind at High Point, the courtship would translate into a long-distance relationship primarily on the telephone. They didn't see each other very often. The future Wildcat mentor had gotten his bachelor's degree in health and physical education, becoming the only one graduated on time among the eight freshman basketball players who arrived at High Point in 1969. With his degree in hand, Tubby found his first head coaching job at his old high school, Great Mills, in Maryland.

During her sophomore year, when a fraternity sponsored Donna for the homecoming queen, Tubby, taking a break from his coaching post, returned to High Point and saw her get the crown. "He came back to be my escort," she said. "That was fun."

She added both of them had never joined the Greek community at High Point. "I was never a sorority (member) and Tubby was never a member of a fraternity, either," Donna said. "When you play sports, it is tough to do both of those."

So she stayed in college for almost three more years while her boyfriend was learning the ropes in coaching at Great Mills High. It wasn't easy for the couple to visit during those years. "That was hard," she said. "(We didn't meet) not once a week because he was coaching basketball. So he really couldn't get away a whole lot. He was pretty busy. I would say maybe twice a semester (when they met), not as often as you would think. (He was) teaching and coaching. He was busy on weekends, especially once his season started. He had most high school games on Friday nights and that was tough to do (to make a visit).

"I used to lie and tell him I would meet him about halfway, but really he ended up doing most of the driving. He would have to drive further than I did because I didn't get a car until my senior year. My dad wouldn't let me have a car until my senior year. So I would borrow somebody else's car to go see him."

* * *

December 27, 1975.

That was the day the couple married. "We got married during the basketball season," she said, "and didn't have a honeymoon or anything until 10 or 12 years later."

Tubby and Donna had wanted to tie the knot earlier. "We wanted to get married before I graduated," she said. "But my mom (Patricia) wouldn't hear of it. She wanted my maiden name (Walls) on my diploma or else. So we had to wait until I had gotten all of my requirements under my belt. I did finish (college) in December of '75 and then came back and graduated with my class in May of '76." Her degree was in human relations with a minor in psychology.

On the long-awaited honeymoon, she said, "We went on a cruise at the very, very bottom of the ship. It was awful. The toilet was inside; it showed. It was so cramped. We went out of Fort Lauderdale (Fla.) and sailed to the Bahamas and then came back. But still that was our honeymoon.

"Eight or nine years later, when we had saved some more money, we went on another one and we had a real nice room. It was fun."

* * *

Former High Point coach Jerry Steele knows a thing or two about Tubby, who played for him as a college senior. They have stayed in touch for years. In recent years, they even met twice at Rupp Arena in 2000 and 2002 when Tubby's Cats dominated undermanned High Point in both matchups. Steele has a favorite story about his pupil.

He said Smith was "smart enough to propose and marry the homecoming queen at High Point, who just happened to be an outstanding lady. He overachieved in his marriage."

Steele retired in 2003 after 31 years at High Point. He once served as the assistant coach and interim coach of the Carolina Cougars in the old ABA in 1970-71.

* * *

In 1977, after four years of coaching and teaching at Great Mills where he compiled an overall mark of 46-36, Tubby moved on. He landed a coaching job in the southeastern part of North Carolina, not far from where Pope Air Force Base was located. He was hired to coach at Hoke County High School in Raeford.

"There was only one high school," said Donna of the Raeford area. "I'll never forget Tubby used to have to scrub the gym floor himself. It was a small, country school. But he loved it. We both did. It was a small town and we really liked it." According to Donna, her husband once coached a Christmas tournament game against Raleigh's Enloe High School when it went seven overtimes.

They stayed there for two years before moving to Richmond, Va., Donna's hometown. Tubby got the assistant coaching job at Virginia Commonwealth, working for J.D. Barnett, his former coach at High Point College. After six years in high school, the VCU post marked the beginning of Smith's coaching career in the collegiate ranks.

* * *

For the most part, the Richmond stop during Tubby's coaching tenure was an enjoyable period, especially for Donna. She will never forget those days from 1979 to '86. Her parents, naturally, were happy about the young couple's move to the Virginia capital.

"Everybody was excited during that time because that put us in my hometown and also it put him two hours from his family at that time," Donna said. "Our kids were real small. Saul was an infant and G.G. was two. When your kids are real tiny, you know grandparents want to see their grandkids. That was the main thing. Our kids were small and they got the chance to see them all the time. So that was fun."

But times weren't always joyful in Richmond, especially when Saul suffered major health problems as an infant. It is a sad story that many casual Wildcats fans aren't aware of.

* * *

Not long before the Smith household moved to Richmond, Donna gave birth to her second child, Saul, in a Pinehurst, N.C., hospital, not too far from their Raeford home. But it wasn't an easy time for the family as Baby Saul and his mother went through a very difficult delivery which resulted in major surgeries down the road.

"Saul's surgery happened because the forceps were pressed against his head," explained the mother. "As they were pulling (the baby out), the bottom part of the spoon of the forceps crushed (one side) right here. When he came out, it was like he had one solid black eye. It looked like he had just been beaten up so bad."

Seeing their unhealthy baby with a black eye, the family was heartbroken, feeling awful for Baby Saul. But they were determined to see that their newborn son would get the best health care possible. The doctor assured them, "We'll send all these x-rays off to Duke University and we'll see what we can do." However, the x-rays came back negative. The images didn't reveal anything unusual.

Anyhow, the baby continued to have problems, crying a lot. There were a lot of uneasy moments. When the Smiths lived in Richmond, they took him to a teaching hospital at VCU and met a physician by the name of John Ward, a neurosurgeon who still specializes in pediatric neurosurgery.

"We had found out that a baby was born in Kentucky without a skull," said Donna. "We learned that Virginia Commonwealth University had made a skull for this baby and the baby ended up doing great."

At VCU, Saul went through a major surgery. Dr. Ward "ended up using this mesh material that was supposed to have been the latest type of tissue that was closest to the human bone tissue available," said the mother. To fix the problem, the physicians had to cut it across the crown of Saul's head from one side to another. After sealing the hole, the baby, however, had a severe reaction to the mesh. "Saul's body rejected it after the first surgery," Donna said.

Saul, who was near death, then came out of it, but not without problems. "So the following eight or nine months, almost a year, they had to go back (and operated) in the same area and this time they used his hip bone (grafted for his skull). That is what they used and this time it was real successful," commented Donna.

"But while you are going through that process, that is the furthest thing from your mind. All you know is that's my baby lying there and my baby is cut up, swollen, has no hair and 158 stitches from ear to ear, and you are counting them over and over again. It was a mess. Oh, it was just awful because every night you are there in the hospital and you don't want to leave. (But) you know we have just been real blessed."

* * *

Before arriving at Kentucky in 1997, the Smith household was living in Athens, Ga., where the father coached the Bulldogs and his son, G.G., who was a 5-11 guard. Tubby took the Georgia post in 1995 after he impressed the school's athletics director Vince Dooley with his four-year performance at Tulsa. He had guided the Golden Hurricane to two consecutive Sweet Sixteen trips in the NCAA tournament with limited resources. He was a hot commodity and Dooley felt fortunate to get Tubby.

But Dooley wouldn't be able to keep Tubby very long. Smith only stayed in Athens for a couple of years where he guided the Bulldogs to two straight 20-win seasons along with NCAA tournament appearances in both years (Sweet Sixteen in 1996). Kentucky athletics director C.M. Newton lured him away from UGA, offering him an opportunity to take what is considered by many the top job in college basketball. Newton liked Smith's coaching experience and his down-to-earth personality. And history will show that Smith became UK's first black head basketball coach, replacing Rick Pitino. The new hoops boss signed a five-year pact with about $1.2 million a season with his base salary of $150,000 coming from UK.

While the school's hiring of a new basketball coach has always been big news, Smith's arrival on the campus was even a bigger event. As far as many members of the national media were concerned, it was a major news-breaking story considering the fact the school supposedly, they said, had questionable racial attitudes many years ago during the days of Adolph Rupp. While it's true that UK didn't have many African-American students back then, many local observers will argue that Rupp was a product of time and many southern coaches didn't use black players mainly because of unrest in the dangerous South.

Nevertheless, despite a warning from a black *Lexington Herald-Leader* columnist, writing in a newspaper column, that the city wouldn't embrace Smith's race, Smith still came to Kentucky. The new Wildcat coach was excited about the biggest move of his career. He was coming to a basketball-crazy state where the Wildcat coach is treated like a Hollywood star.

Interestingly, Tubby wasn't the first one to hear about UK's interest in him. It was his wife, who first learned about it through a telephone call from Newton, who was inquiring about Tubby's possible interest in the Wildcat job. Tubby wasn't around the house. "I knew about the (potential) offer before Tubby did," said the wife. "C.M. called our house first because we were friends with him and his (late) wife, Evelyn. He wanted to call, and get permission from coach Dooley to ask Tubby 'Would he be interested.'"

The Smiths, all five of them, including their youngest son, Brian, talked it over at the dinner table after getting an official offer from UK. "My family came before any job," Donna said. "We looked at the pros and cons and sometimes opportunities don't come around all the time. So you look at an opportunity and you do what is best for everybody. You know some other people may say, 'Oh, that's a no-brainer,' but in our case it was important for us to include our kids because they would be affected, too."

It helped that Tubby had already spent two years as an assistant under Pitino and developed friendships with UK folks from 1989 to '91. Tubby pretty much knew what to expect at Kentucky. The Smith family had no reservations about the pressure-packed job that Tubby was getting into.

"We knew what were coming into," said Donna. "We lived here (in Lexington) before. So we knew the pressure. But it was a good kind of pressure because what happens when you move around as much as we do, (you'll find out that) there are some schools where the priorities are not basketball. You may be at some other school and the priority might be football and basketball is an afterthought. Basketball is secondary. Or they (the media) won't even write articles about basketball in the newspaper until January. Or you, as the head coach at some schools, your radio show won't even start until January and here you have played 12-15 games before then."

* * *

With the rest of the Smith family members in Lexington, G.G. remained at Georgia where he had already played basketball for two years under his dad. The father said it was his oldest son's decision whether or not he wanted to move to the Bluegrass and play for the Wildcats. "He's a grown man, now," said Tubby in 1997. "He's put together two good years and has a good career there. Certainly, I would love to have him here (at Kentucky) but I think he has a great opportunity under Ron Jirsa. He's turned into a pretty good player.....I told him to do what's in his heart."

Said Donna, "The hard part was leaving my son there. But I knew it would help him to grow up and be independent and I'm really proud to say the two years that he was down there on his own, not one time did he call and ask for money from his phone. Not one time did somebody call us and say your son down here is having a party all weekend long and 'Would you please get him in line.' None of that ever. He was always, knock on wood, very responsible and I don't know if it is because he is the oldest son or what, but he has always been very responsible."

While at Georgia, G.G. earned third-team All-SEC honors during his junior year and made Academic All-SEC as a senior. He later got to spend some time in the UK basketball program – a couple of years to be exact -- as a student manager/graduate assistant. He earned his master's degree in sports management from UK before leaving to take a post as an assistant coach for Mike Sutton's Tennessee Tech squad in 2002. After spending one year there, G.G. and his bride then moved to Hawaii where she is in the medical field.

* * *

While playing at Kentucky, Saul Smith was one of, if not the most, scrutinized players in the school's storied basketball history.

And that made his job tougher than what it should be. If the point guard made a mistake, he set off lightning fireworks with tons of criticisms from the Wildcat fans. If he made a good play, he usually got only a lukewarm applause from the crowd or folks watching the game. Some people, especially the ones on the radio call-in shows and the Internet, couldn't stand him, arguing that Saul wasn't good enough to be a starter at a powerhouse like UK. They said he got special treatment because he is the son of the squad's head coach.

However, much of the criticism on Saul was somewhat unfair. Many sportswriters agreed, applauding his efforts on the hardwood court and his demeanor off the floor. Separate interviews with journalists appeared in a sports column written by the author for Middlesboro's *The Daily News* in November of 2000.

"Saul Smith is a good kid who has been put in a difficult situation, the same difficult situation Sean Sutton worked under (his father and coach Eddie Sutton) at Kentucky," said Rick Bozich of Louisville's *Courier-Journal.*

"It's tough being a coach's son – unless you are the best player on the team or one of the guys who rarely plays. Saul is in the middle, always the toughest spot. Nobody can question his effort or how badly he wants to win. He's handled the situation with incredible poise for a player his age. He'll be a success no matter what he does in life. In my opinion, most of the criticism has been of Tubby Smith, not Saul. And in big-time college athletics, criticism is part of the job."

Said sportswriter Mike Strange of the *Knoxville News-Sentinel*, "On one hand, I feel sorry for Saul because he's had to endure a lot of criticism, much of it very personal when, in fact, he always plays hard.

For a guy of decent but still modest ability, he's gotten a ton of playing time at a high-profile program."

Bob Watkins, whose sports columns appear in many publications throughout Kentucky, has a viewpoint. "Saul Smith is certainly getting an education about the American Way," he said. "So far, he has behaved splendidly, steadfastly refusing to allow so-called experts to make him run and hide.

"On the contrary, he has shown grace, determination and grit and will be the starting point guard for one of the country's top-ranked basketball teams. Because there will be better and smarter players around him this season, I suggest his qualities will bring the experts to wax eloquent again. Some will even write in various forms, 'See, I told you' knowing nobody will remember their criticisms."

Saul's mother, of course, didn't like the criticism placed on her son. She wasn't very pleased, either, when her son was booed at Rupp Arena during a game in 2001. However, she understands the booing or criticism is a part of basketball culture and the territory of being in the public eye. "As a mom it makes you feel like people are picking on your kid," said Donna. "But when you are in the limelight or at a school of this magnitude, you know that everything you do is going to be scrutinized. That just comes with it and you can let it bother you or not."

Interestingly, Donna added that no one has spoken harshly of her son in a direct way. "You got to remember no one ever criticized my son to my face, never," she said. While understanding that some folks could have whispered behind her back, Donna said she readily chose not to hear the criticism on various media -- radio, television, publications and the Internet. "Also, I've got to say that we received letters of praise. I would like to say twice as much as the so-called criticism that was out there. I just choose not to listen to it."

After playing for the Columbus, Ga., franchise in the National Basketball Developmental League for two years, Saul returned to UK for the 2003-04 campaign to serve on his father's staff as a manager. While he is looking at the possibility of a coaching profession, the younger Smith still has plans for a law career.

* * *

On a wintry January night in 1998, Tubby and his family went through an unusual emotionally-draining reunion when they visited Athens, Ga., their former home, for the first time since arriving at

Kentucky. It was a special journey the family will never forget.

Only several months earlier, Tubby was coaching the Bulldogs to the Big Dance. But on that night, he would be facing his former players at Georgia, including his son, G.G., at Stegeman Coliseum, once casually known as "The Tub." With freshman guard Saul on the Kentucky squad, that meant Tubby and Donna would be watching their sons battle on the hardwood floor before "Mr. Excitement" Dick Vitale and a national cable television audience. Plus Tubby would be competing against his former assistant, Ron Jirsa, who had been promoted as Georgia's head coach.

Who did Donna pull for? Did she cheer for her oldest son playing against her husband? "I was pulling for Kentucky," recalled Donna, who wore a multi-colored sweater featuring colors of both schools and sat directly behind the UK bench.

The sixth-ranked Wildcats won 90-79 behind a balanced scoring attack with four UK performers in double figures -- Allen Edwards, Nazr Mohammed, Wayne Turner and Heshimu Evans. In a reserve role, Saul drew a defensive assignment on his brother and pumped in two three-pointers. For the Bulldogs, G.G., a starting guard, gunned in eight points, including two three-pointers.

After the game, Vitale interviewed the UK coach, Donna and Saul for ESPN. Very relieved that the highly-publicized family affair had ended, Tubby told reporters that he himself didn't feel much happiness. After all, he didn't feel all that good in beating his son and his Georgia friends.

As for the Smith brothers – G.G. and Saul – they would face each other three more games with Kentucky winning each time. But it was that January night which drew a lot of attention.

* * *

Her youngest son, Brian, is a 2003 graduate of Lexington Catholic High School where he was a 5-11 standout guard. He also played in the Kentucky-Indiana All-Star summer series. Brian was planning to attend a prep school in the fall of 2003. His mother said he will make his own decision on where he wants to go to college, explaining that he's the one who has to live with his choice.

"It's up to him," said the mother. "I don't want him to later tell or say to me 10 years from now, 'Well, I did that because you said....'. So I put the ball back in his court and said, 'You decide where you want to go.' He has seen what his oldest brother did at Georgia and he has been here to go through what his other brother, Saul, has done in Kentucky."

* * *

A very caring mother, Donna is very thankful for her three children. "Once you do get a child, you'll learn that children are a gift from God," she added. "They are on loan. They are not yours; you don't own them. Actually, they are the property of God and God lets you use them for awhile. God lets you enjoy them while he sees fit. The children really are a blessing."

* * *

John Stewart.

He's the kid from Indianapolis who was supposed to play for the Wildcats. But he never did. The 7-footer died after collapsing while playing in a high school game in 1999. An autopsy later showed that Stewart had an abnormal enlarged heart.

The Smiths were saddened to learn of Stewart's tragedy. He was a special guy. They really liked him. Even four years after his death, UK had a tribute for Stewart at the emotional Senior Night ceremony at Rupp Arena in 2003 when he would've been a Wildcat senior. His parents, Felicia and John Stewart, were honored along with UK seniors Keith Bogans, Jules Camara and Marquis Estill.

One of the memorable cookouts at the Smith's Lexington home involved Stewart and his parents. They were touring UK on an official recruiting visit. "The one that stays on my mind a lot is the one when John Stewart's family was at our house," said Donna. "That cookout lasted way into the night and we had so much fun and we laughed. I have never seen a kid that wanted to be at a school more than that boy, John Stewart. His dad was so much fun to be around. So was his mom. But his father had on a colorful shirt and flamboyant shoes and it kind of reminded you a little bit of the '70s. All of the team was there, too. And I'll just never forget that.

"That kid had the biggest heart. He was just such a good kid. I think his major was going to be something working with kids, juvenile delinquency or juvenile something. But it was something working with disadvantaged children."

Stewart's coach at Lawrence North High School, Jack Keefer, said the player's death was the low point of his life, adding Stewart was a remarkable person.

Had he finished college, many observers predicted Stewart would have been a lottery pick in the NBA draft.

* * *

What was Donna doing on the fateful day of Sept. 11, 2001, when the terrorists shocked the world, using kidnapped commercial airplanes to attack two major U.S. cities of New York City and Washington, D.C.?

"At that time, I was with a friend going into the new Bob Evans (restaurant) on Richmond Road," she recalled with sadness. "We were about to have breakfast. Actually we heard about it just before going in to eat. But I honestly thought in the back of my mind there had been an accident that a plane had veered off (into the Big Apple). I had no idea that the plane was going into the World Trade Center. It is just so terrible. It is just so hard to imagine. I can't picture someone having that much hatred that they want to kill children. It is just unbelievable."

What about Tubby? Where was he at that time? Said Donna, "Tubby was in the air coming in from Montreal -- he and Mike Sutton." Both Tubby and his assistant were returning to Cincinnati after a recruiting visit to 6-9 forward Bernard Cote, who is from Canada. But they were fortunate to arrive in Cincinnati by the time FAA banned all flights at airports throughout the country. But both coaches had trouble finding a rental car to take them to Lexington. Instead, they ordered a car service from Lexington to get them home.

* * *

Tubby Smith and his UK assistant, David Hobbs, enjoy a close friendship that dates back to 1979 when they both served as young assistants at Virginia Commonwealth.

And they spent a lot of time with each other, rooming together on the road, and viewing game films. Their wives sometimes hung out while their husbands worked.

While at VCU, both of them coached together for six years before Hobbs took an assistant coaching job at Alabama in 1985. Hobbs then became the head coach at Alabama in 1992, guiding the Crimson Tide to a six-year overall record of 110-76 before he was dismissed in 1998.

In 2000, when Wildcat aide Shawn Finney took the head coaching position at Tulane, creating an opening on Smith's staff, Smith called his old friend, who was without a coaching job. The UK coach asked Hobbs if he would like to come to Kentucky. Hobbs took the offer and is now in his fourth year at Kentucky.

Hobbs, who was promoted to associate coach before the 2003-04 season, has several stories about his current boss. "I guess the funniest story was in the old days when we used to watch reel to reel film," he recalled in an interview after a Kentucky victory at Rupp Arena in 2002. "We were in Wise, Virginia, on this (road) trip and we were watching the film in my room. It got to be like 2:00 or 3:00 in the morning and it was late. In the meantime our wives had gone over to Tubby's room (adjoining room) and just laid down in the bed and they had fallen asleep.

"And I remember Tubby walking and saying, 'Man, I'm so tired and I'm going to bed.' He went over to (the other room) and I heard him (talking to my wife). He said, "Skeet, you either got to get out of this bed or move over. I'm coming in.' So, that was one funny story that I remember about Tubby."

* * *

In 2003, several weeks after Kentucky concluded its remarkable season of 32-4 with a final No. 1 ranking in the Associated Press poll, including a 26-game winning streak, Tubby inked a new lucrative, eight-year pact with UK. It was believed at the time that his contract, worth more than $20 million, possibly made him the nation's highest-paid college basketball coach.

His superb coaching performance had gotten everyone's attention as he also guided the Cats to 19 SEC victories in as many games, including winning the conference tournament in New Orleans. He captured several national Coach of the Year awards. His Wildcats had gone through a complete reversal from the ugly turmoil-filled campaign of 2001-02. In an interview with *USA Today*, sportscaster Jay Bilas praised Tubby's efforts, saying if the Wildcat coach would write a book about what he did in 2002-03, then every coach in the country would buy it.

Said Tubby of his contract, which runs through the year 2011, "I feel quite lucky that my name is on that contract. Money has never yet made a man rich. What makes you rich is the people you have the privilege of working with. We are 100 percent behind (athletics director) Mitch Barnhart and his staff and they have a great vision, along with (UK president) Dr. Lee Todd. We're willing to do whatever we have to do to make that a reality."

The pact is nothing like what Smith had before in his coaching career. Smith's wife remembers the old days in the mid-1970s when they struggled to make a good living. Even before they had children, the couple didn't have a lot of money to spend.

"When we first got married, we had two cars and $200 between us," said the wife. "We didn't have a whole lot. A lot of things we had were given to us by our families. My mom would give us her big pots or something. We got by and that was good. We were just like everybody else. We had, you know, to crawl before we walked, save and scrimp. We turned out okay."

She remembers their first home the couple had bought. It was where her husband was coaching at Great Mills High, not too far from where his parents lived. "We bought a trailer in southern Maryland," she said. "We lived for two years in Great Mills." While her husband worked at the high school, she found a job at a local water and sewer company in nearby Lexington Park.

* * *

When the UK mentor arrives at home after a game, his personality doesn't change much, if any. Donna says her husband stays pretty much the same person whether Kentucky won or lost. As a 52-year-old father and coach, he keeps things in perspective.

"Tubby is pretty good about that when he comes in the house," Donna said. "He is pretty good about leaving stuff at the job. He is not one to come in and dwell on things. He always says you are not as bad as you think you are and you are never as good as you think you are."

So when the contest ends, regardless of Kentucky's outcome, Tubby moves ahead and focuses on the next opponent. "When he first comes home, the first thing he does is put the tape in and he reviews the game, taking notes," Donna said. "And then after that tape, he puts in the tape of the next game's (opponent). A lot of people don't understand, but I think coaches do best by moving on. They know they can't dwell on a loss or they know they can't celebrate too much on a victory because most of the time they've got another game coming in two or three nights (later). So a lot of it depends on when is the next game. For example, during the SEC (schedule), you are pretty much playing twice a week all of January and all of February. So there is not a whole lot of time to dwell on."

When he is not coaching basketball or recruiting, Tubby likes to relax and listen to music, and watch certain programs on television. "He likes good jazz," said Donna. "He likes to listen to jazz every now and then. And he loves the Discovery Channel. There is another one, the History Channel. He loves that, too."

* * *

Donna has enjoyed many good moments at UK, including the time at San Antonio in 1998 when the Cats, led by Final Four MVP Jeff Sheppard, won the national championship before 40,509 fans in the Alamodome. "That was really fun," she said. "Nobody expected us to win and all the announcers picked Stanford and Utah (UK's Final Four opponents)."

Over the years at social functions and games, she has met all kinds of people, including politicians and celebrities. Two of UK's biggest fans are Super Fan Bob Wiggins (who has attended over 1,250 UK games in person) and actress Ashley Judd. When the Wildcats played in Nashville during the 2003 NCAA tournament, Judd invited the team for a dinner at her farmhouse in the Nashville area. Donna says the actress is a true Big Blue supporter who bleeds blue. When Judd attends the UK games, she is often seen sitting next to the coach's wife.

But Donna remembers one unusual experience with a fan who looked familiar. She commented, "There was one guy who was sort of different and we would see him like at every home game. He would always be there when the game was over and many times wanting autographs again and again. So we were starting to wonder, 'Are these really for him or what?' You know when you see the same person asking for autographs over and over again, it makes you wonder. You are thinking, 'That (the autograph) is not really for him. What is he doing?' That is the only one (encounter) that stands out. Other than that, all of the encounters (with the fans) have been great."

About The Author

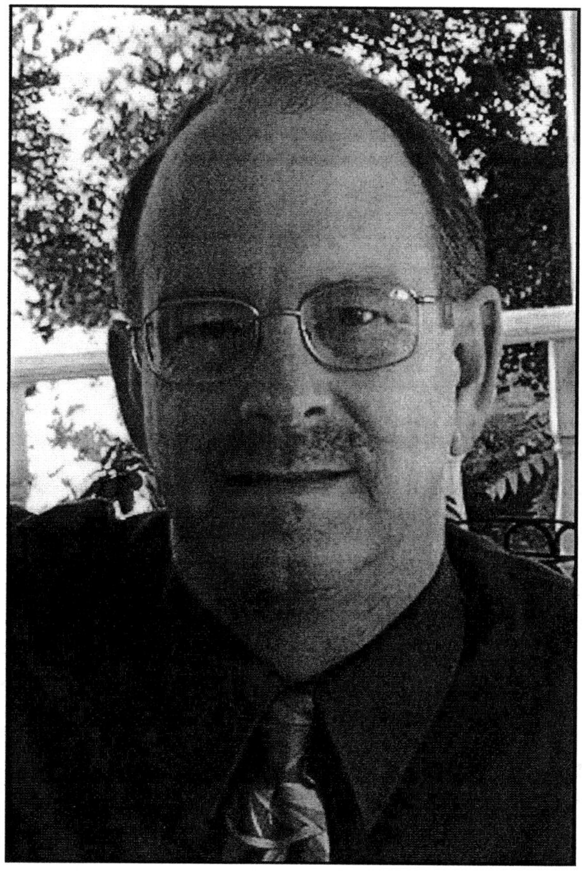

Author Jamie H. Vaught is a respected authority on University of Kentucky basketball. *Krazy About Kentucky: Big Blue Hoops* is Vaught's fourth book about the Wildcat hoops. A former columnist for *The Cats' Pause* magazine for 13 years, Vaught is a sports columnist for several publications, including *The Daily News* in Middlesboro and Lexington-based *Big Blue Nation* magazine. He also has written articles for *Kentucky Monthly* in recent years. A graduate of UK with two degrees, including MBA, Vaught once served as sports editor of UK's student daily newspaper, *Kentucky Kernel*, in the late 1970s. In addition to his writing duties, he is a tenured professor of business and accounting at Southeast Community College in Middlesboro. Vaught, a Somerset native who is hearing impaired, and his wife, Deanna, live in Middlesboro with their daughter, Janna, who was born in August of 2002.

Also by Jamie H. Vaught:

Crazy About The Cats: From Rupp To Pitino
Still Crazy About The Cats
Cats Up Close: Champions Of Kentucky Basketball

(Cut Here)

ORDER ADDITIONAL COPIES TODAY!

Krazy About Kentucky: Big Blue Hoops

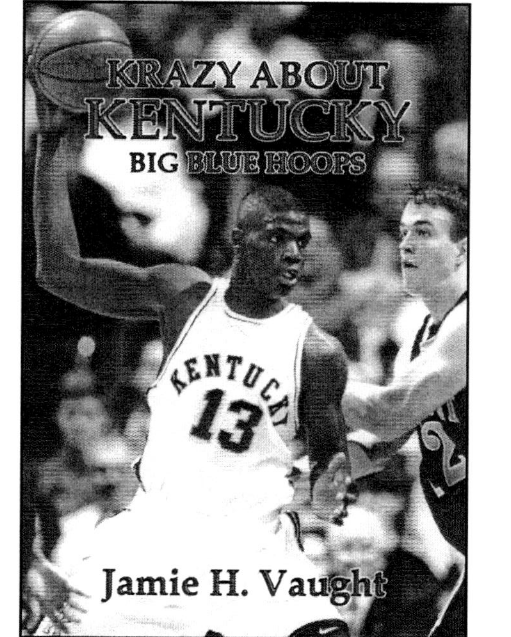

Please send ________ copies of *Krazy About Kentucky: Big Blue Hoops* by Jamie H. Vaught @ \$18.95/copy + \$3.50 Shipping and Handling. I have enclosed a check or money order, made payable to Wasteland Press, for \$ ________

Mail to:

Wasteland Press
P.O. Box 148
Hillview, KY 40129

Name	
Address	
City	**State/Province**
Zip/Postal Code	**Phone**
E-mail (optional)